The First Baseman's Grumpy Fan

A Closed-Door Baseball Romance

Home Run Hearts
Book 1

Rosalie Pease

Editor: Paisley Press Books
Cover Designer: Maria Rosera

This is a work of fiction. Names, characters, organizations, places, events, and incidents are either products of the author's imagination or are used fictitiously. Any resemblance to actual persons, living or dead, or actual events is purely coincidental.

First Sweet Edition

Spicy Edition Ebook ISBN: 978-1-958726-09-9
Spicy Edition Paperback ISBN: 978-1-958726-11-2
Sweet Edition Ebook ISBN: 978-1-958726-08-2
Sweet Edition Paperback ISBN: 978-1-958726-10-5

PAISLEY PRESS BOOKS
WEST WARWICK, RHODE ISLAND

A Note from Rosalie

Hey, reader friend!

Thank you for picking up *The First Baseman's Grumpy Fan*. I hope you enjoy Gale and Finn's story.

This is the sweet, closed-door version of the book, meaning there are intimate scenes described on the page and some swearing. A spicy, open-door version is also available, which includes swearing and on-page intimacy.

After this message from me, you'll find a few content notes on what to expect inside this story if this is the sort of information you prefer to have ahead of time. I'm big into my readers being comfortable, which is why I have sweet and spicy versions available, and these notes (or warnings if you prefer that term, though I've included good stuff for you to expect, so it's not all a warning) are a part of that.

If you like this book and want to be on my ARC team for future releases, I'd love to hear from you!

All the best,
Rosalie

Content Notes

What you WILL get:

- French fry thievery and other potatoes
- Christmas in July
- Humorous wardrobe mishaps and malfunctions
- Strong female friendships
- Blossoming bromances
- Lots of feels
- Kissing
- A guaranteed happy ending.

Here's what you WON'T find:

- Cheating
- Anyone currently dying
- Children or animals in peril
- A third-act breakup.

If you're looking to find out what's in this book to know if it's right for you either at this moment or at all, here are some topics you'll find within the book. I have provided additional detail on my website >> https://rosaliepease.com/what-to-expect-in-the-first-basemans-grumpy-fan/

- Parental (father) death due to skin cancer (recent past)
- Brief mentions of said parent's cancer battle
- Grief related to above death
- A heroine in the process of healing from the above
- Parental divorce (past)
- Absentee/uninvolved parents (current and past)
- Stress from paparazzi and the press
- Visiting children in the hospital (no health specifics or interactions shown) and mentions of sick kids getting special experiences at the ballpark through a Make-A-Wish-type program (again no interactions shown)
- Minor references to a side character's past relationship making her self-conscious about food choices
- Getting locked inside a large room, no threat of peril.

I have tried to be as thorough as possible regarding these topics. If you come across any additional ones that I may have missed or feel the description of any of these could be improved, please don't hesitate to reach out via my socials or through email (author@rosaliepease.com).

The First Baseman's
Grumpy Fan

To all those who have found love during times of grieving and healing.

Chapter 1
Gale

A night at the ballpark with my friends shouldn't make me nervous, yet here I am pacing my bedroom floor as I finish getting ready. Is it too late to back out?

I grew up going to baseball games. Easily sixty a year since birth. Often more.

That's what happens when your grandfather was the founding owner and manager of the team, your dad a player and later a manager for that same team, and your best friend's dad is the team's current manager.

But now, everything's different. We haven't hit mid-season yet, but it's been ages since I've been to a game. None so far this year. And considering I work at the stadium, it's not like I haven't had the opportunity.

A pounding on the front door interrupts my sunscreen application, the only difference in my game-day preparations from my childhood years.

"Gale, it's me!" my best friend Macey shouts, her voice muffled by the door but still audible. She follows this with another knock.

I don't move. Frozen as the reality of going to tonight's game sinks in, sunblock still coating my hands.

"I'm coming in!" Macey shouts again. She's got a key and uses it regularly. Three months into my living here, I got tired of having to get up to answer the door for her.

The door opens, and seconds later, Macey pokes her head into my bedroom. "Oh, good. You're dressed." Her high blond ponytail sways as she gives me an enthusiastic nod.

"I don't know if I'm going to wear this." I turn toward my mirror, hating how unsure my voice sounds. And I hate the knot of unease that lives in my stomach and how much tighter it feels right now.

Macey walks over to me and looks at my reflection before turning back to face me. "But it's what you've always worn. It looks great on you." Considering she's pretty much wearing the same, I could argue that it looks good on anyone.

I rub the last of the sunscreen onto my cheeks, then glance at myself once more, taking in the whole outfit. The team jersey I have on is so familiar to me it's almost a second skin. But now that my dad's gone . . .

"I'm not sure if it's me anymore." I sigh and pull off the jersey so I'm in just a bright-blue T-shirt with the Snowhaven Snowhawks logo on it. "Maybe I shouldn't go."

Macey pulls me into a hug. "I know it's going to be hard, but we're doing this for Dinah. She needs us, and a night looking at hot guys in tight pants is just what she ordered."

Right, Dinah, whose boyfriend recently broke up with her. "You make it sound like we're going to one of those shows in the city to watch men dance and rip off their shirts," I grumble into Macey's shoulder.

I ignore her comment about how hard it will be. Of course

it will be hard. It's the first game I'm going to since my dad died —the first time I've been near the field since his memorial was held there before the start of the season. My office has street access, allowing me to avoid the rest of the stadium until now. It took me a few months to just go back into the office. Thank goodness for the ability to work from home when needed, because it was.

She sets me at arm's length, making me take a half step back, then pats my cheek in an attempt to be cute. "That's step two if this doesn't work. Now come on, we gotta get going or else the concessions lines are going to be wicked long and we'll miss the first inning."

"The lines are never that long. You just don't want to miss certain people warming up on our side of the field."

She gives me a look. "I don't know what you're talking about. It's the only time they're all out there in their tight pants. Dinah deserves to see all of them."

Guess I'm not the only one avoiding things today. "You're right. We're the ones with the tickets, so we need to beat the girls there."

"Now you've got it. So let's go." She motions for me to lead the way, so I do. I learned a long time ago, it's easier to go along with what she says than to try to resist.

As I head outside, I grab my wallet and small tube of sunscreen from the small shelf I installed by the door, then slip both into my back pocket. My former dance teacher always said putting things there and sitting on them was horrible for one's posture, but I can't stand bringing a purse to a game. Not when I only need it for those two things.

The warm sun greets me, improving my mood slightly. We have a tenuous relationship, the sun and I, but with a layer of sunscreen already on, I can enjoy the sun for almost two hours before needing to reapply. Probably right before the anthem.

Macey follows me out of the house, and we walk toward her car, a cute little sedan that she got last year after she practically drove her old one into the ground. No way was it going to last another New England winter. Coupled with a new job, she could afford the payments on something better.

I slide into the passenger seat once I open the door, pulling the sunscreen out of my pocket as I do and sticking it in the cupholder. Macey plops down into her seat a moment later.

"Did you use some already?" I nod to the sunscreen.

"Yes, Mom," she deadpans. Probably the only person I'd let answer me that way. "Mine's tinted. You should try it. Put some color back onto your cheeks."

"The white goes away after a little while." Still, I lower the flap covering the mirror on the sun visor in front of me, making sure there's no excess anywhere. Okay, I'm a little pasty, but it's fine. I'm not trying to impress anyone.

After taking a moment to adjust her rearview mirror, a habit she developed thanks to the old car's mirrors slipping whenever we went over a bump, Macey slides her sunglasses down onto her face and starts the engine.

I let out a long breath. It's going to be okay. I can do this. For Dinah.

Excited, girly squeals give me just moments to brace myself before multiple pairs of arms encircle me from behind.

"Gale!" the girls shout, attempting to bounce around me

without breaking the hug. I stay still. It's easier to when their jumping isn't in sync with each other.

Still, I squeeze their arms tighter. "It's so good to see you. Or it would be if I could actually see you."

They giggle and separate, and Shelby hugs Macey as Dinah hugs me.

"How are you doing today?" I whisper to her. "Are we hating on him or hanging on?"

"I'm so done with him." She scoffs dramatically. "Point me in the direction of the cute baseball boys."

Good. Just what I want to hear. She hasn't had the greatest luck with guys, and this last one was giving us all major red flags. "Di, you don't want a boy." And that's what so many baseball players are. I've seen enough locker room antics over the years to know that. No thank you.

"You're right. I need a man." A glint forms in her eye, which tells me she'll be just fine. Probably didn't even need this girls' outing.

But as Shelby and Dinah switch positions and Shelby gives me a hug, I realize how much *I* needed this outing. How much I needed them to get me here. It's been easier than I thought it would be. Dad's probably up there saying I should have been to a game ages ago. He's right. This feels good.

Shelby keeps me at arm's length once she releases me, studying me with concern. "You look pale." She puts a hand on my forehead, then makes a face.

"It's the sunscreen," Macey tells her. If Shelby is the mom of the group, then Macey is the cool aunt.

Shelby wipes her hand on the front of her jean shorts. "I gathered that."

"It's the extra zinc," I explain, pulling the tube out of my back pocket. "You all put some on, right?"

Shelby nods, but Dinah's eyes go wide. "Please tell me you have some in that bag of yours, Shel. I do not want to look like Caspar's melting cousin."

Shelby reaches into her oversized bag and pulls out not one, but two different kinds of sunscreen. "I've got the spray on sport kind and one formulated for your face."

"Oh, is it the tinted kind?" Macey asks. "That's what I told Gale to switch to."

"Does it really look that bad?" I've seen myself in two types of lighting so far today. Neither of which makes me look like a ghost.

"Relax," Shelby says, "You look fine, just a little paler than I'm used to seeing."

"That might just be my natural color now, not the sunblock." I don't tan without a burn first, and I'm not doing that again.

Shelby reaches up and runs a thumb across my forehead. "There. Got the excess out of a frown line. Now you're fine. Just use one of mine when you reapply, okay?"

I nod. "It was a new one I was trying."

Macey situates herself beside me and takes my arm. "Probably not worth trying again."

She's right about that if it accentuates frown lines I didn't realize were there.

"Now come on. It's getting crowded in here, and you have got to try the new concession stands."

The grand concourse, another part of the stadium I've avoided all year, is filled with new places to eat. There are still the traditional game-day options like hot dogs, burgers, fries, giant pretzels, and pizza slices, but now there's also tacos, gourmet grilled cheese sandwiches, fully dressed potatoes of all kinds, and the list goes on. As I stare at the names of the various stands, I realize, "They're food trucks!"

"Well, they're not technically food trucks right now," Shelby points out, "but all our favorites are here."

She's right, and I eye Macey, expecting her to have the inside scoop thanks to her dad. "How?"

"Ownership loved the food truck event you held here last summer with the foundation, and they decided to give some of those trucks a regular spot on the concourse. Some rotate in and out, but others will be here all season. They all still have their trucks too. It's a win-win. It exposes the businesses to more people, and Frost Field is becoming a bit of a food scene as well."

"How did I not hear about this?" Because I've been hiding from anything baseball that didn't take place in my office, that's how.

Thankfully she doesn't call me out for it. "The event you organized here with the foundation was the inspiration, but ownership went straight to the food trucks for this. Guess they figured they didn't need you to make the introductions."

I frown. "I'd hoped to run that event again this year." But with some of the food trucks already inside, that's going to cut into who will want to participate.

Macey furrows her brow. "No saying you can't. This will allow more trucks in since some of them can set up in here instead of having it closed up like last year. I think it would be even more successful."

As I survey the space, counting the stalls, I realize she has a point. With eight trucks represented in here, I could cast a wider net across the Fiddlefern Fjord region for a wider variety of food offerings. Maybe bring some from as far as Saltair Shores or Sunny Valley.

I quirk my frown into a slight smile at the possibilities, and Macey grins widely. "Now you're thinking like that great event planner I know you are." I'm more than that, but events encompass a lot of what people see me do. "But you have plenty of time to figure out event details later. Food now. It's almost time for warmups."

Chapter 2

Finn

Six hours ago

Coach slams his hand against the door jamb. Not an unusual occurrence for the fiery first base coach, so no one pays him much attention.

"Finn!"

Him yelling for me, however, is not normal. I jerk my head up and look at him straight on.

"Stop what you're doing and head into the office."

I point to my jersey. "Let me finish buttoning—"

"Don't worry about it." The tone starts off harsh, but by the time he's finished the statement, it's lost all bite, sounding more defeated than anything.

All conversations in the locker room stop, and everyone sets their gazes on me. This can't be good.

Coach turns around and walks away as I stand to follow, fumbling with my buttons even though he said not to bother. I'm not the type to walk into the office without looking presentable. Some of the other guys, yes, but not me. But whatever I'm about to walk into has set me on edge. Blast these buttons. My usually agile fingers fumble with the small round disks, and by the time I make it to the office, I've missed one hole and only done three buttons.

It looks better unbuttoned, so I quickly undo it, make sure my team undershirt is tucked into my pants, and knock on the door Coach left partially open for me. All the voices inside hush.

Yeah, this definitely isn't good.

Five hours ago

Being traded was not on my radar at all when I arrived at the Wharf this morning, least of all to the Snowhawks, one of the most storied teams in baseball. I was never mentioned in any trade rumors circulating the clubhouse, nor any floating around online. And I would know. I have alerts set up to tell me when my name appears anywhere online.

The Sailors, the team I've been a part of for the last three years—since their founding—is still up and coming, known more for our viral videos and entertainment value than our ability to win games. But we're a lot better than we used to be. Another year or two, and we could really contend with the other teams for a shot at the post season.

Or, I guess, *they*, not we, will contend with the other teams. Even perhaps against me.

It's a strange thought to have, but it's the truth now.

Three years ago, I was a college ball player who liked filming his . . . let's call them extra practices. After enough videos went viral, I was approached by a scout for the Sailors with an offer that I actually refused. It wasn't that I didn't want the money. What college kid wouldn't? Especially one who had no money growing up. But I was in college on scholarship to play ball, and the team was doing well. I wasn't going to abandon them. Or my studies.

I finished the semester, played through the semifinals, and then accepted a new offer. Less at signing and for the first year since it had started already, but the following years remained the same. And I didn't fully withdraw from my studies either, but pared down my course load to one full course each semester and a few mini courses to fill in the time either after the season or before spring training. It's slow going. I'm still technically a college junior, but that's fine by me. I'll finish my degree even if it takes me another five years. I want to have something to fall back on if the end of my baseball days come sooner than I plan. I have no intention of stopping anytime soon.

My being a Snowhawk now doesn't change that.

After one last social media video with the Sailors to say goodbye, the Sailors' bench coach takes me to the bus station with only the duffel bag I showed up to the stadium with this morning. There's no time to pack. Although I should have seventy-two hours to report to my new team, per the league's collective bargaining agreement, the injury that necessitated this trade means I'm starting tonight. And despite the best efforts of the traveling secretaries for both teams, this is the only way to get me to Snowhaven before the game. The Snowhawks have some vehicles they could have used, but the drive to Saltair Shores and back would take too long. And it seems no one on the various rideshare apps wants to hustle me over to Frost Field a few hours away. By the time the bus gets me to Snowhaven, I'll have just enough time to warm up.

It's been an interesting morning, to say the least. Thank goodness for Coach, who's already set me up with a solid plan for subletting my apartment to another guy on the team or whoever gets called up to fill my spot. Furniture included, at least until the offseason. I won't need any of it right now. Snowhaven State University leases one of its dorms for sports housing for all the local teams. It saves the players from having to rent places around town if they live elsewhere the rest of the year.

"There's a mall there," Coach continues as he waits with me, "so you'll be able to grab some clothes and whatever other essentials you might need until you can come back for your stuff."

"Thanks, Coach. For everything." We'd really hit it off when I moved to Saltair Shores and joined the Sailors. He took me under his wing. Out of everyone here, I'll miss him the most.

Coach reaches into his pocket. "There is one more thing," he begins, his voice almost hesitant.

I hold up a hand, assuming he's going for his wallet. "I don't need any of your money. I've put plenty away." Although I signed a decent contract that would have left me with a lot of spending money, I banked most of it, tying it into various investments. Most of my signing bonus too. And although I bought my ma a house so she'd never have to worry about rent ever again, I rent a cheap apartment and still live as if I'm a full-time college student, living off leftovers and showing up for free food in exchange for manual labor.

"That's good to hear," Coach says, but he doesn't stop what he's doing. "I wasn't going to give you money. Probably make more than me. Or will with your next contract." He hands me a dark-blue permanent marker.

I stare at it in my open palm. "What's this for?"

"Equipment manager on the Snowhawks is an old buddy of mine from our college playing days. Says they have most of what they need to get you suited up for today, but it will take a day or two to get you cleats to fit you. There's a strict policy on the team to look, well, uniform." He glances down at my shoes, not that I play in these. "Yours are gray, aren't they?"

"Yeah, and perfectly broken in. Are you telling me I can't use them now?"

"You can today, maybe tomorrow. That's what the marker's for." I blink several times in disbelief, and a short huff of a chuckle escapes him. "Should give you something to do on the bus."

I'm usually the guy who can see the bright side of anything, but I fail to see the humor in this situation. I'm ruining a perfectly good pair of cleats. Seems wasteful. "Gee, thanks."

The crackle of a speaker interrupts me from saying more. "Now arriving: Route 87 to Sunny Valley, stopping at Snowhaven."

Marker in hand, I pick up my duffel and hike it over my shoulder. "That's me." I stick my free hand out to shake, and Coach takes it before pulling me in for a bro hug. "Thanks again for everything. Have a good rest of the season, Coach."

"You too. Not too good, though." He laughs as I give his back a final hard pat, then I step away as the bus comes to a complete stop and the doors open. With one final nod, I turn and walk toward the bus and an uncertain playing future in Snowhaven.

I find a window seat looking out at the landing, where Coach is still standing, and drop into my seat before heaving my bag to in between my legs to leave space for someone else should they need it. As the bus pulls away, I give Coach a final wave, but I don't look back to see him walk away.

Instead, I zip open a side pocket on my duffel and pull out my small tripod. With its bendy legs, it's perfect for using on weird angles like this one. I wrap one leg around the handle of my bag to keep it secure, then steady it on the bag's end with the other two legs. Then I pull my cell phone out of my back pocket, the easiest place to put it even though it's supposedly terrible for me, and attach it to the tripod's grip. I bring up the camera app and film a quick goodbye video to send to our team's social media manager. Or their social media manager. Since he's not mine anymore. I'm not part of the *our*, not a part of the team. Still, I'm sure he'll post the video. It's for the fans.

After a replay, I decide against using the tripod on the bag for the longer video. It has a terrible angle of me, but it's from the heart, so I don't want to redo it and lose that. I pull the phone free from the tripod's grip and hold it as I record a longer video for my own account.

"Hey, Sailor Nation! Finn Nixon here, and as I'm sure some of you have heard, I got traded today." I draw my face into an exaggerated frown, my attempt to be the funny guy they fell in love with. "I'm shipping up to Snowhaven. I don't think any of us saw it coming. It was all very sudden. So sudden, in fact, this is literally me sitting on a bus with just my duffel bag of stuff I brought to the Wharf today for the game.

"Thank you all for all the love you've shown me since I started my baseball career nearly three years back. But now it's time for me to put on a new uniform and become a Snowhawk . . . just with my own twist, if you know what I mean. Got any suggestions for what I should do to make a good impression? Tell me what some of your favorite moves of mine are.

"Anyhow, don't be afraid to say hi if you come up for a game this season or any. I may not wear the uniform anymore, but I'll never forget my roots. You all mean so much to me, and I'll see you again someday. This is Finn, signing off."

I stop the recording and load it into my social media stories before checking all of my notifications. This is the first time I've looked at them since I found out about the trade. No time before now. Hundreds of notifications are waiting for me, and I can only imagine what the Sailors' social media manager is dealing with.

I scroll through the likes on my previous post from this morning. A simple game-day prep post of me in the locker room. The fans love to see that sort of behind-the-scenes stuff. It's how I've made myself and the team feel like real people. Like friends. When I head into the comments, they go from excitement about today's game to shock or well wishes. A marked difference between before and after news of my trade broke.

The outpouring of love the fans have for me is near overwhelming, and I hope to get even an inkling of that in Snowhaven. I heart what I can, saying thank you here and there. Can't go too fast or I'll get put in time out and be unable to use the platform for a few hours. Don't want that.

New notifications continue to pop up, many on my latest video, including a couple about how the Snowhawks' accounts are now following me. I've been following them for years already, same with the other teams in the league. Always good to keep an eye on what the other teams are doing. And until now, the Sailors have done it best. Let's see what I can do with my new team.

Finally, I check into the news alerts featuring my name. The articles confirm I'm needed there after an undisclosed injury to their first baseman. So at least I'll be in my usual position, which is good for me, but with no timetable for the return of who I'm replacing, there's no telling how long I'll be in that spot.

I pull up the private message section of my social media app and type in the Snowhawks' account handle.

You interested in posting an official hello to the fans from me?

Their icon shows whoever's in charge of the account is online, so it doesn't take long for a reply.

Absolutely! Send it to the email listed in the bio, and I'll post it with you as a collaborator so it will appear on both accounts.

Can do! Give me five.

Wicked! Looking forward to working with you. I think we can liven up this feed a whole lot with your presence.

At least someone up there is looking forward to me joining the team. Replacement trades can go either way. Relief or disdain. I don't have any beef with the Snowhawks and have always played a clean game against them. So I have that going for me. But their first baseman is—was?—a good one, a beloved player, so I've got some big shoes to fill to win them over.

Shoes . . .

And now I have my idea.

I dig out my cleats from my duffel, shoving everything else in there that threatens to come out. Thank goodness this trade came before the game, so everything I have in here is clean and fresh, well, minus the cleats, but I throw deodorizer in those regularly. And at least no one is next to me to catch whatever lingering stink they may have. I prop them on top of my bag, then swipe back into my camera app and press the record button once my face appears on the screen.

"Hey there, Snowhawks fans! Do you all call yourself something beyond fans? I want to make sure I'm addressing you properly." It's probably a good question to ask the social media manager. "This is Finn Nixon, formerly of the Sailors. That's right, formerly, because you're looking at the newest member of the Snowhawks. First, I want to wish Dave Mossen all the best in his recovery and say that I look forward to playing with him on the field in the future.

"Second, I am excited to come play ball for such a great team with a strong history and legacy. Growing up in the region like I did, like I'm sure many of you did, this was the team you watched up here before the league expanded.

"I hope to do you all proud while bringing some of my own flair to the game. So I will see you all later today, but first I have some work I need to do."

I pull the marker from my shirt pocket, stick the cap end in my mouth, and pull the marker free. There's a brief moment where I want to goof off and draw on my face, but first impressions are important. I can't imagine the front office would be appreciative of permanent marker on their newest player's face. I waggle my eyebrows at the camera before switching it to the front facing camera, putting my shoes at the center of the screen.

Carefully, with my marker-holding hand, I pull the cap out of my mouth so I can explain what I'm doing as I put the first lines of dark blue onto my light-gray shoes.

"My shoes and I will be hitting the field very soon, and I can't wait to see you. If you're at the game today, let me know how I did with my efforts when you see me."

I press the button to stop recording, and once it's done processing, I load it into an email and send it to the social media person. A few minutes later, I receive the notification saying I've been added as a collaborator in a story and a post by the Snowhawks.

I'll give it some time before I go in to see what the fans' reactions are. I have some coloring to do.

Chapter 3
Gale

I plop into my seat, tray of concessions in hand, and immediately spot an unfamiliar face standing at first base, a foot off the bag, his cap askew. He does the arm wave, flicking his gloved hand up and wiggling his arm up to his shoulder, then going down the next arm toward his throwing hand as if the movement is traveling from one side to the other. The game hasn't started, the Hawks are still warming up, but what sort of warmup is that? His eye should be on the balls being shagged across the field.

"Who's that?" I ask Macey as she carefully lowers her seat bottom from its folded-up position. "Where's Dave?"

She glances toward the team's first baseman as she takes a sip of her soda, but being the manager's daughter, she likely doesn't need to.

"Oh, that's Finn Nixon. Our newest Snowhawk. He was a surprise trade after Dave was a late scratch this morning. Showed up earlier this afternoon. Dad barely had any warning."

"Is Dave going to be okay?" He's older. Been around for

years on several teams, but he's always found his way back here. One of the few on the team who were here before Macey's dad took over from my own. With only a few years left before his likely retirement, I hope this hasn't sped that timeline up.

Macey shrugs. "With how fast someone got on the phone this morning to make this trade, my guess is he's out for at least a month. Maybe longer."

That's true. A late scratch and missing a day or two wouldn't result in such a hasty trade. "Where'd he come from?"

"The Sailors. We're lucky their team's only a couple hours from here." Saltair Shores isn't the most direct bus ride away, but it's close enough. I remember those trips as a kid, riding in the front of the team bus, the players in their travel suits and probably on their best as possible behavior because I was there. The memories ping at me, little bites into the armor I've put up. When did I say I was too cool to do that anymore?

What I would give to do it again.

Nope, can't go there right now. Not if I want to make it through the game.

Needing something else to focus on, I scan the field, but aside from Dave, none of our regular starters are missing. Neither is anyone else. The whole dugout's busy warming up. "Who'd we lose in the trade?" Maybe someone from the bullpen? Their area is harder to see from these seats.

Macey shakes her head. "Not us. The Snowcaps sent two of their guys over to the Seafarers. Some money too. Sailors called up someone from there to replace Finn."

"Wow." I shove a bite of hotdog in my mouth as I shift my focus back to the first baseman while the team pairs off in lines. Finn has a ball in his hand while Kyle, the shortstop he's paired with, jogs backward away from him. Not unheard of, but our farm team is strong, so, "He must be good."

"He is."

But as Macey says that, Finn lobs the ball toward Kyle, arcing the ball high into the air, and as Finn's arm swings down to complete the throwing motion, his body follows. His feet leave the ground, and he finishes the front flip by landing cleanly.

My eyes widen in surprise as a chorus of chuckles rises around us. "Did he—did he do that purposely?"

"Probably."

Finn's goofy grin cements that truth.

"But, why?" My dad never would have allowed such behavior.

"Because it's fun. Look at everyone. They enjoyed it."

Even Kyle, who has a reputation for being the team curmudgeon. He tosses the ball back to the new first baseman, corners of his mouth ticked upward and slowly shaking his head as he takes a giant step backward.

When Finn throws this time, he flips once more, and again the crowd claps. More this time as people continue to find their seats and those near them tell them what to be on the lookout for.

Macey bumps me with her arm. "You're staring." I shoot her a look, and she wags her eyebrows at me.

"Assessing his flip, I assure you. Not him." It was impressive. Not every athlete can do that, and I wonder if he trained somewhere or simply discovered he could one day. Seems like he'd be the type to just try it. I'd need at least a step or two to give me enough of a push. If I could even still do it at all. It's been a few years, and acrobatics was never my strong suit.

"Mm-hm . . ." she teases.

"Trust me, you can have him. He's a ballplayer and not even a serious one."

She blows a quick raspberry. "Nah, not my type."

Dinah leans forward in her seat so her head is practically between mine and Macey's. "He's not nearly old enough for her."

I laugh. "And how *is* that going, Macey? I'm shocked you haven't switched your season ticket to one along the third-base line." It's no secret, at least not to anyone sitting here, that Macey has had a crush on Ian, the third baseman, who's almost ten years older than her, for the last few seasons.

"And give up one of the best seats in the house near my friends? No, thank you." Her grin turns wicked. "Besides, who says a gal can't have more than one set of tickets? Where do you think I sit when I can't get one of you to come join me?"

"Oooh . . ." Dinah squeals with a giggle, and Macey's cheeks turn a slight shade of pink.

My jaw drops. "Does your dad know?"

She shakes her head. "Bought it myself."

"A season ticket?"

She nods.

"But I get that list of names for the foundation." Many ticket holders donate tickets for games they can't attend to the foundation so I can give them to local charities for fundraisers or to disadvantaged youths. "Your name isn't on it." Not even for the seat she's sitting in now since it's comped like mine is.

"I . . ." She pauses. "I used a fake name." Her blush deepens.

"Scandalous," I tease, picturing her in big glasses and a ballcap to hide her identity. If I'm well known here for who my family is, she's even more so now by being the manager's daughter. But what would her dad think about her dating an older guy, let alone one of his ball players, no matter how decent of a guy he seems to be.

"Your last email about the Christmas in July Gala was well designed, by the way. I'm looking forward to it. Cordelia Smithson, however, sends her regrets about her inability to attend the event. Can we go dress shopping soon?"

"Oh, yes please," Dinah says with a clap. "Sign me up for some retail therapy."

"I'm in," Shelby adds.

"Yes. There's no way I'd get something without your opinions on it." Or without them doing my hair and makeup. I'm perfectly capable of everyday looks, but nothing that's gala-worthy. Things like that are much better with friends. Same for things like this, I think as I look back toward the field. "I've really missed this. Missed you all."

Macey leans in and gives my shoulders a squeeze as Dinah and Shelby lean forward, arms holding containers of food going this way and that in an effort to not spill any of it. Dinah's chicken Caesar salad worries me the most, the arm holding it sticking out over Macey's side, trembling as she tightly squeezes us with the other arm. No one wants to wear a salad.

"We're glad to have you back," Macey says. "Good idea, Shel."

"Okay, let's break this up before one of us ends up covered in food." We all settle back into our seats, but it takes me a minute more before Macey's comment settles in. I turn to her, enough so I can see Shelby and Dinah in my periphery. "Wait, I thought we were here for Dinah."

"Yes, that was part of our plan." Shelby says. "*You* thought we were here for Dinah, but *we* are here for *you*."

Macey quirks a soft half smile. "Baseball is good for the soul, remember?"

I'd grown up hearing that phrase from both my grandfather and my dad. Now I used it every time I spoke at an event for work with the team's charitable foundation. Somewhere in the aftermath of my dad's death, I guess I had forgotten that.

If I was the crying type, and I'm not, the waterworks would be starting right now. And although I'm more the type of person to toss my emotions onto a pile to be dealt with later—or never, if I can help it—even I can feel the weight of the excess moisture in my eyes.

"Oh, they're coming off the field," Dinah squeals. This outing may not have been for her like I thought it was, but she still enjoys a man in tight pants, especially when it looks like the entire team is heading right toward us given the location of their dugout under the section next to ours. She wolf whistles as they draw near, and since we're sitting in the first and second rows, the noise gets their attention.

Most smile, Kyle shakes his head as if embarrassed, and much to Macey's delight, Ian waves. Finn, however, tips his cap to such an extent that it pops off. He tries to catch it with his head, and although he does—I'll give him points for that—it's crooked and nearly slides off. My grandfather would have had a fit at the sloppy look it's given Finn.

As he disappears into the dugout, I find myself wondering what to make of the newest player on the team.

Chapter 4

Finn

Kyle drops down next to me in the dugout as the grounds crew heads out to make the dirt around the diamond look nice for the on-field ceremonies before the game. "I knew you'd be weird when they said you were coming from the Sailors, but that was next level." He shakes his head.

I shrug. "Just doing what I know." These sorts of things were normal on my last team. Made it fun. I'm not sure Kyle knows what that is.

Devon takes a seat on the other side of me. "And what I want to know is how you just flip like that. I only end up like that on accident and with some momentum behind me."

"Yeah," Kyle scoffs as he reaches forward for one of the dangling two-liter soda bottles with a baseball and pen inside it. "And usually you end up on the ground when it happens." He grabs both out and then uncaps the pen before signing the ball.

Kyle doesn't seem like the talkative type, and it's as if everyone's surprised by the comment. Several of the guys burst out laughing after a second, although Kyle never breaks his straight-faced appearance, and Devon blinks at him a few times before cracking a toothy grin. "Wow, man. You don't hold back sometimes."

Kyle's eyebrows raise slightly, the only indication he's heard Devon. Then he hands the ball and pen to me, and I take it, almost like a peace offering for now. Surely he would have had more to say about my weirdness had Devon not come over. But for now, it's done.

Signing stuff for the kids is always a highlight of my pregame. The dugout's lower here, under a portion of the stands, so the kids send stuff down in containers. I scrawl my signature close to the brand information along the stitching. Kyle's already taken the sweet spot on the other side of the ball, and I want to see if the guys have some sort of pattern to where they all sign before I go and stake a claim on a spot. I don't need to ruffle more feathers by signing in the wrong place.

I cap the pen and turn to hand both off to Devon, but he's already got a ball in his hand and another one next to him, so I stand and set it back inside the soda bottle. The milk jug next to it is empty, so I grab the one on the other side sitting on a pile of bubblegum. This kid knows their stuff. Bribing gets even the most reluctant guys to sign, and there are already several names on the ball. I quickly note where the guys have signed already before adding my signature and putting it back.

I move to the next container, this one a Halloween bucket with three balls inside. I peek my head out from the dugout and look up to find three kids looking down at me, two boys and a slightly younger girl in pigtails.

"These yours?" I call up to them. The little girl gives me a full smile, one that's missing several teeth, and nods.

I pull myself out of the dugout and onto the ground. I consider doing a forward roll, but I'll save it for another time. The kids study me, heads cocked to the side, as I reach down for their bucket and pull out the three balls. Let's hope I don't make a fool of myself.

Two balls in one hand and one in the other, I let the first ball from my dominant hand fly, then let the other two go when that one has peaked. The kids clap excitedly as I juggle, drawing attention—and cameras—my way. I maintain a good rhythm for a minute or so before throwing all three high in the air and catching them all in my cap to a loud round of applause. Including some from my new teammates, Devon among them. But not Kyle. He'll come around. I have a way of growing on people.

I wave to the kids before disappearing back into the dugout with their balls. I make quick work of signing them and then place them back into their bucket, letting this one swing so the kids know their balls are back.

"Thank you!" they shout from above.

I sign a few more balls and one cap before a chorus of kids shouts their thanks and the containers slowly rise out of view.

The announcer comes over the speakers and welcomes everyone to the game, saying it's a great day for baseball. It sure is. The mountain air is clean and fresh, and the sky is a brilliant blue. I'm sure I'll miss the salt-tinged air from my old stadium, but this is nice.

A hand claps me on the back as the team funnels through the dugout to head up the few stairs to the field. "Think you can teach me some of your stunts?" Devon asks as he steps away from me and leads me toward the stairs. "I'm not as bad as Kyle says, but I could use some help."

Behind us, Kyle snorts.

I step out onto the dirt. "Show me what you got out there today so I can see what I'm working with." Then I turn around to take in the crowd. Way more people here now than during warmups. We must be near a sellout. I'm used to it from the Sailors, but this is a bigger stadium. Noticeably so.

I scan the crowd for the three kids from earlier but can't find them. They don't bar them from coming from other sections to get autographs, so they could be sitting anywhere.

A microphone stands just off the pitcher's mound, waiting for the national anthem, and as soon as we're all in position, the announcer introduces the singer and she steps onto the field. The crowd goes wild as she hits the hardest notes, and it's only a moment's reprieve until their applause at the end.

If the cheering is even half this enthusiastic when we're playing, I'm going to get spoiled. Not that the fans didn't cheer for us on the Sailors, they did. This is just . . . more.

I'm the new guy, though. No one's really going to be cheering for me here.

As I said my goodbyes to the Sailors earlier, the comment I heard the most from my now-former teammates, aside from how they were going to miss me, was how great it was that I was single. That it's easier being unattached when you get traded. And maybe that's true. But if I had just one person here who was clapping for me—only me—the whole park could be otherwise silent and that would be enough.

For now, I can live with this.

After several official media photos, the singer throws out the ceremonial first pitch. Finally my favorite words echo through the park.

Chapter 5
Gale

"Play ball!"

Those were my favorite words as a kid. Even now, after nearly half a season of finding every excuse to avoid coming here and giving away my tickets to friends and friends of friends, a little thrill runs through me. It doesn't take long for me to settle into my usual routine of game watching, loud clapping and the occasional whoop to cheer for a good play, picking apart stances and strike zones the way my dad once did —from my earliest game-day memories of him as a pitcher, then as a manager, and all the way to watching games on TV with him during his treatments.

And perhaps unsurprisingly, being here feels good, and I'm already looking forward to my next time here.

My cell phone alarm goes off in my pocket during the second inning. Time to reapply my sunscreen. As I do, the announcer introduces everyone to the new first baseman entering the lineup for the first time.

Finn Nixon.

He's so new, his highlight reel on the billboard over the outfield is of him juggling and doing flips during warmups.

It then cuts to a secondary feed taken from the side where you can see he was juggling for three little kids. The entire ballpark lets out a collective *aww*. Then a live feed shows the three kids waving enthusiastically from their seats, drawing a round of cheers from the crowd.

Macey nudges me with her arm when the screen cuts away from them to feature Finn walk up to the plate. "See? I told you it was sweet."

"Okay, so he's won over a majority of the fans with how charming he is with kids, but let's see how he plays."

"Did you just admit he has charm?" She gives me a wry smile.

I roll my eyes. "If you like that sort of thing."

"And we all know you do," Dinah says, leaning forward.

I fight a smile as I glance up at his stats from the Sailors before focusing on the plate where he's waiting for the pitcher of the Nevershade Ravens to throw him the ball. He was batting over .300—impressive—in Saltair Shores. It's a bigger city, but the Sailors have a smaller fanbase because they're a newer team. Dad never managed a team against them, fully retiring from the game four seasons ago when he first got sick. Scratch that, when we first found out he was sick. He'd been sick longer than that.

A new dusting of grief coats my emotions. Every one of them is piled up so carefully with the rest so as not to break free and start an avalanche.

The crack of a bat holds the flurry at bay as Finn Nixon makes solid contact with the ball, fouling it several rows behind where we're sitting.

"Heads up, ladies," I call out to my friends over the excited din of our section as people clap for the kid who caught the ball. "Can't lose focus with this one." One should never take their eyes off the game while it's going on just in case, but if someone routinely lands fouls in your area, that's all the more reason to stay sharp. I've seen what happens when people don't pay attention.

"More like *you* can't take your eyes off him," Dinah quips.

I shake my head since she can't see the accompanying eye roll as I remove my sunscreen from my back pocket, then squirt some into my free hand. Shelby quickly pulls the tube away from me, making me bolt uprights as if I need to prepare for an oncoming baseball, although what the pitcher just threw at Finn was a ball he rightly didn't swing at. Shelby puts my sunscreen into my empty cupholder and shoves the non-spray sunblock that she brought with her.

"At least put this on your face."

"Thanks." I'd forgotten I said I'd try it. I rub the stuff already in my hand onto one arm, working it in as best as I can before taking my tube to do the next arm. I'm not going to use Shelby's everywhere. If I like it enough after doing my face, I'll get my own. And as I glance at my arms—can't keep my eyes off Finn, no, wait, the ball for too long—I'll definitely need to get something other than what I used. I swear I'm even pastier than before. It's as if what was on me from earlier got reactivated and I'm trying out for a new team mascot that's covered in fake snow. No, make it a marshmallow fluff. Gross.

I'm still rubbing the white streaks into my arms as Finn belts a line drive between first and second base. The Ravens' second basemen makes a valiant dive for the ball but comes up empty as it skips into shallow right field. The right fielder beats out the first baseman for the ball and throws it to the pitcher who's now covering first, but Finn reaches the bag with no problem.

"He's got speed, I'll give him that."

"Oh, the compliments are really flowing now," Macey says, going to bump into me again but thinking better of it when she spots my arms.

I make a face. "Hey, I can appreciate a solid at bat and the effort to race to the bag."

"Mm-hmm . . ."

I push her arm gently. "Here, I think you really need to reapply." When I remove my hands, a faint whitish print remains on her arm. She *ewws* but rubs it into her arm all the same. "That goes for you two as well," I add, turning to the girls behind me. Shelby's covered in a fresh sheen that says she applied some already with the other one she brought. She holds up the can and sprays some directly into Dinah's hands so she can rub it on. Not the best method, but it will do in a pinch. I quickly use Shelby's other sunblock on my face, noticing how smoothly it goes on, then check the label so I can look up its rating later before handing it back to her.

A double by the next batter drives in a run, and gets Finn get to third, but the next batter hits a pop fly that the shortstop catches, ending the inning and stranding Finn on base. He starts toward the dugout, but halfway down the baseline, once the majority of the Ravens has passed him on their way to their dugout, he starts cartwheeling down the line.

"Oh brother," I roll my eyes.

"Look at him go!" Macey shouts enthusiastically as Dinah and Shelby let out a whistle and a long fangirl cheer, respectively.

"There has got to be a rule against that sort of thing," I mutter. What would Dad think of this on his team? Grandpa?

Macey quiets and shoots me a look. We both know there is no such rule. Footage of the great Ozzie Smith of the Cardinals doing a backflip still makes highlight reels today. And although he seems like he'd be more at home playing Banana Ball, based on everyone's reaction to Finn's five consecutive cartwheels, it's never going to be a rule.

I settle back into my seat as our pitcher takes a few warmup tosses, and Finn emerges from the dugout with his glove. Just when I think he's going to run out there like a normal player, he breaks out into the grapevine of all things. I think back to the last time the Sailors faced the Snowhawks. Last season, not this season, since I've avoided games on TV as much as I've avoided them in person. Had the whole team been like that? They have a reputation for their fun vibes, but certainly they haven't taken things to this level.

I nudge Macey. "Are the Sailors always like that?"

She shakes her head. "Not so much for away games. You seemed to enjoy it a couple seasons ago when we caught that game in Saltair."

"I did?"

"Yeah. It was before . . . everything." She means before my dad got really sick because it certainly wasn't before everything. We were already deep into treatments then, though my friends had no idea at the time. I didn't tell them until after, encouraged by my dad to keep things normal for as long as possible. Still, I barely remember the outing. Everything from that time exists in this strange haze.

Shelby leans in. "Yeah. We knew something was bothering you, but we didn't press it, and you lightened up as the game went on. You even laughed."

Dinah gasps in mock surprise. "You laughed? It's like I don't even know you."

I do what any rational non-laughing human being would do and stick my tongue out at her.

She laughs. Of course she does. Because if I'm the non-laughing friend, Dinah is the exact opposite. Cheery, quick to laugh, quick to smile and clap, overall bouncy. Her enthusiastic attitude makes her a great personal assistant for one of the big wigs at the Fiddlefern Broadcasting Network. Sadly, it does not always bode well for her relationships with men, which is why their excuse to get me here worked so well. It was all too believable.

"I can only imagine the Sailors have upped their game in more ways than one since then," Macey says. "They had a winning record last year, and they're huge on social media. Bet they've added a bunch of new tricks to their home games."

"But he's not on the Sailors anymore," my gaze lands on Finn once more as he dances, yes, literally, behind the base. His footwork isn't half bad, but there's something about it—about him—that I can't put my finger on.

"He isn't, but obviously he's going to bring a bit of the Sailors with him. He's trying to make a name for himself and find his footing in a new place on a new team. And it's working. You can barely keep your eyes off him."

"Just trying to figure him out, that's all," but her words stick with me through this inning and the next and the one after that too.

I'm back in line at the concessions stand during Finn's next trip to the plate in the fifth inning. I always grab another round of food at this point of the game to avoid all of the people trying to beat the rush of the seventh inning stretch by going during the sixth inning. Considering I'm still out here watching the TVs set up around the concourse at the bottom of the inning shows me how much I misjudged the popularity of the new concessions. It's both annoying, because now I'm missing our guys bat, but good, too, because this is the sort of update that will keep the stadium fresh. Both my dad and grandfather would have loved it.

As I make it to the front of the line to order, Finn draws a walk.

I'm back in my seat before he's brought home after the next three batters get a single, a walk, and another single. This time, Finn's footwork allows him to avoid a miscalculated sliding dive by the catcher, and Finn reaches home plate for a run before the catcher can adjust course and tag him out. In celebration, Finn flips forward to a raucous applause. The cheering only grows louder as the cleanup hitter hits a grand slam, clearing the bases and ending the pitcher's night early with one out left to go. Although the new pitcher allows our number five batter to reach first base, he strikes out the next batter. This ends the bottom of the fifth inning and sends us into the top of the sixth.

Shelby and Dinah take this as their opportunity to grab food. With the way lines were for me, maybe they'll be back by the next inning. I'd offered to get them food when I left, but Dinah had refused. She was never one to turn down food until this last boyfriend. No doubt he was filling her head with nonsense about her looks. But her resolve broke when she saw what I came back with. Or more like smelled. Sausage and peppers stuffed inside a salty baked potato. Perfection.

Several minutes later, Macey and I have barely made a dent in it. It's one of the biggest potatoes I've ever seen. And among the most delicious. But when the crack of a bat has our heads whipping up to watch the ball arcing high up above us, I shove the potato her way so my hands are free to hopefully catch my first foul ball.

Chapter 6
Finn

I take a few steps back as I track the ball high in the air. It's drifting foul along the narrow first base side of the field. I might run out of room to catch it here before the field gives way to the stands, but if it does that, it's a foul and the batter gets another chance. But if I catch the ball, it's an out. Doesn't matter where I'm making the play.

How high is that wall? I glance back. Totally jumpable. Eyes back skyward, I bound over to the wall, my glove hand outstretched as I hit the dirt with my feet. Another quick look at the wall, and I leap. I stick the landing and take one giant step toward the armrest of the seat behind it to make the play, right as the fan sitting there stands up to reach the ball I'm about to grab.

Her shoulder bangs into a part of me that makes me grateful for protection, but it still stuns me enough that I lose my footing on the transfer to the armrest with my other foot. It slides into the cupholder, squirting white goo in a stream toward her T-shirt. What is that, sour cream? She drops back into the seat at an awkward angle as I pitch toward her. I throw one arm out to catch myself from toppling too far over and onto my head in the aisle next to her or to my side on the cement floor between her seat and the wall. Hopefully it keeps me from putting all of my weight on her too. At six feet tall, I'm not a tiny guy.

Her hands press against my chest, fully resisting and supporting me as if she's done this before.

"Whoa, there. I got ya," she says, flustered but not strained. Light-blue eyes that nearly match the wings of the Snowhawks logo meet mine, and man, if I don't feel like I won the falling on a fan lottery. She's beautiful.

I shout to be heard over the roar of the crowd, including someone shrieking very close by. "Are you okay?"

Someone's at my side now, and a few hands grab for my jersey as if they intend to haul me off her.

"I'm fine." It's matter-of-fact. As if this doesn't faze her at all. But then she yells, "Nobody move!"

The hands trying to help me go still but don't let go.

"Where are your feet?" she asks.

I tilt my head to the side. "What?"

"Your feet," she shouts back as if she thinks I couldn't hear her the first time, but that's not it at all. What kind of a question is that? "When I lift you off me, I don't want you to break an ankle. Last thing I need on my first game back."

I dial up the charm and give her my best smile. "Come here often?" She must if she's got first-row seats. Those only go to season ticket holders or special guests.

"Did you just use a pickup line on me?" She doesn't sound amused as she raises a skeptical eyebrow.

"Trying to lighten the mood."

She scoffs. "How about lightening the load? You're not a tiny guy."

I want to laugh at how she's echoed my thoughts. "Sorry. Let me get my foot out of the cupholder. I'm going to need to put a bit more weight on you for a second."

"I can handle you." Louder, she yells, "Dinah, calm down! I'm fine."

"Make some room," a gruff male voice commands, and several hands disappear let go of me. I glance up. The angle's awkward, but I can make out the bottom half of the word *security*.

I try lifting my stuck foot, but it won't budge. Instead, I have to pull my foot out of my cleat. That's how wedged the toe is into the cupholder. Then I use my foot to search around for a flat surface to stand on, eventually locating a spot on the seat she's sitting on. There's just enough room for me to put the ball of my foot onto it.

"Step back to the next seat," a second voice offers, this one female. "Seat's empty."

The owner of the second voice puts her arms under my shoulder as the security guard takes the other, lifting me off the fan I tried to crush in my misguided attempt to get an out. So much for making a good impression with the fans on my first day. They guide me to the empty seat next to the now not-squished fan. I lower myself to a squat in the seat as she sits upright and looks down at her shirt, a large white streak now running vertically up her chest.

"Ugh . . ."

"Did you get it?" a third voice rising above the noise of the crowd asks.

The fan's attention moves from her shirt to the umpire standing in front of the wall. "After all that, he better have."

"Get what?" I ask dumbly, too busy taking in the gorgeous young woman beside me.

"The ball!" she says exasperatedly, her intense gaze locked on me before she looks away. Not to me, she adds, "I don't think he hit his head." Though maybe I did with the way I can't stop staring at her. Or maybe that's all thanks to the talk in the Sailors locker room earlier about me being single. And now I've let their comments get to me, wondering if this pretty girl is also single.

I slide onto my butt so I'm sitting properly on the seat and look at my clenched gloved hand. The ball. It's there. I hadn't realized I'd made the catch until seeing it right now. I hold it up for the umpire to see.

The crowd erupts as the umpire yells "Out!"

"Not bad, huh?" I toss the ball to the ump with a look I hope he recognizes. He nods and slides the ball into his back pocket.

"At least it wasn't for nothing," the gorgeous fan says.

"Impressive catch," the second fan, the one who helped me off the first, says.

"Thanks." My gaze flicks toward her, and I smile before turning my attention back to the woman I'm next to. "Are you okay?"

She's wiping the sour cream off her shirt and rubbing it into her arm. Okay . . . "I'm fine. You?" She seems genuinely concerned.

I nod again.

"You should probably get back out there, then." She presses her lips into a tight line.

"Right." I pull off my glove so I can yank my shoe out of the cupholder, and once it's free, I notice the tube that I'd squeezed when my foot slipped. Sunscreen. Not sour cream. Way less weird to rub into one's arm.

I shove my foot back into my cleat and stand. "Um, thank you."

She furrows her brow in question. "For what?"

"For not letting me fall." The smile I give her is smaller this time, genuine. She really did save me. I owe her big time.

Her face takes on the slightest hint of pink, and man, if that doesn't make all of this worth it. Seems I do have an effect on her after all. "I've never dropped anyone before. Don't intend to start now."

What sort of an answer is that? This whole encounter has been . . . different. She's different. Someone I'd like the chance to talk to a little more. But right now, I have a game to get back to.

"Okay, well, bye." I nod at her, then her friend, then climb back over the wall. The ump offers me his hand. I don't need his help, but I take it. There's no need to pretend I'm some bigshot. With her, I think I need to show her I'm the exact opposite.

"Can you get word to team relations and ask them to put something together for me to thank her at the end of the game?" I ask the ump. "I'll sign the ball."

He gives me a knowing grin with a chuckle that suggests he knows something I don't. "Can do." He walks away, talking into the mic on his headset.

I double-check and make sure my cleat's secure before trotting back to first base, and the game resumes after what was only a few minutes' pause but felt like forever frozen in that moment.

Although I'm still not sure how I caught the ball to get the second out, when the next batter grounds out to third, the inning's over. I head to the dugout with the rest of the team, slowing the closer I get. The guys run past me, a couple slapping me congratulatory-like on the back, others paying me no mind, like Kyle.

"Nice one, man," Devon says as he continues down into the dugout. He's first up to bat this inning. I'm third, assuming I don't get benched. My manager looks pissed, his gaze locked on me.

As I hold my hands up in front of my chest, my thoughts flash to the fan and how her hands had been in almost the same spot not too long ago. I shake the thought away. Not the time or place for that. "I'm sorry. It was dumb of me to go after the ball like that."

"But you caught the ball." He crosses his arms, but he doesn't sound mad, more restrained.

"I did." I stop a few feet away from the steps to the dugout, allowing Devon to come bounding back onto the field with his bat, followed by our right fielder, Noah, I think his name is, who's on deck.

"Impressive save after all that." He lips curl into a smile, not unlike the one the umpire gave me. "You must have given Macey and her friends quite the surprise. Gale seemed only a little worse for wear after getting stuck under you."

"Macey? Gale?" Does he know the name of all the front row ticket holders? They are pretty close to the dugout. Easily within chatting distance, not that I've seen him head up there today.

"Macey is my daughter. And Gale, her best friend, is a Frost."

I blink. Several times. "A Frost? You mean a Frost Field Frost?" My gaze darts in her direction, where security is talking to her and her friends. I continue down into the dugout so she doesn't catch me looking.

"Ah, you pieced that together quick," my manager says with a single slow nod.

"Anyone who grew up in the region knows that name. Dustin Frost was a fantastic pitcher."

"And an even better manager. Led the team to multiple championships during his tenure. One of my best friends too, God rest his soul. Gale is his daughter."

I hang my head.

"She keeps a low profile these days, so I couldn't have expected you to know that, despite her famous family." He puts a hand on my shoulder. "But let's try to keep all the fans, no matter who they are, in one piece, all right?"

I groan. "It's not that." A raised eyebrow is all I get in response. "I asked for security to have her meet me after the game so I can sign the ball for her and get her whatever else team relations gives people when baseball players land on top of them." She must be swimming in signed baseballs.

He snorts. "Not sure if there's a standard fan package for when something like that happens, but I'm sure the girls will get a kick out of it. You'll do all right here, Nixon." The hand that had been on my shoulder gives me a hearty slap.

"Thanks, sir. I'll try not to let you down."

"See that you don't."

Chapter 7
Gale

The game ends with a Snowhawks' victory, and as the throngs of fans make their way through the grand concourse to leave, one of the security guards meets up with us at a locked doorway that opens onto the maze of hallways connecting the stadium's offices, some of them underground. It's faster getting to team relations this way.

"You really don't need to lead the way, Bob. I know my way around." Possibly even better than he does even though he's worked here for years. "I played hide and seek down here dozens of times." If not hundreds.

"Humor me," the older man says, trudging onward through the labyrinth, as I've heard it called numerous times. "If you won't let me treat ya like regular guests who gotta go the long way around while I regale them with random facts I've picked up during my time here, then you gotta let me walk you through the maze. What will the new first baseman think if you just pop out of a staff-only door instead of coming down the hallway as expected? Might scare the poor guy."

"No scarier than him crashing on top of me, but I see your point."

He barks a deep laugh, and if he had a long white beard and maybe another fifty pounds on him, he'd make a perfect Santa with a hearty *ho-ho-ho.* "Feels good to see you back down here, Miss Gale. Been a long time."

My mouth goes instantly dry as my throat tightens from his change of topic. Macey must sense this, as she wraps her arm through mine. "No need to walk these halls when you have an office door that opens onto the street." She squeezes my arm with hers.

I mouth her a quick "thank you" for saving me from responding, even if what she said isn't the whole truth. Even after my dad stopped managing the team, I was regularly down here for work purposes. But memories of him loom large down here, and these last several months, my assistant, Phoebe, has been my gofer if I've needed anything this way.

Dinah comes up on my other side. "And thank goodness for that street access. I'd never find you if your office was down here. Your lunch would probably get cold before it ever got to you." Since she works around the corner at the main office for the regional broadcasting network, Dinah and I regularly get together for lunch, swapping who picks up lunch on the way to the other's office. "Speaking of, lunch Tuesday?"

"Sounds good to me."

"Jealous!" Shelby says.

Dinah turns to look back at her. "You need a job closer to us then so you can take part. That goes for you too," she adds to Macey. Macey, for as often as she's here, doesn't have a job with the team.

"And what am I, chopped liver?" Bob asks with another hearty chuckle, and the comment sends me back to something my grandfather would say if I didn't say hello to him fast enough when I'd visit the team as a kid. Not in a mean way, of course, but it became a thing between me and him. I'd drag out my hellos and special handshakes with all the guys my dad played with before making it to my grandpa's side for the best hug. The memory doesn't cause me to seize up like mentions of my dad do. Grandpa died years ago, and the memories with him are warm and welcome, not painful and barely scabbed over.

Knowing the team doesn't have a home game then, I ask Bob, "They don't still have you working on non-game days, do they?" What I don't say is how that's usually a job for the younger guys.

"Nah, stopped doing that about three years back. I like my game-day schedule. I like working with the public, but then I get to be with the grandkids the other days and help my wife watch them while our daughter and her husband are at work." We turn another corner and are faced with a plain-looking door about twelve feet away. With no windows in it to provide privacy and added security, this door opens out into the hallway used by game-day personnel, including the players.

"Well here we are," Bob states as he reaches the door and turns the knob. "Now, cut the new guy a break, Miss Gale. Like I said before, I'm not sure he even knows who you are."

"I can be nice," I say, a bit of incredulity seeping into my voice. Plenty nice. My people skills are on point when work at the foundation requires it. I can turn them on when needed, but the rest of the time, I don't have that sort of persona. Never have. "And it's just Gale. I'm no one special."

"Aww, sure you are, Miss Gale. I owe your family a whole lot. Including this job."

"It was good to see you, Bob," I say before he can add more.

He gives me a kind nod, then opens the door and steps through it before telling us to follow him.

"That was so exciting!" Dinah says. "I've never done that before."

"Make sure I never have to do that again," Shelby says with a small shudder. "Especially not alone."

Dinah laughs, not entirely picking up on Shelby's unease. "And you used to play hide and seek down here, Gale? How did you not get lost?"

I shrug. "I have a good sense of direction, I guess." And a willingness to go through all the doors to help find my way. "But who said I never got lost?"

They think about this for a moment. "Good point," Dinah finally says. "Was it scary?"

"For everyone looking for me since the sound travels down there in weird directions? Probably. I thought it was fun."

Only a few yards down the hallway is the office for team relations. Beyond that is a door leading to the manager's and coaches' offices and the team's locker room.

Growing up, I was down that way all the time, but that's not my place now. Every so often, though it's been several months, I go through with kids who have chronic illnesses who wish to have a behind-the-scenes experience. We show them everything during those sorts of tours. Nothing held back. I love working with the kids and making them smile, giving them a bright spot in whatever is going on in their lives. Their families too. I know all too well what it's like to have a loved one go through something major like that.

Bob knocks on the door to team relations and a voice from inside the room hollers for us to come on in.

"This is weird," I state. "I've never done this part before. Been the expected visitor."

Bob opens the door and steps inside, pushing the door to its limit with his back so that my friends and I can walk inside.

"Hi, Eva," I give the woman in charge of team relations a polite smile and a small wave before setting my sights on Finn Nixon once more. "And hello to you too, Finn. I think getting up close and personal like that puts us on a first name basis."

He smiles broadly, a different smile than either I've seen on him up close, the fake big one and the real one that sent a wave of warmth running through me that made me blush. "It's nice to meet you too, Gale."

My rebel heart thrills at hearing him say my name. "Oh, so you know my name."

"You should have seen the ribbing I got after learning who you are." He turns slightly toward Macey. "Your dad especially."

"He's a big jokester once you crack that exterior. He means nothing by it." She sticks her hand out. "It's great to meet you. Quite a surprise you were today."

He places one hand at the back of his neck. "Yeah, you're telling me."

"Oh." He extends his other hand toward me. "Probably should have done this first." As I take his offered hand, his smile falters, but he quickly recovers it, his hazel gaze wide with . . . I'm not sure. Nervous energy? Or is it only me who has that right now? And why do I? Gosh, his hand is warm. And although his grip is firm, it's unexpectedly comfortable. In another life, his hand would be nice to hold on a regular basis. But I don't date baseball players. I've lived by that rule for years. Dinah, however, has no such rule.

"No worries," I say, dropping his hand that I've now

awkwardly shook for way too long, and then tug Dinah toward me. "This is Dinah. I'm sure you heard her, and this here is Shelby, who was next to her also getting an earful."

"Got a powerful set of lungs there, Dinah." He has no problem smiling for her, but it's different somehow. The nerves, if that's what was there, seem gone.

Dinah blushes. Why is she so starstruck? Maybe this really is our chance to set her up with a baseball player, despite it not being why we came to a game tonight. My gut clenches at this thought of them together, tightening the knot that's already there, although it shouldn't. He's off limits to me, not her.

"You meet ball players all the time," I tease her quietly, trying to get a read on her feelings for Finn as he shakes Shelby's hand. I'm not sure how I want her to feel.

Dinah leans in and matches my volume. "It's the tight pants. Usually when I see them this close, they're in jeans or dressed up for one of your events."

The comment has me looking. I'm only human. But as I follow the navy-blue line down his light-blue pants, appreciating the view, I gasp at the sight of his feet, mortified. "What is up with your cleats?"

Chapter 8
Finn

I glance down, doing my best to hide the telltale signs of my embarrassment over being called out like that. Thoughts of my childhood, when my shoes regularly drew attention for how ratty they were, run through my head. Not that I believe she was pointing them out to poke fun at me at all.

"I wish I could say it was a result of them getting stuck in your cupholder, but no, this is all thanks to my coloring them."

"Excuse me?" She seems completely lost, her brow furrowing. Clearly, she hasn't seen my video, or else she'd know all about it.

"Yeah," I begin, "These were mine from the Sailors. Guess they didn't have any my size stocked here." If I knew her better, or at all, I'd crack a joke about what they say about big shoes (big socks, what else?), but she doesn't seem the type who'd appreciate that. She made me chuckle a couple times with her comments earlier, but I get the feeling that witty, not funny, is her style.

Brows still drawn together, she says, "Oh, well, that's unfortunate."

"So anyway," Eva starts, cutting the growing awkwardness, "Gale, we wanted to present you with the ball that Finn, here, was going after when he crashed on top of you. He's signed and dated it, and there's a certificate of authenticity there too. In addition, there's the usual T-shirt and some playing cards in the bag, which I'm sure you have a ton of, but I put this together before I realized who I was doing it for." She nods toward a gift bag on the office coffee table made-up nicely with tissue paper flowing up from it in team colors.

Gale brightens, and the spark of life I see there further piques my interest. How can I get her to do that because of me? "I don't have this year's set of cards, actually. I'm sure I could have grabbed some eventually while doing foundation work, but I've always liked getting the set on opening day, and" —she deflates—"I obviously wasn't here for that."

Eva smiles understandingly, and Gale shakes off whatever she was thinking and continues at a much more level but conversational tone, "And I could use a new shirt after this one met its end thanks to the sunscreen." She swoops an open hand, palm up, in front of her shirt as if it's on display, once again showing me a bit of that spark from earlier. Much like how she eyed me a few minutes ago before noticing my shoes, my gaze slowly travels over her, and I like what I see. The faded white line trails up her shirt, getting lost in the Snowhawks logo, but it will probably leave a grease stain once it's washed.

"I thought it was sour cream at first," I admit, hoping she finds the truth funny.

The other girls giggle at this, but Gale raises an eyebrow at me. "Why would I have sour cream in my cupholder?"

That's a very good question, but luckily I have an answer and point to Macey. "I saw the baked potato in her hand."

Gale makes a face. "Sour cream does not belong on a

sausage and pepper stuffed potato. Nope." She continues shaking her head.

"Yeah, I probably wouldn't go for that either." Not that I wouldn't try it first just to be sure. But are we really talking about potatoes now? None of this has gone how I thought it would go. "But it does make a lot more sense as to why you rubbed it into your arms after wiping it off your shirt."

Her friends lose it at that comment, their giggles turning into full on belly laughs. At least they like me. But why do I care that they do and she seems not to? Because I find her interesting, that's why.

"Well, thank you for all of this. You really didn't have to." One corner of Gale's mouth ticks upward slightly. "It was one of the more . . . unique games I've been to."

That's probably an understatement given how many games she's no doubt seen, but there's something in the way she says it. "You sound unsure."

"No, I'm quite sure of that," Gale says matter-of-factly, and she crosses her arms, checking to see how they cover the stain. She lifts her gaze back up to me, blue eyes thoughtful and smile soft. I swallow hard as she studies my face, hoping she likes what she sees. "But I'm not sure how I feel about it, that's all. It was different."

There's something loaded about her statement, but it's not my place to unpack it. Especially not right now. "Well, it's not every game you have to catch a baseball player. That's certainly different."

"I'll say." She releases a puff of air through her nose as she half shrugs. "Maybe that was it."

It's not, but I won't pry. But whatever it is, my comment's loosened her up a bit, letting a bit more of the girl who caught me shine through her beautiful but guarded exterior.

Eva claps her hands, "Okay, how about a picture for social media?"

Gale drops her arms to her sides as she glances down at her shirt once more, shakes her head, then sighs before turning on her smile. It's pretty but one that's clearly put on for the cameras. "Okay." She walks over to my side but stops short of pressing up against me, keeping her distance and angling her body in what I assume is an attempt to hide the stains on her shirt.

Eva first snaps a photo of me handing Gale the baseball, my signature visible inside the sweet spot. Gale's arm is positioned awkwardly but strategically, and I get it, just for different reasons. When my shirts had stains on them growing up, I just had to deal with it. Couldn't afford new ones. Didn't make it any less embarrassing sometimes.

"I have an idea." After making sure Gale has a solid grip on the ball, I let go and take a few steps forward and then reach into the bag on the coffee table before pulling out the T-shirt. "How about one with this too?"

Holding onto one of the shirt's sleeves, I return to my spot by Gale's side and wrap my arm around her, pulling her in closer and confirming how well she fits next to me, only a few inches shorter. She smells of sunscreen and ballpark food, which combines to smell like summer fun.

Her breath catches, her eyes widening, and she noticeably stiffens against me. "What are you doing?"

"Hiding the stain," I say quietly, my face turned toward her ear so only she hears me. "I noticed it bothering you."

"Oh." Her tone warms, and she relaxes. "Thank you."

I reach around the front of her with my free hand to grab the other T-shirt sleeve, momentarily pulling her even closer. Her breath hitches once more, but she stays relaxed this time, and it thrills me that maybe she's finally warming up to me. I lift the shirt, covering up the entirety of the stain. "Hold the ball above the collar and you'll get a bit more coverage."

As she does, there's a subtle shift in her smile. I doubt the camera will even pick up on it, but at this distance, I can see the start of crinkles at the corners of her eyes. They weren't there before.

Eva takes a couple more photos before I say, "Now one with all of us. After all, they were all right there when it happened. Thanks to a particular shriek, my ear drum might never let me forget that." I chuckle. In truth, they probably deserve shirts as well, though they probably don't need them.

Thankfully, none of Gale's seem upset to not be getting a goodie bag. In fact, they're all laughing again, including Gale. The sound of hers is a personal victory because I made it happen. And want to do it again.

Gale's friends gather in, pushing around us hard enough that I need to brace myself to keep steady as Gale moves even closer to me.

"Okay, smile, everyone," Eva says, snapping away. She could do this for the rest of the evening and I wouldn't mind, but all too soon, she puts her camera down. The girls step to the side, and Gale shifts in my arms.

"Um, Finn?" she asks, and I focus on her. "Can you let me go now? You're kind of holding me in place."

I let go of the shirt and drop my arm that had been around her down to my side. "Oh, right, sorry. Here." I hand the shirt to her.

She folds it almost instinctively as she says, "Thanks again."

"Absolutely. And I'm sorry, again."

She nods. "Well, it's not chasing me away from my front-row seats. And I did get a new shirt out of it too, so don't feel too bad."

"So you'll be back?"

"Yeah." She glances back at her friends, who are chatting away with Eva as if they're all friends with her. Maybe they are. Gale's smile turns wistful as she says, "I've missed this."

"Well, I'll try not to fall on top of you again."

"That's probably for the best," Gale replies, no hint of teasing in her voice. She almost sounds sad. Then she reaches for the paper bag and slips both the T-shirt and baseball into it.

Ouch. I totally expected some sort of witty one-liner from her there. Not something that feels almost like, *yeah, please don't. I would rather this be our one interaction.* For a guy who happily makes a fool out of himself for views and likes, I'm not sure I've ever felt this foolish. Was I reading into things earlier? Does she really not like the shirt?

My shoulders slump, but I try to recover. "Well, have a good rest of your night."

"You too, and uh, welcome to Snowhaven. I hope you get your new cleats soon." She gives me a small smile, then turns and heads back to her friends before I can respond, leaving me to stare at how her ponytail of light-brown hair swishes across her back with each step.

The girls say a chorus of goodbyes, all talking over one another as they give me a wave while Gale leads the way out the door, casting a lingering look my way that gives me more hope than it probably should. The security guard follows them out, closing the door behind them but not before I hear him say something about team policy to them.

Eva clears her throat and holds her camera halfway up when I turn her way. "I'll look through the photos and figure out which one is best to use for social media. Clips of the play are already going viral, so I'm sure our fans will eat this up. All the better that it's Gale you landed on. She's practically royalty around here with how important her family has been to this team."

"She doesn't act like it." It comes out harsher than I intend it to, but I don't think Eva notices my tone as she clicks a button once and then again on her camera, its screen visibly bright. "Like royalty, I mean."

"No, she's never really been one for the spotlight, much happier to put others in it, though she's not afraid to wield her name for good causes."

"She mentioned something about a foundation? I take it she wasn't talking about the physical ones that support houses." I'm fishing for information, but Eva's still focused on the camera screen to realize it.

"Right. The Frost Foundation. It raises money for all sorts of causes. Gale's the driving force behind it. No one ever turns her down when she calls. If there's a cause you're particularly invested in, you should tell her. I bet she'd be glad to have your support."

"And she works here, at the ballpark?"

"Uh-huh." Still flipping through photos. "Her office is on street level, between gates four and five over on Frost Street, the pedestrian one that's closed to vehicular traffic on game days. Do you know it?"

"I'll find it. Ballpark's only so big. Thank you for this, by the way."

"Of course! I'm always happy to do this sort of thing." She looks up at me then. "And giving Gale something to smile about was nice too. Her dad died last year. We had a big memorial here for him on the field before the season began."

I never knew my father. He chose not to be a part of my

life. I have no idea if he's alive or dead, and it doesn't matter to me. Not anymore. But I can't imagine how it must be to lose someone close and then be surrounded by their memory daily on a scale like this. Maybe that's why she seemed reserved. Maybe it wasn't me at all.

Eva scrolls to another photo. "Oh, this is a cute one." She holds the camera out to me. "Do you want to see?"

I step toward her, my hand outstretched. "Absolutely."

She hands me the camera, and I turn it so the screen is facing toward me. This is the one before her eyes crinkled. I'm looking at her as her face is softening. Not all the way there, but reacting. I flip to the next one and see the genuine smile that crossed her face so briefly. We shared a moment. I'm not imagining it. "Can you send me these two?"

She nods.

"But use one of the group shots for social media. If you say she likes staying out of the spotlight as much as she does, then she'll like one of those best. Less attention on her."

Eva's face smooshes as if she's thinking *aww, that's so sweet.* And you could call it sweet, I guess, but if this photo would make Gale happiest, then that's what I want too. Why? I can't say exactly. I'm attracted to her, sure, she's gorgeous. Yet, this goes beyond that. There was just something about her, about that moment. I want to see her again. See if we can have another moment. "Thanks, Eva. I owe ya one."

"Just doing my job."

"You have a good night."

"You too, Finn. And good luck with whatever you just decided in that head of yours. Looks like you're on a mission."

Oh, I am.

Chapter 9
Gale

"Oh, this was the best night ever!" Dinah squeals as we leave the ballpark, her hands clapping together excitedly.

"I wouldn't call it the best night," I start, keeping my eyes glued to the sidewalk in front of us as we head to where Macey's car is parked. Although she has special parking privileges as the manager's daughter, she refuses to use it on game days. Can't say I blame her. The area around the park gets so crowded it would take ages to get out of here despite the prime parking. Not worth it. So we park a few blocks away, where the crowds have already thinned out and it's much easier to navigate out of by car. The fact it's close to one of the best ice cream places in town is only a coincidence, but a welcome one.

We walk into the ice cream shop, it's door already open in an attempt to lure customers in with the smell of fresh waffle cones and hot fudge.

At the rear of the group, Macey replies, "Sure it wasn't. Okay, little miss flirty pants. Spill."

I make the face made famous by that surprised blink meme

gif thing. "Me? Flirting? With who, Bob?" The alternative is even more ridiculous.

"No! With Finn, of course." She punctuates her statement with a sigh of exasperation.

"I was not flirting with Finn." I try to cross my arms, but the bag from team relations gets in my way, so I drop them back to my sides.

"Oh, I saw that look you gave him when you first walked in. You could have eaten him up until you got to his shoes."

We let the others get in line ahead of us, and I try to make myself appear engrossed in the menu of flavors as if talking about Finn doesn't faze me whatsoever. But let's just say Dinah isn't the only one who likes a guy in fitted baseball pants, though I prefer jeans. And although I won't date a baseball player, that doesn't mean I can't admire them when they're right there. The Snowhawks might not have had the right shoes for Finn tonight, but his pants fit him perfectly.

"Yeah, what was with the shoes, anyway? And I didn't forget about the whole coloring them in thing. I get that. But how do we not have shoes in his size?"

Macey shrugs. "Odd size? Common size and someone on the team already grabbed the last available pair? Sheer dumb luck? That trade happened quick. We weren't prepared. Given his own surprise about it, trying to blend in with the marker was a smart idea. Just be glad the Sailors have gray shoes and not bright-yellow ones like over in Sunny Valley. Can you imagine what a blue marker would have done to those?"

I picture the bright-green mess that would have been. "No thank you. But how do you know he was surprised by the trade?"

"It's on his social media page. He posted a video saying

goodbye to the fans of Sailor Nation and mentioned it. Hang on, I'll pull it up."

While she does that, I order a simple two-scoop cup of lemon and black raspberry ice creams, and as we wait for both of our cups to get scooped, she shows me the quick clip.

"Oh, wow. Look at how many reactions he's gotten to it. If only the foundation could get that sort of traction." Try as I might, I've never been able to get social media to work for me. Maybe because I barely use it as an individual. Phoebe often takes care of the foundation's accounts for me.

"You could always ask him for pointers. I bet he'd be all too happy to help."

I shake my head. "He gets all of that because he's a baseball player. He's famous."

"Kind of like someone else I know . . ." Macey eyes me as if her hint is obvious, which it is.

"I'm not that level of famous, and I don't want to be." Too many people reaching out because of who my family is. Dad dying made it worse. Although I appreciate that people were moved enough to write after his passing, I didn't need strangers coming into my personal inbox and tagging me in their comments to the official statement on the team's accounts.

Macey shrugs just as our ice creams are placed on the high counter running along the top of the ice cream coolers in front of us. She takes both and hands me mine. "Still, he had to start somewhere."

"I'll take it under consideration." We join the others at the table they picked out in a back corner, as far away from the street noise as possible. After several hours at a game, where we have to sometimes shout to talk to one another, quiet is just what we're looking for. Though, we're anything but as we continue to catch up with each other.

I'm scraping the last of my ice cream out of the cardboard cup several minutes later when the conversation once again turns to my encounter with Finn.

"So it was nice of him to get you that shirt," Dinah begins. "How many do you have now?"

"Well, once I retire this one"—I point down at the stain on my shirt with a chuckle (when did I reach the point of laughing about what happened?)—"at least enough for a week."

"Or three," Macey quips, and I eye her. She holds up her free hand in surrender. "All I'm saying is I know how many I have, and there's no way you only have a week's worth of shirts."

Once upon a time, I had way more, back when I couldn't be caught dead in the same shirt too soon after wearing it. Teenagers. College living, especially the need to haul my laundry up and down multiple flights of dorm stairs, taught me the benefit of downsizing my wardrobe. "I donated a lot of the stuff I used to wear but don't anymore. So some have gone on to new homes. And I don't count the ones I won't wear for sentimental reasons." Those, usually created for special events or anniversary years, stay in a bottom drawer. I have some going back to when I was a baby.

As a family organization at its core, the Snowhawks always include players' significant others and kids when it comes to commemorative gear. Staff too. I still haven't taken the one from this year out of the bag, though it's in my drawer. The design incorporates a silhouette of my dad's profile on one arm, his last name—my last name—across the shoulder blades, just above his number from his playing days. It was touching, what the team did, even going so far as to make a few extra to raffle off for charity at my request, but it's a little much for me to look at, let alone wear.

"So are you actually going to wear this new one, or is it going straight to your sentimental pile?" Shelby asks.

There is not nearly enough ice cream left for where this is going. But since my friends aren't going to let me drop this subject, I head directly for it. "Why would it be sentimental?"

"It marks the occasion of you meeting the swoony Finn Nixon," Dinah answers for her and Shelby nods. They all eagerly await my response, their eyes wide with merriment.

"Oh, he's swoony now? His tight pants must have done a number on you, Di."

"Don't think we didn't catch you checking him out as well."

"Told you," Macey teases under her breath.

Dinah leans in as if she's ready to hear a juicy secret. "So tell us, how were those muscles?"

Hard. Very hard. "I was too busy trying to keep him from falling to notice."

Shelby shakes her head with a sigh. "And how about when his arm was wrapped around you for the photo? There was no threat of falling there. You two looked mighty cozy."

"Oh my gosh, we were not." Why did I blow through all my ice cream so quickly? I need to cool my rapidly heating face down.

Macey pulls out her phone and swipes the screen repeatedly before turning it back to us. "Oh, no? This looks cozy to me."

I stare at the photo on the team's social media page, fighting a small smile from creeping onto my face. "That's actually a cute photo . . . Of all of us. Of course it's cozy, we're trying to squeeze in and make room." I think back to our postgame meet and greet. Had I said anything about not liking being the center of attention? No. Neither had the girls. Eva would know, and it was probably her decision as to which picture to include on the post, but Finn was the one who had requested the group shot in the first place. And he'd been the one to suggest the pose that would prevent people from seeing the stain on my shirt. How could he tell I was uncomfortable?

"Earth to Gale." Macey pulls the phone out of my hand. When did I even take it from her? She points to the corner of her mouth. "You've got a little something right here."

Thinking it's ice cream, I wipe my mouth with a napkin. But it comes away clean.

Macey smirks. "Sorry, thought there was a bit of drool."

"Drool? What? No. I do not drool."

"You and I both know that's not true." She laughs. "Years of summer sleepovers prove you do. But I'm talking about drool from the way you zoned out staring at his picture. Admit it. You think he's hot."

Macey always has been able to see right through me, and our decades-long friendship from our dads' playing and coaching time together means there's no point in trying to deny it. But I don't need to fully admit it either, not when it doesn't matter.

"I can appreciate a ball player in tight pants just like anyone else can," I reply, shooting a glance Dinah's way, hoping she'll back me up and we can get off this topic.

Instead, she squeals with excitement. "You should go for it. He was totally into you."

"There's nothing to go for, and he totally was not. He was being nice because it was a meet and greet."

"And there were four of us there, and he could barely take his eyes off you," Shelby points out. Great, now even she's getting on my case about this. As both the designated mom of the group and having dated someone on the team before, she usually stays out of relationship drama. Not that this is a relationship.

"Et tu, Brute?"

She shrugs. "What? It's a fact."

I sigh. "Even if there is a mutual physical attraction there, and I'm not saying there is, nothing is going to happen between us. We're way too different."

"How so?" Macey asks as if the answer isn't obvious.

"You saw him out there doing flips and dancing whenever he got the chance. Before and after his risky play to catch that ball. One wrong step and he could have broken an ankle, and then where would the team have been? Or if it hadn't been me to catch him when things went sideways? That could have been an arm or a neck right there."

"Oh, come on, it was fun. You can have fun too, you know. You do when you let yourself."

"Today was fun." Even with whatever happened with Finn. I'm not going to lie about that. I take my bestie's hand and give it a squeeze. "It was great to be at a game again, and I love you all for tricking me into it. But you know my stance on dating baseball players. He is not the type of fun I should falling for. I have the foundation to focus on and an image to maintain for that. It's my family's legacy. Allowing myself to have fun with Finn—or any ballplayer—would only detract from that. I don't need the sort of attention that comes from dating players." As I drop Macey's hand, I turn toward Shelby, looking for her to back me up about that statement.

"I dunno," she says a little too wistfully. "It wasn't all bad." When did she change her tune about that? She used to hate the cameras that popped up whenever she went out with the team's second baseman.

This is the topic we should be focusing on, and I try to

catch Macey's attention so she can jump on it, but she's on her phone again.

"Cassie just texted." The mention of our long-distance bestie draws my attention away from Shelby's comment. "She's already seen the photo. And if you're trying to avoid gaining attention from this, I have some bad news for you."

My eyes widen as the constant knot that lives in my stomach tightens and loops back in on itself.

"Finn's stunning catch is going viral, and right behind it in popularity is the photo of us all at the meet and greet."

This time, I snatch the phone out of her hand. Regional news outlets have already picked up the photo released by the team, showing it right after the clip from the game. Beneath it on the site Macey's on is the caption: *Finn Nixon meets with Gale Frost, daughter of late Snowhawks manager and pitcher Dustin Frost and granddaughter of her namesake and Snowhawks team founder the late Gale Frost; Macey Brockmann, daughter of current Snowhawks manager Mack Brockmann; Shelby Hillard, former girlfriend of Snowhawks second baseman Toby Sutton; and Dinah Scholand, an employee at our own FBN office, after Nixon's successful catch of a pop foul resulted in his landing on top of Frost in the stands.*

This is my worst nightmare.

Chapter 10
Finn

The locker room has mostly cleared out by the time I get back from meeting Gale and her friends. I unbutton my jersey and hang it on a hook inside my open locker. It's more like a cubby, but it fulfills its purpose and is much faster to put my stuff away. Or to shove my head into like I do now. That did not go how I expected it to.

I take a deep breath, finding my resolve to figure Gale out. There's something about her, and I'm determined to win her over.

"Meeting with Frosty not go so well?" Devon asks as he slaps me on the back, causing my head to wedge further into my cubby. Great, now I'm stuck, but that's not why my annoyance rises into the back of my throat, causing me to clench teeth.

"Frosty?" I grit out. And I thought he was a good guy up till now.

"What? You're muffled."

I place my hands on either side of the cubby, finding enough leverage to pull my head out of the space. My cap stays momentarily suspended between the sides of my cubby before plopping on top of my very squished duffel bag.

"Frosty?" I repeat once I face the half-dressed Devon, crossing my arms. He's roughly my height, maybe has a few pounds on me, but I'm all muscle and could take him. Who says that about someone, let alone a Frost, especially on this team?

And whoa, why am I so bothered by it?

"Relax, man," Shane Montclair, our catcher, says as he comes walking into the locker room dressed in his street clothes. "It's a childhood nickname. One I gave her actually."

I drop my arms, relief making them feel lighter. "You grew up with Gale?"

"Yeah, she hung around with my best friend's sister." He slings his much smaller duffel over his shoulder.

"You two ever . . ." I don't finish the statement. It's a good idea to find out if she's off-limits before I think of something better than a T-shirt to give her. Don't need a teammate think I'm encroaching on his girl.

Shane snorts before barking out a single laugh. "Gale and me? Oh, no. She's all yours if you can get her to break her rule about dating ballplayers. Just don't go calling her Frosty until you get to know her better."

"You like Gale?" Devon says enthusiastically, his face brightening like a kid who just saw his presents from Santa under the tree, before growing quiet. "Oh . . ." he continues as understanding dawns on him. "You thought I was insulting her? Nah, I mean, if you didn't know her, she could come off as a bit chilly, but Gale's great, though she could stand to relax a bit. She's always so serious."

Serious but intriguing like a present when you have no idea

what's inside it beyond the little you've seen after carefully lifting the tape at one end to peek inside.

Ugh, what's with the Christmas analogies tonight? Probably that flyer about the foundation's Christmas in July gala coming up. I noticed the first one when I set foot into the locker room before the game this afternoon, but since then, I've spotted a few more scattered around the team's space.

Christmas comparisons aside, Gale gave me a peek of who she is under her serious exterior when she laughed with her friends and as she tried to make me feel better about such a generic gift from team relations. Despite what she said, she's probably got a ton of T-shirts and signed balls from everyone who's ever been on the team. I can do better than that. And maybe our next encounter won't be so awkward.

"Curious about her, is all," I'm finally willing to admit. "Not every day I fall on top of the granddaughter of the team's founder. Felt dumb giving her a team T-shirt once I learned who she is."

Shane shrugs. "There's always flowers."

"Isn't that a little cliche?"

Shane shrugs again, his bag slipping down his arm. "Girls like flowers. Send them to the foundation office."

"Oh, yeah," Devon says as if this is the greatest idea ever. I'm glad he wasn't making fun of Gale and is the decent guy I thought he was when I met him. "Then you can see if she puts them out for everyone or keeps them in her office. There's a whole language to flowers."

Flowers have their own language? He seems serious, so I'll take his word for it. "Got it. Flowers I can do." Though they still don't seem personal enough. I glance at the flyer for the foundation's gala on the wall beneath the clock, and an idea materializes. I point. "You guys go to this?"

Shane seems to already know what I'm referring to. "A lot of us do. It's good PR and helps draw interest from the fans. More interest means more tickets sold."

"You just have to show up?"

"Show up and look good," Devon replies, drawing out the word *good* and dropping his voice. He pretends to pop the collar of his non-existent shirt, then shines his knuckles against his chest.

Shane rolls his eyes as if embarrassed for our teammate. "At least for the gala. Some of us show up at other events to help out and donate to the various causes. Gale always makes sure to keep us in the loop." He hikes his bag back onto his shoulder.

"Got it, thanks. I won't hold you up any longer."

"See ya around, Finn. Good work today. Try not to show us all up next time." To Devon, he adds, "See ya at home for breakfast tomorrow, cuz."

I whip my head back to Devon. "You two are cousins?"

"Yeah, on our mom's side, so different last names."

I unbutton my shirt, then hang it on a hook in the cubby. Team services will come by and wash this one. Then hopefully have more for me for future games. And some team issued cleats. Hopefully they're as comfortable as my old ones. Knowing I'll never wear them again, at least not past tomorrow, I step on the back of one to pull it off, then do the same with the other. But these I put in my bag. Call me sentimental.

"What's that like? Playing with family."

"I love it. And I love that he grew up here and that my aunt is a good cook. Home-cooked meals are the best."

A twinge of jealousy pangs me as I nod as if understanding that fact completely. Home-cooked meals weren't a common thing for me growing up in my single-parent household. My ma was always so busy working multiple jobs. I try my best to make stuff now, but I don't find it as fun to cook for myself as I imagine it would be for someone else. Gale's image flashes in my mind. What sort of food does she like? Potatoes obviously. Sausage and peppers too. Sour cream is still an unknown.

"I barely do more than heat up frozen food or call for delivery," Devon continues when I don't respond. "Where you staying?"

"The college dorms."

"I'll wait for you to shower, then I'll go with ya."

Good because no one told me how to get there. "You don't stay with Shane and your aunt?"

"Nah. Don't want to crowd them out of the one bathroom." He smiles. "I do my laundry there, though."

I grab my street clothes out of my duffel. "Does the college not have laundry?"

"They do. But you gotta pay for it."

"So you go to your aunt's so she can do your laundry for free," I joke.

"I'm perfectly capable, but my aunt enjoys taking care of her boys. Home-cooked meals and free laundry. You should come with me sometime."

"Yeah, I might just do that, thanks." I grab my stuff, then head to the showers, which I have to say are much nicer than what the Sailors have. Being an established team with a bigger bankroll has its perks.

Fifteen minutes later, I'm heading out of the ballpark with Devon playing tour guide in his SUV. He points out various places as we drive by, where to get the best tacos, the best Chinese, the best pita pockets, the best pizza—guess he really wasn't joking about how often he calls for delivery—and ten minutes later, we're turning onto a winding road uphill toward the college campus I'm about to call home for a while.

"How many of the guys live here?" I ask as the car climbs to the third tier of the campus, a good couple hundred stairs above the first tier, which is raised above street level. There's one more tier above us, leading to the athletic area if the football goalposts are anything to go off. I can only imagine the workout everyone must get walking around on campus.

"Most of us first season players. Several veteran players who live elsewhere during the offseason do too, though some rent apartments together just for the season." He laughs. "Kyle has a place of his own, to get away from the rest of us, I'm sure.

Once Devon parks the car in the lot, it's a short walk to the campus security office. For as rushed as my trade was, I'm relieved when the guard there says they've been expecting me. I'm in and out within a few minutes, swipe card in hand to get into the building and a key to get into my room.

From there, Devon and I head to a three-story brick dorm building across the lot, stopping quickly to grab our stuff from his trunk.

"We're on the first floor," he tells me as he waves his card in front of the scanner by the door. Thank goodness there aren't more stairs. I can't imagine finishing a night game, then having to trudge up extra flights of stairs to crash.

He invites me out with some of the guys for a late dinner, but I excuse myself on account of the day it's been. There will be plenty of bonding time later. I open the door to my room. It's fully furnished with a mini-fridge, microwave, and coffee maker. The bed's already got sheets on it too. If it weren't for the cream-colored cinderblock walls and cheap laminate tile floor, it could almost pass for a hotel.

I drop my duffel onto the floor and pull my phone out of my pocket before flopping onto the bed. This day has been one for the books, not least of all my now viral highlight of falling onto Gale. For someone who tries to avoid the spotlight, she's probably upset I thrust her into it. No doubt this will be on my highlight reel all season. I owe it to her to do something that will pull it off the Jumbotron sooner rather than later. And I owe her something better than a T-shirt, and that is something I can take care of tonight.

Chapter 11
Gale

I fly solo to the day game on Sunday. Somewhat solo, anyway. Somewhere along the third-base line sits Macey in disguise. I hadn't told her I was coming, and when Finn's first time up at bat highlights his catch yesterday afternoon, the cameras find me in the stands. With a tight smile, I flick my wrist to the side once for a wave.

Once upon a time, I ate up this attention. My mother thrust me into the spotlight, both on the pageant stage (which I hated) and the dance one (which I loved). I wouldn't put it past her if she's the reason the cameras first followed me in the baseball stands too, highlighting me as a cute kid waving excitedly in moves large enough to catch my dad's attention on the mound—not during the active parts of the game, of course. After my parents divorced, creating a media storm, and my mother left, the cameras found me yet again as a teen finding her way in the world and trying to make a name for herself by looking cool.

Even as a college student, finally twenty-one and able to live it up a bit in the stands, the cameras continued to show me attending games because of who my family is. Unfortunately, those times resulted in some of my not-so-finer moments, and I was told as much. "Frosts have an image to uphold," they said.

Now? I'm happily running the team's charitable foundation that my grandfather started. I'm not just some figurehead put there because of who I am and who my family is either. I went to school for nonprofit management. Utilizing my experience, the Frost Foundation supports charities and causes that directly benefit those in the local community. And while I may hold a lot of sway in what charities the organization supports and what events get held, I don't have the only say. I have a board to answer to, so I don't always get my way. It almost makes me feel normal in what is not a normal situation.

But now, thanks to Finn's spectacle of a catch, I'm front and center once again. Maybe Macey is right and I should use this to my advantage for the good of the foundation.

My phone buzzes with an incoming text.

MACEY

You didn't tell me you were coming.

ME

Last-minute decision. How is Cordelia's seat?

She sends me a photo of her view.

Better for watching third base but farther from the field. Want company?

And put your foolproof disguise to waste?

Good point. Did Finn see you?

I cast my gaze to home plate, where he's squaring up for a 1–1 count.

> He waved earlier. Or at least I think he waved.

I don't tell her that while everyone else was focused on his highlight reel as he walked to the plate from the on-deck circle, he was looking at me, seeing what my reaction was to being on the big screen again. How my cheeks that the cameras showed in all their pink glory are that way more from his gaze than embarrassment.

> What do you mean you think he waved?

> There was a waving motion, but it was definitely part of a larger warmup routine. When he repeated it, not looking at me that time, the wave part wasn't there.

Finn swings and misses, making it a 1–2 count.

> PLEASE tell me you waved back and that it was better than what I just saw you do up there.

> I used my fingers. Is that better?

> All of them, right?

> YES! Like I'm going to be mean to someone on the team. Who do you think I am?

My dad and grandfather would have chewed me out for even thinking about it. And for the record, I was not.

> Just checking. I know you aren't happy about going viral.

The crack of Finn's bat pulls me away from my phone. It's

a short grounder that sends the first baseman for the other team scrambling to get it, then it's a footrace to the bag. Tie goes to the runner, and I clap my hands together loudly, nearly dropping my phone. With two outs, he's kept the inning alive and moved the runner before him to second.

Everyone's cheering along with me, so there's no way he'd be able to hear me over the noise, but as our leadoff hitter takes his position at the plate, Finn's gaze finds mine. It freezes me for a beat, my hands together around my phone in an awkward prayer-like pose. A flash of a smile breaks out across his face as if he knows the effect he has on me. As the pitcher winds up for his throw, Finn turns his attention back to the game, breaking the spell.

I drop my hands but not my full focus on him, only partly aware of what's going on at home plate. The batter's range is typically between third and second base, so I don't have the same worry about foul balls on this side of the field. On a 1–0 pitch, he makes solid contact. The ball bounces once before the left fielder catches it, and although Finn's already made it to second base, the inning ends with an out at third.

Finn glances my way as he jogs back to the dugout, and I nod in acknowledgement.

My phone buzzes in my hands once more.

Man he's good.

He's something.

What does THAT mean?

And in truth, I'm not entirely sure. But as he comes running back out onto the field, backwards, before doing a back tuck, I have to wonder if that move was so he'd have another chance to look this way, and what it means that this sort of stunt doesn't bother me the way it did just yesterday.

The ballfield is bustling with activity when I get into work on Monday morning.

Last night's game ended with the Snowhawks losing by one. We can't win them all, although I wish we could. But with having won Saturday, today's getaway game is a rubber match. The game starts at eleven, which means I can sneak away from my desk for my lunch break to watch the game. With food from the concessions stand of course.

No more than ten minutes into my workday, Phoebe, my assistant, knocks on my partially open door.

"Come on in," I tell her, pulling up my calendar for the week. The Christmas in July gala is three weeks away, and I need to finalize some of these plans. The final count of attendees is due soon, and I'm meeting with the baker in Heartwood Hollow to choose cupcake flavors for our dessert table. With the gala raising money for the mobile skin cancer screenings offered by the hospital located there, it only makes sense to use their local baker. Plus, her cakes are simply magical.

Phoebe steps into my office, half hidden by a large bouquet of red and white flowers with sprigs of holly and pine boughs.

I stand from my desk to help her. "I thought I had received all of my flower samples for the centerpieces last week."

The back of the bouquet shifts slightly back and forth. "Not a sample. There's a card. It's for you."

"Me?" Who in the world would be sending me flowers? I take the vase of flowers from her and set it on a side table so I can read the card. I lift the flap of the small envelope and pull out the single-sided cardstock.

Gale,
Thought these might be nicer than just a shirt for falling on top of you. I'm sorry for that, by the way, again, but I'm glad I got to meet you. Hope to catch you at another game, not the other way around.
Your friendly first baseman,
Finn

I smile at the witty line about catching me at a game. He must have arranged to have these sent on Friday because there's no way he didn't see me yesterday. But why? The T-shirt was perfectly fine, and there was a signed baseball as well. Sure, that's now wrapped in a sock in my drawer to keep it safe until I can fit it in my display with the others, per instructions from my friend Cassie, who works at the regional baseball museum, but it will be out with the rest soon. Those were enough. But now flowers too?

"Secret admirer?" Phoebe asks, breaking my concentration.

I shake my head. "Definitely not a secret. Admirer, maybe?"

"Well, whoever it is must know about the gala because, you're right, had this come last week, it would have blended in with the rest of them. This is too specific for some random bouquet. Right now, all of the flower specials are Fourth of July themed, which this definitely isn't. The very Christmassy poinsettias steal the show in this one. So whoever it was is trying to impress you and not taking the easy way out."

"The easy way?"

"Red and white roses. Not one in sight."

I file away that statement, unsure of what to make of it. "Thanks for bringing these to me. Do we still have vases?"

She blows a raspberry. "Only about a dozen. They're under the sink. Want me to grab you one?"

"No. I'll be right out, thanks."

Phoebe spins away and out of my office, and after placing the card from Finn onto my desk, I leave as well, heading for our little break room. It has little more than a small fridge, a sink, and a microwave. Across from the narrow countertop with a tiny sink is a high bistro-style circular table with two tall chairs on either side of it. No one actually sits there, not when the main room of the foundation's office has a couch and coffee table that work just as well for eating, but it's a great place for leaving snacks.

I open the cupboard door under the sink, and pull out a swirly clear vase. It reminds me of a candy cane, just without the added color, and it will go great with the flowers.

Back in my office, I grab my phone and snap a pic of the overwhelmingly large bouquet. I want to remember how beautiful they look. Then I arrange half of the flowers into the second vase. Once I'm done, I have two respectable bouquets and can still utilize part of my side table. I carry the one in the swirly vase out into the main room and place it on the coffee table.

"Oh, how pretty!" Phoebe says from her desk. If she had more room, I'd have put it there, but even an arrangement this size would block her view of nearly half the room.

"I know we typically donate the bouquets we get to the nursing home, but since this one was a gift to me, I figured it's okay to keep here. It was just way too big to not share."

"It looks great," she says sincerely. "I think it's wicked sweet of whoever to have gotten them for you." She gives me a pointed look, trying to break me down so that I'll tell her, but I am not going to make Finn's flowers a big deal. Though, keeping it from her probably is doing just that.

I sigh. "Finn Nixon."

Her eyes light up. "Oh, he's a cutie."

"Is he?" I try to play it up as if I hadn't noticed.

"You have seen him, right?" She laughs. "Of course you have. All close and up in each other's business."

"We were not up in each other's business. I kept him from falling after he, well, fell. My hands were firmly on his chest. Not his business." My cheeks heat and no doubt they're rivaling the color of the poinsettias right now. "Ugh . . . That came out all wrong."

Phoebe's glance turns wicked. "Or completely right. So . . . why's he sending you flowers?"

"Because he said a team shirt seemed silly because of who I am and how many I must have."

"He clearly hasn't seen you at work before."

I glance down at my team T-shirt—yes, the one he gave me —and professional white blazer combo paired with gray dress slacks and navy flats. "How could he? He just got here."

"You know what I mean. You live in your shirts. Or you used to. I have to say, it's good to see one back on you." She gives me an understanding smile over the unstated reason why I wasn't wearing them for a while.

"Thanks. I'm maybe finally starting to feel like me again." I owe the girls so much for getting me to a game. "Are you joining me for lunch today?"

"There's no way I'd miss a getaway game."

A couple hours later, I'm about to leave the office to head to lunch and an hour of baseball. My blazer's off, too dangerous of a color to wear with all of that concessions food, my sunscreen is on, and my stomach is growling. On a whim, I grab a red carnation from the vase on my side table and snap the stem so it's not unwieldy, then tuck it above my ear.

Phoebe's waiting for me by the door, her jacket off, revealing a short-sleeve navy blouse, and her hair's pulled back into a quick ponytail. She taps the empty spot above her ear when she sees me, and a Cheshire grin appears across her face.

"I like the new accessory," she teases.

I shrug. "How else am I supposed to let him know I got his flowers? You remember sunscreen on the back of your neck?"

"Sure did." She shows me the tube in her purse.

"Great let's go." I open the door, turning the sign hanging from it from *Open* to *Enjoying the Game* along with a number to call that will send a message to Phoebe's phone. A quick glance at the street-side door reveals Phoebe already flipped the sign there. That one doesn't have a number, though. We learned that lesson the hard way with too many crank calls a couple summers back from people just walking by.

I let Phoebe leave first, then close the door behind me, already able to smell the food on the grand concourse.

Chapter 12
Finn

Three innings into the game, I've got to face facts. She's not coming today. Not that I should have expected her to come to every game, but after her appearance yesterday, I had hope. Seeing her on the big screen, looking less than thrilled by the attention drawn to her, made me glad I had ordered those flowers to be delivered today. Has she gotten them by now? I wasn't given a specific time, and I only arranged for a workday delivery.

Which is probably why she's not here. She's working. I sigh.

"Chill, man," Devon says as he stands in front of me in the dugout, rolling his shoulders to stay loose during the bottom of the inning. He's seen me glance to where she sat the last two games enough times in the last two innings to guess what's on my mind. "If you take a fast shower, you'll be able to see her before we head out. She'll be here past game time at the foundation offices."

I stop bouncing my leg. "I'm not heading out with you all, remember?"

"Oh, right."

I'm not looking forward to the trip to grab my stuff, but fortunately, there's not a lot I need to grab. The Sailors player called up to replace me is going to sublet nearly everything, including my furniture, so it's just my personal effects and clothes that I've got to take care of. Shortly after the game, I'll grab a rental car and drive down to Saltair Shores. Tonight and tomorrow morning, I'll load the car, then I'll drive back to Snowhaven and take a commercial bus to meet the team.

When the number six hitter, our center fielder, returns to the dugout after getting an out, Devon grabs his bat and helmet to head up to the on-deck circle, leaving me with my thoughts once more.

Focus on the game, Finn.

I stand, joining some of my team at the metal fence that protects people from falling into the recessed dugout.

Devon takes a swing, then adjusts his gloves. With the latest rules in place, he doesn't have the same sort of time to do all that between pitches, so he's getting comfortable now. He brings the bat up behind his neck, grabbing on to it with his free hand and puffing out his chest as he walks in a circle, staring out at the crowd.

As he turns back to the dugout, he's got a Cheshire cat grin, and he's staring straight at me. Waggling his eyebrows, he quirks his head to the side.

I pull myself up and out of the dugout to try to see what he keeps glancing at, going partway underneath the lowest rung on the fence, but the angle of the wall is too steep from here and I can't see anything. I drop back onto my feet as Kyle, our number seven hitter, earns a walk. He jogs toward first base, and Devon releases his hold on the bat with one hand, letting it swing down as he lowers the other before approaching home plate.

That's my cue. I head toward the stairs, barely stopping to take my bat and helmet, putting the helmet on in one fluid motion with my left hand while sticking the knob of the bat onto the palm of my right so that it's sticking straight up. To the fans, it looks like I'm balancing it there, and I am, but only partially. My palm is slightly cupped, giving me a bit of a hold as I follow the sway of it toward the on-deck circle, keeping one eye on home plate to stay aware of what's going on and another on—

She's here.

In my distraction, the top of my bat leans too far forward and begins to topple. I grab the knob, pushing it away from me to over correct and guide the bat onto my shoulder. It's messier than I would have liked, but hopefully comes smoother to the unknowing eye.

That must have been what the strange look Devon was giving me meant.

But her being here isn't what catches my eye the most. She's wearing the shirt she got the other night. Blue really is her color. It works with everything about her, from her barely sun-kissed complexion to her light-brown hair pulled up in a pony-tail to her blue eyes. It even works with the wrapper for the burger she's chowing down.

Devon slices the ball to center field, entering a no-man's-land that sends three fielders scrambling for it. He easily gets to first, and now it's my turn to bat.

I cast one last look toward Gale as I head to the plate, and this time, we make eye contact as she sips a drink. She smiles around her straw and points up to her ear, where a bright-red flower rests.

Guess that answers my earlier question.

I nod in her direction, flashing her a smile before turning back toward home plate, feeling lighter than I have all game.

With a 3–0 count, I dig in. Most would tell me to take the next pitch no matter what it is, but Coach always told me to act on instinct because mine was good. So when the pitcher releases a fast ball, I go for it and swing.

When contact is made just right, there's a sound that indicates you've hit the sweet spot of the bat. The crack echoing away from me tells me I got it, that the ball is going far. Still, I take off running to first. As a kid, I'd watch how some players would stand there watching the ball go when they knew they'd hit it out of the park before breaking into a trot around the bases. I don't have that luxury. Although my batting average is solid and my home runs are up this season, I don't know the field well. This could easily be a long fly ball, ready to be caught for an out, or it could take a lucky dive onto the field, and then I'd have to beat out the throw.

It's not until I'm steps away from the bag that my first-base coach waves me on, his arm circling with his finger pointing up, that I can slow down a bit and take this moment in, so I do.

Up in the first row of the stands is Gale, on her feet, her hands framing her mouth as she cheers . . . for me. I've never had that before. No family or significant others or friends that were only mine at a game. Although this must be something Gale does all the time, with that flower in her hair, this is the closest I've come to having someone be there for just me.

A warm sort of excitement swells in my chest as I hit second, round third, and high five Devon and Kyle when I reach the plate. Then I grab my bat and head toward the dugout, spotting Gale, still standing, still cheering, but this time turned toward me. She extends her hands forward as I approach, still clapping, a full-fledged smile on her face. She's gorgeous.

I tip my helmet toward her before lifting it up and waving first to her and then to everyone. With any luck, this is one for the highlight reels. Then with a wink in Gale's direction, which earns her a friendly elbow in the side from the girl she's with, I head back into the dugout, where the guys greet me by smacking my helmet as I pass by. Note to self: take the helmet off before I reach the base of the stairs.

The bottom of the inning ends after two more batters but no more runs. We're up by two. I race up to the field with my glove, throwing it high in the air and spinning around, clapping my hands once. I do it again, only this time, I clap my hands twice. And again, three times. The second baseman's signals he's ready to throw. I slip my glove on, and he tosses me the ball. I flip as I throw it back. Usually I keep that to pregame warmups, but Gale's here now. I gotta show off a bit. Whether it's my imagination and wishful thinking or not, it's like I can feel her staring at my back, cheering me on.

We make it through that inning and the top of the next, keeping our opponents from scoring. After fielding the last out of the fifth inning, I smile at Gale. She taps at her wrist where a watch would be, then waves, only half of her mouth curved up into a smile. Her friend who's with her stands, and she does too. Did they come here to catch only a few innings?

Then I remember what Devon said about her working. A lunch break. And now it all makes sense. I'm bolstered by the fact she seems disappointed to leave. I hold up my hand with the ball inside it, splaying my fingers to wave while keeping the ball steady with my thumb. That sends the crowd around Gale cheering. It takes a moment, but I realize they think I'm going to toss the ball toward them, so I jog up to the railing separating the stands from the field, and that's what I do. With my hand free now, I wave properly at Gale and her friend.

"Back to work?" I call to her as she walks into the aisle.

She nods. "Unfortunately. It's shaping up to be a great game. Congrats on the home run."

"Thanks. Was saving it until you got here."

Her cheeks flush slightly, and she smiles gently, but her friend looks ready to burst with excitement over our interaction.

"Nixon!" my manager yells from the top of the dugout.

My eyes widen. "Gotta go."

"Me too."

"Have a great rest of your day!" I spin on my toes and rush down into the dugout as my manager shakes his head from the base of the stairs, eyes closed.

"I'm watching you, Nixon," he warns, low enough so the rest of the team can't hear him over the bustle of activity down here.

"Nothing to see, sir. Just saying hello to some fans."

He doesn't buy that for a second, and his glare from one open eye suggests as much. "Uh-huh. Not just one fan in particular?"

I step to the side to allow one of the guys to get to the on-deck circle. "I have no idea what you're talking about. There's a lot of fans in that section who were very excited by me throwing the ball their way."

"Mm-hmm. Just know I promised her dad I'd look out for her. So don't do anything to hurt her." Both eyes are open now and leveling me with an intense glare.

"No intentions of that at all, I swear." I take a step toward the bench as a spot at the opposite end opens when Shane stands up to grab his bat.

"Good. Because I like you, Nixon. I'd hate to make good on my other promise to her dad."

I swallow hard. "I think I would also hate that."

"You would." He nods once in satisfaction, then turns back toward the field, dismissing me.

I walk toward the railing and stand next to Devon.

"What was that all about?" he asks.

"Told me to not hurt Gale."

"So he just gave you the green light."

"What do you mean?"

"He didn't say to stay away from her. And believe me, man, he is not afraid to put his foot down." He bangs against the railing with an open fist as our batter sends a long fly ball to the base of the outfield wall in celebration. After he reaches second, Devon continues, "Anyway, you should go for it. You saw her here, right?"

"Yeah." My chest warms at the thought of her. "She got my flowers. Had one in her hair."

"See? That's your sign right there. Frosty doesn't make grand gestures. Likes to stay anonymous." He claps loudly when Shane hits a single, driving our number three hitter to third.

"I'll think about it."

But I don't need to think about it.

I want her to be mine.

Chapter 13
Gale

I keep the game up in a browser window on my computer while I work, muting when necessary but always keeping an eye on what's happening. Games during the working hours don't happen all too often, so I allow myself this small distraction when they do. Starting now. After all, isn't it good, as the director of the team's charitable foundation, to stay as up to date as possible on how the team is doing? For purely professional reasons, of course.

Not to keep watching the new first baseman. Nope. Not at all. But it is an added bonus.

There's just something about him that lures me in, even though nothing about him is what I usually go for. A lot of that has to do with how he draws attention to himself. Showy actions, lots of flair, a big personality. If that's all it was, I'd probably not be interested. Guys like that come through the clubhouse every season and often leave me rolling my eyes with how they yuck it up for the cameras. It's all about them. I don't need that in my life. But even in my few, short interactions with him so far, Finn seems different. Able to cater to a whole audience yet still make you feel special as if you're actually the only one who's important, not him.

And the flowers. No one has done that before. Not even my ex-boyfriends when they screwed up.

Finn might think it, but he didn't mess anything up by giving me a T-shirt and a signed ball. Yet still he's trying to make it up to me.

He certainly seemed happy to see the flower in my hair. As if it wasn't some throwaway gesture. Maybe he is different.

The chorus of one of my favorite songs filters through my computer speakers. Sung in between the top and bottom of the eighth inning, it's a game-day tradition nearly as old as I am.

When I was born and—surprise!—wasn't a boy like my parents thought I would be, one thing reporters always asked my dad was if I was going to play softball and carry on the family dynasty that way since I couldn't play baseball in the big leagues. But that was never my path. If I wasn't at the ballfield with my grandfather, dad, and the team, I was on the dance floor (or a pageant, but I'd like to forget those). This song was my first recital song, and it first got played as a guaranteed way for me to practice my steps at least once while I was here. Usually focused on watching my dad pitch or playing with the team in the dugout or sitting with my grandfather, once that music came on, I dropped whatever I was doing to dance.

It doesn't take long for something to become a tradition in baseball, especially when the game they first played that song during started a nineteen-game win streak. The team went thirty-two out of the next forty. I was two when I danced to this song at my recital. I'm twenty-seven now. Twenty-five years. As a result, I'm also probably the only twenty-something who still knows her recital dance from toddlerhood.

And now the camera isn't focused on a little me dancing in

the dugout, or teenage me when they wanted to flash back to those days and show how I was growing up, or me like they did two nights ago, or even the dancing fans that they regularly highlight on the big screen. They've cut to Finn on the field.

The first night, he hadn't been prepared and was already in the dugout when it played. The second night, he'd danced a little, but it wasn't anything special. He must have asked about it being played two games in a row, because today he's ready. Sashays punctuated by arabesques, tendus, and plies as he moves around on his toes right on the foul side of the first base line. I doubt he was formally trained, his form needs a bit of work, but he gets major points for doing all of that with spikes. And I'm sure the grounds crew is happy he hasn't tried to spin and tear up the basepath or grass as a result.

"You're smiling again," Phoebe says, making me jump in my seat.

I rub my face and try to gain composure. "I am not."

"It's a good look for you. Keep doing it."

"Did you need something?" I ask in an attempt to change the subject, biting my cheek to keep from smiling again. It's not that I don't ever smile. She saw me do it at the game. I just need to stay composed for what's going on around me here. The causes that the foundation supports deserve that sort of drive and focus.

"The contract for Santa and his elves just got faxed over, and I need you to sign it." She hands me two sheets of paper.

I skim over it and find it to be in order. I grab a pen off my desk, click it, then sign my name. Santa will be appearing not only at the gala, but he'll be making the rounds through the children's ward at the hospital beforehand. I want to give everyone a chance to have a bit of Christmas in July, not just those attending the foundation's event. "Here you go."

She takes the papers back from me before she turns and strides out the door, calling, "Think about what I said."

And I do, but I also think about how I owe it to my grandfather and dad to do the family proud. Some of my dad's last few words come back to me. "Guess you're in charge now, Gale." I told him I wouldn't let him down, and I meant it. They gave me a great life but also showed me that we have a responsibility to serve others who need it too. It's why I went into nonprofit management for school, it's why my grandfather started this foundation, why my dad served on its board until his health determined otherwise. As much as baseball is my family's legacy, so is this. I'll never get to play ball and live up to the family name in that way, but I can do some good this way.

I glance back at my computer screen. Top of the ninth, and although it was a quick bottom half of the eighth, we're still in the lead. Our best closer is on the mound, and although the first batter gets on, he strikes out the next two and the third forces the out at second with an infield dribbler handled by the pitcher.

Game over. Snowhawks win.

And now the ballfield will fall quiet for the next nearly two weeks in what is the team's longest stretch of away games. Then it's the mid-season break for the All-Star Game. A handful of our guys are headed out to play in the game, and Shane's going to see if he can win the home run hitting contest.

Also during that time? It's the Frost Foundation's Christmas in July Gala. I should probably send the team another reminder to be on the safe side. With the long road trip ahead of them, it's likely not on their minds.

I stand from my desk and head toward the main part of the

office. Phoebe's head lifts as my door opens. "Just got the received receipt from Santa Paul. Should be all set."

"Paul's a wonderful Santa. Has his own cottage in Heartwood Hollow each season." Going to see him was one of my favorite childhood traditions. I smile. The event is shaping up just how I want it to.

"You're smiling again," Phoebe teases.

I roll my eyes, but I don't try to hide my smile. "Santa makes me happy," I admit freely. And when she looks at me, expecting more, I add, "Team won."

"And how did your new friend do for the rest of the game?"

"He did fine."

"Mm-hmm . . . that man *is* fine." She waggles her eyebrows.

"Phoebe, stop," I say, exasperated, drawing out the word so it sounds more like *stahp*. But I can't argue with her. He's more than fine. "It's not professional to talk about people like that in the office."

"Fine. I won't talk about him like that in the office. The next girls' night, however . . ."

"You're incorrigible. Anyway, I should probably make sure he knows about the gala, though given the flowers—"

"I know all about the gala," Finn says from the doorway that leads to the concourse, a duffel bag hanging from his shoulder. "And I wanted to talk to you about that."

Chapter 14
Finn

I don't miss the way Gale startles when I speak. I'd had every intention of knocking or clearing my throat to announce my presence, but when they brought me up, it was a perfect opportunity to jump right in.

"Finn, I—" Gale begins, then stops. Her mouth opens a couple times as her gaze rakes over me and my street clothes before she settles on "Hi," her voice softer than a moment ago.

I can't help but chuckle at her reaction and hope I come off as charming. In no way was I expecting her to be tongue tied. A witty remark, sure, even aloof professionalism, but this? This is better than I ever could have expected. "Hi."

"What are you doing here?" she finally asks, turning to fully face me. Her friend, the one from earlier in the stands, sits behind a reception desk, an amused look on her face as she flicks her gaze between Gale and me.

I hike my bag further up on my shoulder. "I wanted to talk to you about the gala."

"Right, but shouldn't you be on the bus by now? I thought the team was leaving tonight for the road trip."

"Everyone but me."

Her eyes widen. "What do you mean? You're in regular clothes. What happened? Is Dave back already? You just got here."

I hold my hand up to stop the rapid fire, though her worry over me is appreciated. "Nothing happened, and no, Dave isn't back." It does something to my insides that rivals the one caused by the look she's giving me. "I need to head back to Saltair Shores to get my stuff from my apartment. Team headed out a little while ago. I'll join up with them tomorrow before the game."

Her shoulders sag in what I can only assume is relief. But why? Is she feeling the same sort of connection to me that I do with her? "Oh, okay. Good. That's good. Do you want to step into my office?"

Her friend sits upright. "Oh no, please continue this out here. Let me just grab some popcorn."

Gale's cheeks redden as she glares at her friend. There is definitely something going on here between us.

Her friend cackles.

I take a few steps toward Gale, spotting the flowers I bought her on a coffee table toward the front of the room. So much for them meaning something despite the carnation still tucked above her ear. Something seems off about the bouquet, though. It's smaller than I expected. They say cameras add ten pounds, but I didn't think that applied to flowers too. Guess I won't be using that florist anymore. "Your office is fine."

She holds her hand out in an *after you* motion toward the only room that has a door to close it off from the rest of the space, and I proceed to cross the room and walk into her office. There on a table to my right is the reason the bouquet out in the main space looked much smaller than what I had ordered.

It was. About half the size. And here's its match. I smile, a tingly warmth flooding my system.

She closes the door behind her, giving us some privacy. "So what about the gala do you want to talk about?"

I pivot on my heels to face her, resisting an urge to lift my hand toward her face. "You still have the flower in your hair."

Her hand moves to above her ear, tracing the petals of the red blossom, and her fading blush deepens. "Thank you for these, by the way. You didn't have to."

"Wanted to." I step closer, and she doesn't move away or tense the way she did the other night. Progress.

"I hope you don't mind that I split the bouquet in half. It was beautiful but so big it overtook my table. Do you want to see? I took a picture." Without me answering either way, she pulls her phone out of her back pocket and brings up the photo. Instead of handing it to me or turning the phone screen toward me, she comes to stand next to me, our arms nearly touching. Wow. Even better than what I saw online. Okay, I take back what I said about the florist. I would absolutely use them again.

Still by my side, Gale looks up at me. I feel it, my cheek actually tingling, before I look down to meet her bright-blue gaze. I've never paid much attention to eyelashes before, but wow, they're long. She could bat her eyes, and I'd be lost to her for sure. She blinks slowly as a shy smile crosses her face while she studies me as I do the same. "Why a Christmas bouquet?"

"I saw the flyers for the foundation's gala. Christmas in July, right?"

For a brief moment, Gale's gaze remains locked on me before she shakes her head in quick short movements as if snapping back into reality. She looks down at our closeness and takes a step back. My arm instantly feels colder in the air-conditioned space.

"Right. It's a fun theme. And it's not likely to get snowed out like the actual Christmas events sometimes do." Her gaze lifts toward the ceiling, and her lips draw into a straight line with only one corner barely turned up. "Welcome to Snowhaven. It earns its name."

"One of our games up here last year was postponed due to snow," I tell her to remind her I'm well aware of Snowhaven's reputation. "We had to get back to Saltair Shores for our game the next day. We made up for it with a double header later in August the next time we were up here."

"Oh, I remember that. We put out a call to our fans to help shovel out the stands the following day so we didn't have to miss any more games. You didn't dance and flip then. I would have remembered."

"The Sailors are more mild mannered when on the road. There was minimal dancing." I chuckle. "More of the keep warm kind than anything."

"Nice moves today, by the way."

"You saw that?" I tick my head to the side. "But you'd left by then."

She slides her phone back into her pocket before walking around her desk. She points to the computer as she taps on the keyboard, bringing the monitor back to life. "Watched it on here. You could extend your lines on the arabesque a bit more, but I don't imagine it's easy in cleats."

I let out a burst of laughter. "Thank you?"

"Sorry. I danced for years. Never really leaves you. Did you ever take classes?" She motions to the seat in front of her desk, then sits in hers.

"Only through videos on the internet." Actual dance

classes would have been too expensive as a kid for my family to pay for. Not that I would have taken them then. I take the seat she indicated and lean forward, trying to stay as close to her as possible. "Danced as in past tense? What made you stop?"

Something crosses her face, and she loses a bit of the light from her eyes. "Life got busy."

"I can understand that. Would you do it again if you had the opportunity?"

Her response is immediate. "Absolutely."

"You love it, don't you?"

The spark returns to her eyes, and her face softens. "I do. I danced from the moment I was old enough for Mommy and Me classes. My first recital was at two years old. Danced all the way through college. It's shaped me just as much as baseball has."

I want to ask why she doesn't allow herself even one class a week. They're what, no more than an hour long? But something about the way her face changed when she said why she doesn't anymore keeps me from opening my mouth.

"That's what, twenty, twenty-five years of dancing?" Her age doesn't really matter, but I am curious.

She nods. "I danced for twenty-two years. Stopped just about three years ago."

"So you're twenty-seven now?" She nods. "I'm twenty-five."

"Oh."

She says nothing more, so I say, "You seem surprised."

"You act younger."

"Is that a bad thing?"

"No. I guess it's not."

"I was a junior in college when I got signed by the Sailors," I offer. My phone buzzes, and I pull it out of my pocket. The text has gone to spam, so I ignore it. But it is getting late, and I need to pick up my rental car soon, so I guide us back to why I'm actually here. One reason, anyway. The other reason is to see her. "So is your love of dancing why you picked a gala for this event?"

Gale smiles warmly. "Any chance to dance nowadays is welcome. I think that's true for almost everyone. And the people who come to these events want to dress up and have fun while helping a good cause. I'm glad to provide that opportunity."

"What cause are you helping with this event? It wasn't on the flyer."

"Mobile skin cancer screenings in partnership with Barrett Hospital in Heartwood Hollow." Her face falls slightly, and it's easy to see the cause hits home.

"Wow. That's really great."

"Thanks."

"It makes sense now."

She raises an eyebrow. "What does?"

"The sunscreen the other night. And why there was a brand-new tube of it in my locker when I got here. Why all the guys use it." I study her for a reaction, but there isn't one. "You or someone else?"

She sags just enough for me to notice and to feel bad for asking. If it's not her, it was someone close to her. "My dad. He died at the end of last season."

"I'm sorry. I knew he had passed, but I didn't know the cause. He was a solid pitcher. I remember watching him play as a kid."

"You saw him play?" She brightens momentarily.

"Only once in person. But on TV all the time."

"I wonder if I was at the game you went to. Wouldn't that be something?"

"Yeah, it would." Her gaze darts around my face as if she's searching for something. I hope she likes what she finds.

"I owe you an apology," she finally says.

"For what?"

"For how I acted the other night. You did something nice for me, and I was borderline rude."

"You weren't rude." A bit awkward, maybe, but not rude.

"Well, we can disagree on that, but you were right. I was uncomfortable."

"The stain?"

She nods. "I'm used to having to look a certain way at all times, and when I don't . . ." She pulls a face.

"Got it. And then you had to take pictures like that."

"It's okay," she starts, but the small twitch in her expression tells me otherwise. "I'd do anything for the team." The conviction behind that part of her statement, said the same way as when she said she loved to dance, warms me over.

"So speaking of the team, how would one go about working with the team's foundation to help a cause that they support?"

She sits up straighter. "Put in your time. When I started here, I took on other people's causes too often, and sure, some helped, some continue to help, but there were those who barely even did their part despite them asking me to support their cause. I need the promise that you'll be a part of whatever it is that we put together."

"Done. That seems obvious to me." Why it wouldn't for others is mind-boggling.

"And you have to be a part of other events too. You're expected to be at the gala, by the way. Or to donate something that can be auctioned or raffled off. A lot of the guys do signed gear. Both is preferable, even if just for a short time."

My mouth turns up into what I hope is a flirtatious smile. "Will I get to see you dance? If so, I'm there."

Her gaze flicks toward mine, capturing mine for a moment, before it darts away. "Oh, I don't really get a chance to dance at these things. I'm usually so busy."

I adjust how I'm sitting to catch her gaze again, then straighten. She follows, not looking away. "But if you were asked to dance during a quiet moment?"

She blinks a few times, her cheeks flushing. "Are you asking me to dance with you?"

Chapter 15
Gale

I can't tear my eyes away as I wait for Finn to answer. I don't tell him that I don't dance at these things because no one has ever asked. There was my dad before he got too sick, of course, and I'll treasure those memories forever, but as for the players on the team? No. Just no.

But that was before I wanted to dance with someone. Before Finn. And because it's just a dance, not a date, it's within the bounds of my rule.

"What if I am?" His question is obviously flirty, but the look in his eyes causes me to swallow hard as my stomach flutters. Oh my word, is he really causing me to have butterflies?

My voice wobbles as I answer, "Then it's a definite maybe." Or an absolute yes, but just like with giving his cause some support, he's gotta work for it a bit first. "But you should know I don't date ball players."

"Noted." He looks like he wants to say more but doesn't. The tension in the room grows as we take one another in, his eyes sparkling. Apparently, the butterflies in my stomach really like sparkles because they're still there.

"So what is this cause?" I finally ask. At least it came out even.

The intensity of his gaze on me lessens with his answer, "Shoe Soles for Souls," though his tone is no less passionate, just in a different way. "To give kids new shoes for sports and for school. As a kid, my ma could never afford new pairs for me. Everything was hand-me-downs and rarely did anything fit right. My first cleats came from the donation bin that the rec department had. So did my second pair. And my third. Well, you get the picture."

I do, and the thought of it tugs at my heartstrings. I was never that kid. It was always my stuff ending up in the donation bin for those kids at the slightest bit of wear or discomfort. Or simply because I didn't like the particular strap or wanted the buckle versus the snap. "My senior project in high school was a big donation drive for dance shoes and costumes. So often those costumes are one and done after recital season. Even competition costumes don't get worn more than a handful of times depending on the season. But they're fine for someone else to use the next year. Shoes too. Once, maybe twice a week for ten months, if that with the way kids' feet grow. It never failed that I'd need new shoes right before recital because I'd gone up a size. And then again before the season started back up." I don't say that to my mom, image was everything, and heaven forbid my barely scuffed from class shoes would end up on stage . . . at least on *my* feet. Sitting back in my chair—when did I lean so close to him?—I wave my arm around the office. "It's one of the things that got me into wanting to do this sort of work."

He smiles, and the boyish grin full of excitement matches the hope in his eyes. "So we can do something for them?"

"It's not that simple. In addition to putting in your time

with the other events we have going on, I need to bring it to the board. It's not just me making these decisions, though I do have sway."

"I'd imagine so. Your grandfather established this foundation, didn't he?"

I doubt he means anything bad by the comment, but any suggestion of nepotism grates at me no matter the source. "Yes. And every day I try to prove that I'm worthy enough to be running it."

He holds up his hands, eyes widening. "I mean no disrespect."

I take an audible steadying breath. "Sorry. I'm sure you didn't. But you wouldn't believe the people who first thought that. And I'm still trying to prove some of them wrong. It would be one thing if I had no credentials, but I have a master's degree in this. Internships. A portfolio I still update. I'm trying to do it the right way. I could have taken the figurehead spot my dad held on the board, never worked yet been the face of it all, making sure I'm in every photo of events we sponsor or hold, or running with my causes only. But I didn't want that. I sit on the board as the top employee here, but I get no more say than anyone."

"I think you're doing great," he says placatingly.

"You've seen nothing yet."

He must take my statement as some sort of flirtation. That grin of his comes back as does some of the heat in his eyes. "Oh, but I'm looking forward to it."

His gaze lights something within me that goes beyond just butterflies. If I don't tamp these feelings down, I'm going to be in trouble. I probably already am. It's been so long since a guy has shown interest. Since I've let myself be interested, even if he is a ballplayer. I lean in, close enough I could kiss him if I was daring enough, and my voice drops as I reply, "So am I."

I want to say more, but his cell rings. "Sorry, need to check that." He half stands, sending the top half of himself further across the table and giving me an up-close view of how well his shirt fits his lean but muscular build as he pulls the phone out of a back pocket and then glances at the screen. "Car rental place."

He stands completely and turns away, heading for the opposite corner of where my desk is and putting me at eye level of how well his jeans fit him too. Dinah might prefer a man in tight pants, and while I can—and do—appreciate a man in baseball pants, give me one in a pair of dark wash jeans any day. And thanks to Finn, that day is today.

"No, that isn't going to work," Finn says, still on his call, bringing my attention back to him and not his assets.

"That barely has any trunk space." I can't help but glance back at his bum with that comment.

"Sure, I could make more trips, but who has time for that? I'm supposed to be returning it tomorrow." A pause. "I appreciate the added time, but I'm not going to be able to use it as I'm going out of town for work, and no, I do not need the car for that."

He sighs. "Yes, please cancel my rental reservation. I'll figure something else out. Thank you."

Then he hangs up, slides his phone into his back pocket, letting me admire his tush one more time, and turns.

I straighten and try to look busy and not as if I've just been looking at his behind this whole time. "Is everything okay?"

He tries to mask the frustration on his face with a small smile. "Yeah . . . no. There isn't another car rental place in town, is there? The one by the bus station only has some sporty coupe left, but I reserved an SUV."

I glance at the clock, and the offer flows out of my mouth. "Take mine."

"I couldn't."

I face him head on. "You can, because I'm lending it to you."

"No, really. It's okay. I'll just wait until the All-Star break to get my stuff."

"And have one set of street clothes until you get done with your road trip?"

"Devon took me shopping already for a couple of things before yesterday's game." He spins, flirtatious grin back in place. "You like?"

Remind me to thank Devon for today's eye candy. "Not bad. But seriously, take my car. I'll need to cancel an appointment I have to leave for soon, but it's no biggie." I'd just have to pay for another set of tasting cupcakes.

"Where do you need to go?" His face is soft in his curiosity.

"I need to go taste test cupcakes at a bakery in Heartwood Hollow. Figure out what to serve at the gala."

"Can I come?"

I press my lips together in a straight line as I tick my head to the side. "I thought you had to get on the road."

"I do. Don't get me wrong, but if you're doing me as big of a favor as you're going to, the least I can do is go with you so you don't miss your appointment. And you said the magic word. *Cupcakes.*"

"Got a sweet tooth, do you?" A smile tugs at my lips, but I'm trying to not let it show.

"Most definitely." He presses his palms together. "Please, please, please."

There's no use fighting my smile when Finn asks like that. I shake my head slowly as I chuckle. "Okay, you can come."

"Yes!" He pumps his fist in a celebratory manner, keeping his twinkling and heating gaze on me as if waiting for my reaction to change. It doesn't. I'm still smiling. Only now my cheeks might be turning pink if the heat I feel in them is anything to go by.

I close my browser, then shut down my computer. We'll be a few minutes early if we leave now, but it will give Finn more time. "Do you need to get anything before you go?"

He shakes his head. "Got everything I need in the bag."

"Then we should go." I grab my purse from a drawer in my desk. As much as I don't like them on game days, purses are helpful at other times, and meeting someone on foundation business is one of those times. It gives me a more professional look, as does the planner and matching pen inside. This bag has the added benefit of fitting a full-size sunscreen bottle inside a separate, interior pocket, protecting everything else should any accidents occur. And given what happened the last time I was with Finn near some sunscreen, I can't be too careful.

Finn picks up his duffel by the door, then opens it and motions for me to go first, but I point to him. "Gotta lock up." He nods, then heads into the main office. I follow, pulling the door closed behind me and lock up.

Phoebe looks as if she's done nothing but stare at the door to my office since we went in. What did she think was going to happen? I meet her gaze, and she waggles her eyebrows while I roll my eyes. She's gonna love this.

"We're heading out to Heartwood Hollow."

Her eyes widen with delight. "Together?"

"Yeah. He's putting in his time helping me with gala stuff." She arches an eyebrow, her skepticism working overtime. But she doesn't need to know the whole reason right now. "You want your usual?"

She brightens. "Yes, please. I love those black and white cookies."

"You got it. See you tomorrow."

Finn and I wind our way through the basement tunnels, making small talk and casting glances at one another. Walking side by side, the conversation's easy, especially since I'm not being distracted by certain physical attributes, though I'm finding that I like other parts of him just as much.

We exit the building into the staff parking lot. Finn spins on his heels as the door closes behind us, the boom reverberating through the large garage.

"I'm that one over there." I point to a dark-gray SUV I bought a couple years ago because driving small cars through our regular snowy winter weather makes me nervous and it can carry whatever I need for foundation business. In a few weeks, its backseat and trunk will look like Christmas came early.

I click a button to disengage the alarm. "Think she'll be big enough for you?"

Finn eyes the SUV, assessing its size. "Absolutely. Thanks again."

"You're welcome."

He runs his hand along the bottom of the hatch, then pops it open, lifting it only enough to place his bag inside before closing it.

I head to the driver's side as he goes to the passenger side, and we open the doors and slide in almost in one synchronized move. We reach for our respective door handles, and he chuckles. I can only assume he's noticed our timing. But I close my door a fraction of a second before he pulls his closed too gently. It doesn't latch.

"You need to use a little more force than that. I've seen you swing that bat; you have it in you."

"Didn't want to hurt her." Even if he's just humoring me, I like how he's calling my SUV a *her* after I called her a *she*.

"You don't have to be gentle."

"I want her to like me, so no harm in easing into things." Finn stares at me with an open, soft gaze that simultaneously freezes me to my spot and fans the flame I now carry for him, causing me to melt.

I open my mouth only to close it again, unsure of what to say because I don't think we're talking about my SUV anymore.

Chapter 16
Finn

Gale tries once more to speak, but she says nothing. She stares back at me, and I can't get a read on her. Maybe comparing what I was doing to her SUV to what I was trying to do with her was too much. Or maybe it wasn't enough.

I thought if she knew I was serious about helping her with the gala, about wanting to dance with her, and about her herself, she'd . . . I don't know. Say yes to going out with me?

After another moment, Gale's brow furrows, and she lets out a hard breath through her nose as she presses the start button. The SUV revs to life, and Gale backs out of the parking space.

Still, I'm not giving up. You don't land every trick on the first try. Not that Gale's a trick or that this is a trick, but the fact remains. I'm not done. I want more than a dance.

Gale's intriguing, the walls she's put up only makes her more so. Through the cracks and gaps in the mortar, she's kind, and caring, determined, and passionate. And gorgeous on top of it. How she's still single is beyond me.

But back to the SUV analogy, I need to ease into things.

You're bound to have a few false starts when you're learning. And I could study Gale for days, probably the rest of the season if not longer, and still learn new things about her.

"Does your SUV have a name?" I ask once we're out of the parking garage and heading toward the stoplight at the intersection leading away from the ballfield. Small talk seemed to work fine as we walked to the lot, so it's my safest bet to regaining some ground.

She comes to a stop at the red light. "Clara."

"What's that from?"

"*The Nutcracker*. She's the little girl who receives the nutcracker as a present from her godfather."

"Is that the one with the rats?"

"Yeah, that's the one. Though it's mice in the original story." The light turns green, and she accelerates forward, heading north according to the state route sign. Turning left would have put us on the path toward the college dorm I'm currently calling home.

"You're really big into Christmas, aren't you?"

Her lips curl upward, but she doesn't look at me. Probably for the best since she's driving. And this way, she can't see how much I can't keep my eyes off her. "I love Christmas."

"So beyond the dancing, you really chose to have a Christmas in July gala because of how much you like it, didn't you? Once a year wasn't enough?"

She shakes her head, her smile growing and the corners of her eyes crinkling, erasing all traces of a freckle she has there. "It's never enough." She sighs wistfully. "The lights, the smells, the cookies, pies, and chocolates, the promise of snow, the excitement. I love it."

"And is this why you don't mind the nickname Frosty?"

A burst of laughter escapes from her. "Oh my gosh, who

told you that? Devon? It was Devon, wasn't it." It's not a question the second time. "Shane would never."

"I thought he was making fun of you at first. It was probably a good thing Shane was there to set me straight."

She glances at me then, turning her head toward me slightly. "Were you trying to defend my good name, sir?"

I shrug nonchalantly, but keep my gaze on her steady. "You just don't seem frosty to me. You're anything but."

"Some would argue with you." She focuses back on the road. We're almost to the edge of town. "They say I'm wound too tight."

"Then they don't know you."

"And you do?" The eyebrow closest to me arches with skepticism. "We met two days ago."

"And in that time, you've tried to make me feel better about giving you a shirt you probably already have, have split a bouquet in half to make the other portion of your office all cheery, and spoken about dance and Christmas with enough warmth to melt even a hint of chill if there was one around you. And there isn't by the way. That's all without going into the passion you have for your foundation work, which is evident the moment someone talks to you about it. If anyone says you're frosty, they've got you all wrong."

At first, I don't think she's going to say anything. She's doing the open mouth, then closing it again thing. I don't know if I've touched another nerve that will send her retreating back behind her wall, but after a moment, she quietly says, "Thank you." She's not facing me, but her eyes are darting from me to the road, more me than road.

I clear my throat, a bit self-conscious after my declaration. So much for easing into things. "So since we've established you're anything but frosty, how did you get the nickname? Is it just because of your last name?"

"No, not because of my last name, but I'm not going to tell you either." Her lips curls upward once more. "You're going to have to work for it. And don't go running to Devon or Shane either. They're sworn to secrecy."

I raise my brows and dip my chin as I look at her. "Are they really?"

She half snorts. "No. Well, kind of. But if Devon revealed my nickname to you that readily, he'll spill the whole story at the slightest provocation, and what's the fun in that? I want to see you work for it." Her smile widens enough that, never mind the disappearing freckle by her eye, her ears move.

"More foundation work?"

Her smile falls as she scrunches her nose. "Oh . . . Maybe. Not sure. I'll have to think about it. So tell me about yourself."

It's clear she's done talking about her, or maybe this is part of the work I need to do to earn the story behind her nickname. I feel the pressure to give her something good, something meaningful.

"Tell me how you got into doing all those tricks," she prompts when I don't speak right away. "You didn't take dance lessons, so maybe gymnastics?"

I shake my head. "Never had the money for that either. Ever since I was little, I was always jumping off stuff. Stairs. The picnic table in the backyard, first from the seat then the table top." I try to make my voice sound younger. "Look how high I can go! Hey, watch this!"

I shrug. "I liked the attention. The other kids thought I was funny—then cool. Adults worried I'd hurt myself. Telling me to stop never worked. I always found something else to try. Eventually, they just learned to embrace it. Then things like parkour and ninja courses got popular, and my friend group was all about those. The only times I wasn't out there with them trying new stuff on the playground or the skate park in town was when I was playing ball."

"Was baseball your first love?"

"One of them. It was also the thing I could do cheaply thanks to the rec center's donation bin and waived fees for families under a certain income threshold. As I got older, I learned it could also get me into college. So I made sure my grades were passable and focused most of my attention on doing as well as I could when I played. It paid off."

"I'll say. Now look at you. Last week you're the star first baseman for the Sailors, then you become the center of a bombshell trade to the Snowhawks. How are your new shoes, by the way. You didn't have your old ones on today."

"A little stiff," I answer truthfully as we pass a field with cows. Not the first I've seen around this area. "They'll be broken in enough after tomorrow's game."

She seems hesitant as she asks, "And how do you feel about the trade?"

"Part of the game, I guess." I shrug. "I won't say I saw myself with the Sailors for my whole career the way some players do, but it was a surprise."

"Good or bad?"

"I met everyone three days ago," I reply with a chuckle, using part of her earlier answer to me. "It's a little early to say, especially when it comes to certain guys on the team, but other things"—I look at her pointedly—"have been better than I could have expected when I got here."

She swallows hard and gently sucks in her bottom lip to wet it before letting it go, and I can't help but stare, wondering what it would be like to have her lips against mine. "I'm glad. I, uh, think you'll fit in well here."

Hopefully *here* includes herself, but I won't push for that. Not when she just told me she doesn't date baseball players. Yet. "With Devon and Shane, for sure. Kyle . . . not so much."

"You'll grow on him. Or vice versa."

We spend another fifteen minutes driving to the bakery talking about the guys on the team, the coaches, the manager. I do not tell her how he warned me that he's watching me when it comes to her. Maybe someday, but for now, that might scare her again, and I'm enjoying whatever this is too much.

Finally we arrive at a small bakery on Main Street next to a little town square that's not much more than a few benches and an information booth. It's cheery pink awning and open door greet us. And before we're inside, the delicious smells of baked goods and chocolate nearly have me salivating.

Somehow, the baker, Joanie, knew to make two of each cupcake, surprising Gale who'd only booked the tasting for herself. She was ready to share with me, but here we are, each with our own cupcakes as Joanie watches us intently, a warm smile on her face.

And oh my. Gale had said these cupcakes were magical, but these are next level. The cupcakes we try are exactly how Christmas should taste. Gingerbread with a light cream cheese frosting, peppermint with a red and white swirled peppermint frosting, hot cocoa with a marshmallow cream frosting, and eggnog with a light nutmeg-spiced frosting.

I moan around another bite of my gingerbread cupcake. "You have to get all of these. How could you choose?"

"Amazing, right?" Gale says, her eyes closing as she takes the last bite of her peppermint cupcake. "You've outdone your-self this time."

Joanie's smile brightens. "That's so kind of you. I always love the free rein you give me for these events of yours."

"I have to agree with Finn. Can you do all four?"

"Of course we can. I'm so delighted."

"I'm thinking a few display pieces," Gale begins, "standard tier type is fine, and you can mix them all up. They'd be so pretty bunched up together."

I clear my throat as I set down my napkin. "If you don't mind a suggestion . . ."

Gale's gaze is questioning, but she nods, and I smile appreciatively when she says, "Go on."

"What if you made the displays like Christmas trees?" I move my hands in a stereotypical pine tree shape. "That's how the tiers are already usually, yeah?" The baker nods. "But maybe instead of flat, you angle them out? If the display itself was green, then these would almost be like ornaments."

Gale sits blinking at me, taken back by the suggestion. I'm not sure if that's good or bad, but she's not smiling. "I think that would be really pretty, Finn, but that's a custom build sort of thing, and our budget—"

"Ah, I get it. No worries. Was just a thought."

She reaches for my arm and gives me a small smile as her hand squeezes my forearm.

Joanie leans forward. "No, no. I like where he's going. Let's run with that."

Gale's eyes widen. "But the budget—"

Joanie waves her off, but not to dismiss her. "I have a friend. A furniture maker. Already does a lot of stuff for the hospital. This sort of cause is right up his alley. I have no doubt that he and his girlfriend would be happy to do this for you at no cost."

Gale's jaw drops. "Are you serious?" She grips my arm

tighter, and I bite back a grin as I watch her reaction morph from surprise to excitement.

"Oh, yes." The baker smiles again. "I'm so certain of it, I'm not even going to call him until after you leave. Think of it as a very early Christmas present."

"Oh my gosh. Yes! Thank you. Can I give you a hug?"

"Of course!"

They both stand from the table we've been sitting around, so I do the same. I don't like feeling towered over. Gale and Joanie hug, and when they're done, Gale spins toward me, bouncing slightly on the balls of her feet, then throws her arms around me.

When she doesn't pull back immediately, I relax into her and wrap my arms behind her back, breathing in the scent of her hair. Either my senses have been completely overtaken by the peppermint cupcakes we ate, or her hair is minty too. It's rocketed up to one of my favorite smells ever. Right next to the smell of freshly cut ballfield grass. I clench my hands into fists. It's all I can do to not run my fingers through the end of her ponytail.

"Thank you," she says on a breath that tickles my ear and sends a delightful thrill down my spine. "The idea is perfect."

And now I'm the one left speechless as she squeezes me, fitting perfectly against me. But all too soon, she releases me and steps back. All I can do is look at her, the pink spreading across her cheeks, the shy smile she gives me as she casts her gaze from me to the non-existent crumbs on her shirt.

Gale turns toward Joanie and extends her hand. "Thank you, so, so much for everything."

Joanie takes Gale's hand in hers. "Happy to do it. Let's go get you taken care of. I'm sure you have a few deliveries to make."

"Like you wouldn't believe." Gale laughs and heads to the counter while I shake Joanie's hand, and she ushers me over to the cases of other baked goods. If everything tastes as amazing as the cupcakes do, this will become a regular haunt of mine during homestands.

Gale keeps Joanie and her assistant busy for the next few minutes, placing orders for friends back in Snowhaven. Then I get a few things for the road and to thank a couple of ex-team-mates for helping me move my stuff.

Then, with full bellies and fuller boxes of treats, Gale and I are back on the road.

Chapter 17
Gale

We chat about this and that the whole way home. The conversation comes easily. I'm not sure if it's the sugar high or the excitement over Finn's great idea for a cupcake display and the bakery owner's wonderful offer, but I can't keep from smiling. It can't possibly be from the lingering smell of cupcakes mixing with whatever soap Finn used after the game that I got a noseful of when I hugged him at the bakery. Nope, not at all.

What in the world was I thinking when *that* happened?

I am fully blaming it on being told I won't have to pay for the fancy displays being made for the cupcakes. Any money I don't have to spend means more money for the foundation's charities.

And Finn's idea is perfect. I never would have come up with it. Am I really glad he came along? Yes.

Have I shocked myself by making a public display of affection toward someone who isn't one of my besties? Also yes. The idea of PDA has always seemed strange to me. But hugging Finn didn't feel strange at all. Almost normal. Though it's anything but normal for me, so maybe *normal* isn't the right word. But I liked it. A lot. His muscly arms wrapped around me. Who knew that could feel so good. I could easily get used to it, have it become my normal if I let it. But I shouldn't.

I pull into the driveway of my small house in the suburbs. Two small bedrooms and a larger living room that has always proved its worth when it comes to girls' nights—and I am going to need one ASAP. The house probably isn't what one would expect from the heiress of one of baseball's great dynasties, but it's also all I need.

When my dad first got sick, he insisted on getting me a house so he could continue providing for me and any eventual grandkids of his even long after he was gone. I'd refused for a long while, but I broke down about a year into his treatments, when a new procedure failed to get rid of everything.

Then when I found this place, he'd argued it was too small and wanted to get something bigger, further out from town where the yards are bigger and the houses grander. But I like blending into the neighborhood, being a part of it, and knowing my neighbors. Something that I really didn't get when I was a kid being raised by a famous father and a mom who was all too aware of maintaining a pretty image that extended from home to, well, me. Thankfully my friend Cassie's house was within walking distance for when I needed an escape. Playing with friends in the yard, like I did with her, is something I've always wanted for my own kids.

When my dad finally agreed to come see the place with me, after he made me go to all of these other showings with him, he saw its charm. The original hardwood floors and arched open doorways, the porch out to the backyard from what would become my bedroom, the laundry chute so I don't have to carry everything downstairs and thus only need to worry about getting it back upstairs. We all have that one chore we don't like, and laundry is mine. I'd let that dirty laundry pile grow out of control if I could. I used to. It's another reason why I had so many team shirts at one point.

I grab my keys out of my purse sitting on the center console next to me and slide the SUV's dongle off the key chain. I dangle it in front of Finn as if I'm waiting for a cat to bat a toy. "You're going to need this to start the car. Do not lose it. They cost way too much money to replace."

"Got it." He gently takes the dongle from my fingers, brushing my fingertips with his, his gaze never leaving me. Mine flicks between his and his fingers as he slowly pulls his hand away, jolts of awareness from each touch and separation surging up my arm. He tucks the dongle into the small pocket in his jeans. "I won't go anywhere without this. It will be safe."

And I'm still just sitting here with my hand suspended in the air, the feeling of his fingertips still on mine, though his hand is now back on the pastry box. Awkward . . . I lower my hand and place it on my bag. "Well, since you have to be getting out on the road, I won't keep you any longer."

"You haven't kept me. You might have even saved me time."

I undo my belt. "How do you figure?"

"Everything from paperwork at the rental place to"— chuckling, he pats the pastry box on his lap—"providing me with dinner so I don't need to stop on the way."

"Happy to oblige." I pop the door open, and Finn does the same. As I slide out, he does too, then puts the pastry box on the seat he just vacated. He buckles it in.

I lose it. When was the last time anyone made me laugh like this? The girls have, sure, but never a guy. But with Finn? It comes so easily. Just like that hug. Just like our conversation.

But I do not date baseball players. I cannot fall for a guy on the team. It's bad enough we're already on media's radar after our viral meeting. Somewhere, my mother is getting a kick out of that. The thought sobers me.

Finn gives me a sheepish grin through the open doors. "I'd put it on the floor, but then I wouldn't be able to grab anything out of it. I wasn't lying when I said it was going to be dinner. And I am not going to get food all over Clara."

I bite back a smile over his use of my SUV's name. Even I barely use it in conversation. Not that my vehicle comes up a lot. "Thanks. I appreciate it."

"And I appreciate you letting me borrow her." He's staring at me again. His gaze soft, taking me in as if I'm some precious treasure.

I step away from his line of sight, closing the door behind me. The noise of mine is immediately met with the closing of his. More solid than the first time he tried and had to do it again.

Finn meets me at the nose of the SUV. "Think I'm finally getting a handle on how careful I need to be with her." He chuckles as if he's joking, but the look in his eyes says he's not talking about Clara. His gaze drops down to my mouth.

I suck in a breath, and he looks back up into my eyes. Once again, I'm rooted in place by his gaze. "Be good to her," I say softly on the breath as I let it out, no longer sure if I'm talking about me or the SUV. "Don't take too many risks."

He takes a step closer to me, shaking his head in a slow, fluid motion. "Not too many." He glances back down at my lips. "Just one for now."

If he kissed me now, I don't think I'd stop him. Don't think I'd want to. I won't date baseball players, but I think I'd kiss one. My heart's pounding. He's so close I can smell the bakery mixed with his soap again. "Just one?"

"Can I have your number?" Finn steps back, fresh air replacing his heady scent and smacking me in the face.

"My number?"

He lifts his hand up behind his neck as he clears his throat. "Yeah. You know, in case I need to reach you. About Clara." His tone is friendly now, the heat from a moment before dampened but not out completely.

"Right . . ." I dig out my phone, sighing. It's a steadying breath more than anything. "Right." I hand him my phone, his fingers once again trailing along mine as he pulls it away from me, and he plugs in his number before giving my phone back to me. I'm careful to not touch him as I take it because I'm unsure if I could stand the way I'm all too aware of the sensations he sends running up my arm again.

"Thanks."

"So I'll, uh, bring this back to the ballpark tomorrow?"

"Yeah, I'll get a ride in from Phoebe. Wait, how are you getting from there to the bus station?"

He shrugs. "I figured I'd walk or take a rideshare or something."

Though there are still a couple dozen full-time staff at the field when the team's away who could easily bring him, the offer slips from my mouth much like the one to use my car did. "I'll take you."

"You've already done enough for me. I couldn't ask you to."

I hold up my hand. "And once again, you aren't. I'm offering."

He gives me a lopsided grin. "Thanks again, then. Anyway, I should get going."

"Drive safe. Text me when you get there."

"I will." He seems like he's going to say more, but then he sets his jaw and gives me a single nod before getting into my SUV.

After a moment, he sets Clara in reverse and backs out of the driveway. I wave as he puts her in drive, and then he heads down the road and out of sight.

I walk into the house, place the pastry box in the fridge, then make two texts.

The first is to Finn.

Hey, it's Gale. You better not be looking at this while you're driving. That is not the risk I want you to take.

The second is to Phoebe.

Can you pick me up for work tomorrow?

When I click back into the main text screen, the preview of my text to Finn catches my eye. Not the whole thing. But three words.

I want you.

And in that moment, I know it's true.

I want him.

Chapter 18

Finn

The drive down to Saltair Shores is relatively uneventful . . . if you don't count the car's voice assistant reading Gale's text to me a few minutes after I left her at her house.

That is not the risk I want you to take.

I pump my fist, then stupidly remove both hands from the wheel in a celebratory clap, coming way too close to driving across the center line of this too narrow suburban road. Thankfully, no one is coming in the opposite direction.

That is certainly not a risk Gale wants me to take either.

But she does want me to take a risk.

Hands firmly back on the wheel, it takes a lot of willpower to not turn back around, march up to her door, and kiss her like I've been wanting to since that hug at the bakery. I'd hoped for another one as we said goodbye, but between the pastry box she was holding and making sure I got her number, it didn't happen. And I didn't want to scare her away, not when we'd had such a good ride back to Snowhaven.

But now?

This is my green light.

Tomorrow I'm going to kiss Gale Frost.

The thought excites me more than it probably should while I'm driving, and I make it to my old apartment in near record time. The more I get packed tonight, the sooner I can get back to Snowhaven tomorrow to see Gale.

And to rejoin the team, of course.

I wasn't lying when I told Gale I could wait until the mid-season break to do all this, but getting it over with now frees up the head space it currently occupies. Then I can fill that space with other things. Probably Gale.

I pull up in front of the old two-story house that I'd called home for the last two years. From the front, it looks like a typical house for the area. A Queen Anne, I think they called it. Wood shingle siding, a front porch, and the peak of the roof facing out because the lots are narrow but long. It's the lot shape that hides how much work has been done to many of the houses around here, and as I walk up the unfinished driveway —I will not miss shoveling this in the winter if I don't come back here in the offseason—the rest of the house comes into view with multiple additions tacked onto the rear.

And mine is in the very back.

I've still got my key, but despite this, I knock on the door. The team has a day off today while their opponent travels to town, so I have no idea what state I'll find the guys in. They know I'm coming, but that doesn't mean I won't walk in to them half dressed having a video game tournament, or dressed in camo T-shirts and having an epic squirt gun battle. Both of which would probably be streamed for fans. I am not the only baseball player who has a unique way of connecting with our following, not when it comes to the Sailors. Though, having been the first one with a viral following on the team, I helped a lot of these guys go viral for the first time.

I pull out my phone to see if any of the guys are live now, then remember to text Gale to say I made it here.

But there's her text again, and this time, I'm reading her words, not hearing them from her car's smart voice.

GALE

That is not a risk I want you to take.

The corner of my mouth ticks upward in a half grin as I text back.

ME

And what sort of risk do you want me to take?

The response is almost immediate.

I think you know.

Oh, I think I do, and my pulse quickens.

No one's come to the door yet, so I knock again. This apartment's never had a bell.

I take a deep breath and let it out as someone finally stirs inside. She told me I know, but it's still Gale. One wrong move and she could clam up.

Is kissing you on the table?

Kissing is acceptable. No need for a table.

I chuckle.

Noted. I'll see you tomorrow.

I hit send as Conner, my former roommate and teammate,

opens the door. A gaming headset is slung around his neck, and behind him, the TV has the latest RPG paused on screen.

"Who's the girl?"

I pocket my phone and play dumb. "Girl?"

Conner eyes me. "Finn, cut it. I have seen that same look on a bunch of guys over the years, but in the three years I've known you? Never. You're always thinking about the next thing. Now come on in and tell me who's got you focusing on the present for once." He retreats into the living room, leaving the door open so I can walk in behind him.

"Okay, but not while you're streaming." And I'm not telling him who it is either. Never mind who she is and what family she was born into, for all that she does that could put her in the spotlight where she rightfully deserves to be, Gale is a private person. I am not going to have her name floating around the Sailors' locker room for any reason, even in connection with me. Or maybe especially in connection with me. She doesn't need to be the focus of jock gossip, fodder for the next time our teams face off on the diamond during the second half of the season.

He puts his headset back on but only briefly as he saves the game before going to the main menu. In the corner of the TV, a small box shows the lower portion of his legs where his head would have been while playing. "All right, I'm cutting this sesh short. Catch me on socials to find out why. Later!" He ends the streaming connection, pulls off the headset, then grabs the remote and turns off the tv. He digs his phone out of his sweats and holds it up. "Come on, dude. For the fans."

I was a regular during his tournament streams whenever we had time for them, so I strike a pose. And by that, I mean I flop over the couch arm in a position I regularly gamed in, half upside-down. My buddy snaps a pic and swipes across the screen a couple times before typing something into the phone.

"And done."

Moments later, my phone dings with a notification. No doubt I've been tagged in the photo, so I don't bother to check. It's not a text, which means it's not from Gale, and that's the only thing worth looking at my phone for right now.

Conner slides his phone back into his pocket. "Now spill."

It doesn't take him long to realize I'm talking about the girl I fell on top of during my first game with the Snowhawks. Given how viral it went, it doesn't surprise me that the Sailors have all seen the video at least once. He doesn't mention anything about who the girl is. They probably only saw the highlight, not the full video naming her. Fine by me. With the way she tries to go unnoticed nowadays, someone would have to be pretty a big fan of the Snowhawks to recognize her and then link her to her dad and thus the team.

"Have you two hooked up yet?" he asks, and I shake my head. "Why not? She's hot."

"She is, but she's not like that. I'd like to get to know her first. It's been two days."

"And this is baseball heading into the trading deadline. What happens to you when the guy you're subbing for gets better?"

His comment hits me right in the gut. Could all this really be so short-term? I roll over into a sitting position on the couch. "You really think I'm being rented?"

He shrugs. "Maybe not for a week or two. The trade to get you there would have been a little extreme for that, in my opinion, but renting you until the end of the season? Totally possible. Have your fun while you can, Finn."

But I'm not that type of guy. "I don't want to just have fun."

"You mean you want a real relationship with her?"

"Yeah, I'm pretty sure I do."

He blows out a hard breath. "This isn't like some preexisting relationship from before you went big and she's going to follow you through your career. You expect a random fan who probably lives pretty close to the ballpark to stick with you once you leave?"

I want to tell him Gale's not random, but with her, that almost makes it harder. She's very settled in Snowhaven. Even if I went to another team in the region, it's not like she'd pack up and make that her home base. There aren't other Frost Foundations to transfer to.

"All I'm saying," he continues, "is that there's a reason why some guys have a girl in every city."

The thought of that roils my stomach, and my hand clenches. I would never do to someone what my so-called father did to my ma, leading her on and leaving her when she got pregnant because—surprise!—he already did the whole family thing once and that wasn't his thing anymore.

He puts up both hands in surrender. "I'm not saying you're like that because you're not. But not everyone is like you. And it's hard being a young, single guy sometimes. We have needs, ya know."

"Even you?" He was never the type, and that's not changed in the two games they've played since I've left.

"Needs, yes." He chuckles. "A girl in every city? No. That's too much to keep up with. My new roomie, however . . ."

My stomach sinks, but at least it doesn't feel sick anymore. "You are okay with him subletting, right?"

"Yeah, yeah. He knows the rules. But where do you think

he is now? Figured he'd give you some space tonight." Looking at the ceiling, he chuckles. "Rookies. He did say he'd be here early to help us move your stuff and sign the sublet agreement."

Phew. Nothing he can't handle. "Thanks. The earlier I can get back on the road, the better." I tell him about the rental mishap.

"And this girl is letting you borrow her vehicle. After two days?"

"Yeah."

Both of his eyebrows rise, impressed by the gesture. "Wow. That's big."

Devon's comment about how Gale doesn't do big gestures immediately comes to mind. "Yeah . . . It is."

"Maybe I'm wrong about this chick, then. What do I know about women anyway?"

"You think?"

"If you think she's worth the chance for as long as you might have it, then go for it. Like I said, I've never seen you like this before. You deserve to be happy. But make sure it's what you want." Conner pulls his phone back out and brings up his social media app, then scrolls through his notifications with the screen facing out so I can see it too. "Look at this. All I did was tag you, and it's the biggest post I've had in weeks. Yet you've not even pulled yours out once since you got here. You used to be all about that. Don't forget who you are because of some chick."

He has a point, but not the one he was trying to drive home.

Can I bring Gale into my world if I'm not going to be a part of the team for long? Should I even try?

Chapter 19
Gale

I greet Phoebe at my door with a giant half moon cookie from the bakery. The rest of the pastries from the bakery remain in the box inside my fridge, waiting for the girls to pick them up later.

"Come here, you delicious cookie." Bouncing on her feet in excitement, she practically yanks it from my hand with extreme eagerness. She immediately takes a bite. A crumb spills out of her mouth as she speaks. "Thank you. But don't think my early cookie will distract me from the matter at hand. Why am I picking you up at your house? Where is your car? How did your night with Finn go?"

I motion for her to give me some room, and when she does, I step out of the house and onto the stoop, closing the door behind me. "Finn is borrowing it."

"You lent him your car?" Her mouth parts in surprise.

I walk down the few cement stairs to the flagstone walkway leading across my yard to the driveway. "He needed one to help him move his stuff up from Saltair Shores. Something happened with his reservation with the rental place, and they didn't have anything he could use."

Phoebe follows me toward her silver sedan. "But you don't even let your friends drive your car, and suddenly you're fine with someone you practically just met borrowing it?"

"It's not that I have a problem with other people driving my car. I just don't enjoy being a passenger when it's happening. As long as I'm not in it, I'm fine." I open the passenger-side door, then slide onto the seat, buckle up, and wait for her to get in before I continue. "And what was I supposed to do, Phe? He left everything but his duffel bag with one set of street clothes behind when he got traded."

"When are you supposed to get it back?" She buckles up and then starts the car, throwing it into reverse.

"Later today. He's already texted to say they've started loading it up."

She half *oohs*, half squeals. "I see that smile. You like him, like him. Just what happened in your office yesterday afternoon? Start there and then tell me all about your field trip to the bakery."

As we drive the few blocks past the college campus where some of the team lives during the season and into the heart of town, passing the cat café, bus station, and the television network building where Dinah works, I tell her everything that transpired, right down to the way his fingers against mine sent tingles all the way up my arm.

Although she's known to tease me about any number of things, Phoebe's worked with me almost since the beginning, coming on as the foundation's administrative assistant a few months after she graduated, so she knows when teasing isn't going to work. A gentle ribbing when Finn comes into the office?

Totally okay. The squealy *ooh* when she saw me smile? That's fine too. But now she listens quietly until I'm done, knowing that if she stopped me, I'd build a dam to hold back a waterfall of words.

We're pulling into the staff parking lot as I finish my story.

She parks in her usual spot and cuts the engine. "That was a lot more than I was expecting."

"Uh-huh."

"And, wow, you are really bold by text sometimes." She undoes her seatbelt.

"Uh-huh. I don't know what came over me."

"You're freaking out a bit, aren't you?"

I still haven't moved to unbuckle myself. "Yeah."

"You do like him, though."

"Yeah, I do." I let out a long breath.

"And you do want him to kiss you, right?"

I don't hesitate. "Yes."

"When was the last time you kissed someone? I don't think you've dated anyone since I started at the Foundation."

"That's because I haven't." I pull a face as I half shrug, lifting only one shoulder. "There's never been time."

"Or . . ." She lets the word hang in the air a moment. "Have you just never found anyone worthy of your time?"

Finally I undo my belt, jolted to action by her hard-hitting question. "I . . . I don't know."

"You make time for the foundation and all of its causes. You make time for all of us when we need it. Heck, you only met Finn because the girls tricked you into thinking you were going to the game for Dinah's sake. This has been a strange time for you with everything that happened with your dad, and I get not wanting to add someone new into the mix, but you've always made time for those you think are important."

She reaches for her purse sitting on the center console

between us. "What I'm saying is, the time is there if you allow it to be. So if you like him and you want to kiss him, you can make the time for him. And you already are without even realizing that's what you're doing by taking the time out of your day to bring him to the bus station. So just think about it, okay?"

Oh, there is no doubt about how much I'm going to think about it. "I don't date baseball players."

"But you'd kiss them? You're not a casual hookup type of person. If you were, having time for a relationship wouldn't matter."

She's got me there. I don't do casual. "You don't think there's a problem with dating someone on the team?" Not that my rule is specific to the team.

She shakes her head. "And there's nothing anywhere in our employee handbooks that says we can't date someone on the team or within the organization."

I whip my head to face her. "Why were *you* looking in the employee handbooks for *that*?" All departments within the ballpark share an employee handbook for the overarching team organization. From players to concessions, security to ticket takers, us to other office staff. Everyone.

Her eyes widen. "No reason."

"Oh, there is absolutely a reason," I call out to her as she opens her door and quickly gets out. She shuts it hard and is already halfway to the door leading to the tunnels before I can even get out of the car.

I hurry to catch up with her, but she's got a good lead. If she's looking through the employee handbooks for the rules regarding relationships within the organization, there can only be one reason. And if she thinks I'm going to let this little tidbit of information go, then she has another think coming.

A buzz in my purse stops me, and Phoebe disappears around a corner as I dig my phone out of my bag. I let her go. After all, I know where she works. She can't escape.

FINN

Leaving now. ETA thanks to traffic is three hours.

ME

Drive safe! See you soon.

Before I hit send, I change my punctuation around. I contemplate changing only the second one, but that seems like too many exclamation points for me in such a short text. I am not that type of person. But I'm also not the type to want to seem short with people because of my perceived lack of enthusiasm.

Drive safe. See you soon!

And I very much want to see Finn.

He doesn't text back, so he's probably already on the road. Two hours and fifty-nine minutes. But who's counting?

I slip my phone back into my purse and head toward the office. No doubt Phoebe is halfway there by now.

I will get an answer out of her one way or another. She must like someone on the team, but who? I hope it's not Shane. That would make things awkward with Cassie. Or Toby because of Shelby. She's been best friends with Kyle for years, and he's friends with Noah and they were roommates with Josh for a while, so maybe it's one of them. She's never said anything to me before, and based on her reaction, that had not been a planned confession either. If I can't pry the information out of her, Macey and Dinah can at our next girls' night.

The office is locked when I get there. Did Phoebe get lost? It's not unheard of that someone gets lost down in the underground maze, though it's usually new hires not people who have been here for a few years. Have I riled her that much?

I unlock the door, flip the lights on, then head to my office to turn on my computer and store my purse.

As I'm sitting down to check my email, Phoebe calls out to me. "Help me out with this, will you?" Her question is followed by a loud thud.

I jump to my feet and hurry out to meet her and the rolling cart she's struggling with. I open the door wide for her.

"Mail call," she says as she backs in through the doorway, pulling the cart. "Carson from the mail room texted me on my way to the office. Figured it made sense to go there first."

The handful of boxes on the cart are all from the craft store. "Our snowflakes!" Or what will be snowflakes. The offseason sparkly paper had been on clearance when I found it online and was way cheaper than premade, pre-strung snowflake garlands, even taking into account the time needed to make them.

Phoebe wheels the cart to in front of her desk, and she plops her purse on top of it. "Guess this is what we're doing today. You bought extra scissors, right? I don't want to destroy mine on all of this." She walks behind her desk.

"Sure did. And yes. Gives us plenty of time to chat about why you ran off on me." I raise an eyebrow at her reddening face, which she hides as she ducks down to grab something out of her desk. I throw out the last name she mentioned. "It's not Carson, is it?" The handbook dealt with all employee relations, not just those involving players. I'd just assumed he was a player because of the Finn situation.

She stands. "I'm not saying anything to confirm or deny."

"But he has your number."

She shrugs and extends her arm over her desk, a box cutter in her hand. "He's got most of our numbers, the various office assistants. Faster than email sometimes." Her face is calm, the blush reducing. It's not him.

I take the cutter from her. "Oh. That makes sense. Are you sure it's not him?" I open the blade, then slide it through the tape on the top two boxes sitting side by side on the cart.

"Positive," she says with a laugh. "When is Finn due back?"

"Three-ish hours." I lift the flaps of the first box and pull out the supplies.

Phoebe does the same with the other box. "Looks like we have plenty to keep us busy until then."

Chapter 20
Finn

The three-hour traffic estimation did not take into account extra traffic thanks to an accident a mile up the road according to the GPS on my phone. We've been at a standstill for half an hour as emergency vehicles make it to the scene. It's another fifteen minutes before I inch forward and begin the crawl up the road, all the lanes needing to merge from three to two.

I'll be cutting it close to catch my bus to meet up with the team. There goes trying to convince Gale to get lunch with me when I get there.

I did a lot of thinking after Conner reminded me how long I'm going to be with the Snowhawks is an unknown. How serious can Gale and I get if I'm not here? Sure, she and I could have fun. There's obvious attraction there on both sides, but she's not the have fun and forget about it type. And I don't want to be that for her either. She deserves someone who can match her passion for everything she does with that same sort of commitment to her. How can that be me if I won't be here once the team's real first baseman gets better and I'm traded away? As much as I hate it, I need to tell her that.

As if she knows I'm thinking about her, my phone rings with the tone I set for her, part of the "Dance of the Sugar Plum Fairy" from *The Nutcracker*. I answer through the car's Bluetooth connection.

"Hey," she begins. "I didn't want to text since you should not be reading your texts. Too risky remember?"

The smile in her voice twists in my gut yet warms me all over at the same time. "I remember."

"Where are you? I thought you'd be here by now."

"Traffic," I grumble. "Still a half hour out." At least now I can see where the traffic clears after it gets past the accident. Oh, if people could just figure out how to properly zipper merge, we'd be out of this mess by now.

"Oh no! Have you eaten?"

Guess I wouldn't have had to try to convince her to go to lunch. The thought makes me smile, but barely. "No, but I don't think I'm going to have time to eat."

"I'll call and order it. Most places should have it ready in twenty. Dinah's stopping by for lunch today, so she can pick it up with ours. It'll be here when you get here."

"I'll have to eat it on the bus."

"But at least you won't go hungry. So what are you in the mood for?"

"What's good around there? I've had ballpark food, fast food, and Devon got takeout from the barbecue place after Sunday's game."

"I think I have a place in mind. Anything you don't eat?"

"Mushrooms." Oh, thank goodness. I'm finally through the traffic jam. I step on the gas, grateful to be moving at the speed limit again.

"Got it. No mushrooms."

"Thanks, Gale. I owe ya one."

"What are friends for, right?"

"Right." Friends. Sadly that's probably all we'll get the chance to be. "I'll see you soon."

We hang up, and I continue my drive back to the ballpark, arriving with little time to spare. Once I park in the staff lot, I do not trust myself to find my way to the foundation office through the tunnels, so I exit the garage and jog down the street to the foundation's door.

Gale's pops her head up the moment I enter. Her face brightens, a smile blossoming across her face. With sparkly paper fanned out all around her while she sits almost cross-legged, she's like the center of a shimmering flower, and I can't help but stare, drawn in by her beauty. If this were some nature documentary, this would be the part where the voice over warns viewers that the flower is dangerous, its looks having evolved over many years to lure its prey. I might be calling myself a bug in this comparison, but how can they—or I —resist?

"You made it!" she says brightly.

"What is all this?" I ask as I step inside the office, letting the door close behind me while the one across the room opens.

"This," Gale says, waving her hand over the makings of a massive paper cut waiting to happen, "is snowflake central."

"And this," Dinah says from behind me, "is lunch." She comes up next to me holding two medium-sized brown paper bags.

With grace that only a dancer could have, Gale effortlessly stands from the floor without using her arms to push her up, then captivates me all the more as she straightens and rolls her neck. "Perfect timing." She leaps over the rows of paper, and I can see now that many are large snowflakes cut from the rectangular paper.

"Is this all for your gala?"

"Uh-huh," she answers over her shoulder as she takes one of the bags from Dinah's outstretched hand. She spins on the balls of her feet to face me, and I smile at how her white flats have red lacing like a baseball does. As she walks toward me, I let my gaze roam up her dark trousers, the fitted baseball tee, and her loose light-brown ponytail hanging gently over one shoulder. "Like what you see?"

I nod, not trusting my voice.

Gale opens the bag, checking it. She pulls out a thin Styrofoam container and places it on the coffee table where Dinah and Phoebe have gathered to go through the other bag. Seemingly satisfied, she closes the bag, folding the top over.

"Are you ready to go?" Her voice is light. Happy.

I nod again.

"Have fun," Phoebe, now sitting on the couch in front of the coffee table, singsongs. Next to her, Dinah giggles.

For a moment, it seems like Gale is going to take my hand before thinking better of it. She smiles shyly at me instead and tells the girls, "Back in a bit." She walks past me, close enough that I can smell the mint from her shampoo once again as I turn to follow her. Then she pushes open the office door, holding it for me as she steps outside. "You coming?"

It only takes me two steps to catch up to her, and we walk side by side back toward the staff lot in the parking garage.

"You're quiet. Everything okay?"

I nod yet again. What am I, one of those promotional bobbleheads they give away at games? "Morning rush took a bit more out of me than I expected."

She sticks her arms out, gently tapping my stomach with the bag of food she's holding. "Then you should get started in on this. Hope you're hungry."

"Starving." I take the paper bag from her, a Boston Terrier's head emblazoned on the side under neon-light-style letters that read Dawg Pound. I open the bag and am greeted by multiple hot dogs rolled up in white paper, an open cup of curly fries, and another of onion rings. "Is all of this for me?"

Gale pivots toward me while still going forward and reaches into the bag, then steals a fry. I part my lips in surprise, not expecting this light-hearted behavior and finding this new side of her highly attractive. The fact she's showing me this part of herself makes it all the harder to show restraint. But the likelihood of being a rental weighs heavier, keeping me in check.

"I know fried food typically isn't the go-to before a game." She pops the fry into her mouth, raising her eyebrows playfully as she looks at me. "But this is one of my favorite places for a quick bite, and I figured it's still early enough to work a lot of this out of your system before batting practice and warmups. They have such a variety that I got you a few different things to try. And don't worry, no mushrooms."

I reach into the bag and grab a fry. It has the perfect amount of salt and is still crisp unlike so many other to-go fries that wind up in a closed container. "This is more than I expected."

"If it's too much food—"

"No, not like that. Thank you. This was really kind of you. All of it, from you letting me tag along to the bakery to letting me borrow your car, and now a full lunch?"

She shrugs like it's no big deal.

"Seriously though." I don't deserve it all. Or her. Not when I can't return the affection if I'm going to be leaving again. She deserves someone who will be able to call Snowhaven home.

"You're welcome."

We step into the parking garage, and I shove a couple of

onion rings into my mouth as we head for her SUV. My hand's in the bag again when she asks about her keys.

"Oh, um, hang on." I stuff the fry into my mouth and take the bag with that hand to grab the keys out of my back pocket with the other. I dangle the keyring in front of her, but she's looking at my lips, not the keys, a hopeful expression lighting up her beautiful face.

Now would be a perfect time to kiss her. To take that risk that she talked about, but time is already slipping away from us, and that is one thing I do not have in more ways than one. I clear my throat. "We should probably get me to the station."

Her gaze clears, and her cheeks turn slightly pink. "Oh, right. Yeah." She takes the keys from me, then clicks a button on her fob, unlocking the SUV. She opens her car door, and I do the same, but she stops when she looks inside. "Are you bringing all of this stuff with you?"

"Ugh." I drop my head back and look up at the ceiling. "I forgot to stop off at the dorm to drop stuff off. The traffic really threw me."

She waves it off, but I don't miss the long, silent exhale. "It's fine. I can look after it all while you're gone." She shakes her head quickly, more at herself, before asking, "There's no plant that needs watering hiding somewhere in here, is there?"

"No, nothing like that. Clothes mostly. Better bedding than what the dorm has. Some school books."

She tilts her head to the side as she steps up into the car. "School books?"

"Just because I signed with the Sailors to play ball before my junior year does not mean I stopped going to school." I click my seatbelt into the clip. "It's taking me longer, sure, but I'm not giving up on it."

"Oh." She buckles up, then presses the ignition button. "What are you studying?"

"Psychology. With plans to specialize in sports psychology."

"That's impressive."

It's not a long ride to the bus stop, but my hunger and desire to eat as much of this food as possible keeps it a quiet one. I manage to scarf down two "dawgs," one with salsa and melted cheddar cheese and the other with honey mustard, bacon, and cheese. There's a third one in there, but more probably wouldn't be a good thing right now.

"There are more fries still if you want them," I tell Gale as she pulls into a spot at the bus station. "Thank you again for everything."

"You're welcome." She looks in the rearview mirror at all my stuff behind her. "Do you need help getting anything?"

"No. It might not look it, but I've become a pretty efficient packer." I open the passenger door and get out, then open the back seat door behind it to where I shoved my bag before I got into the car. It's heavy, but I won't have to tote it so far on my own once I've met up with the team.

Gale's standing next to me when I step back to close the door. "Let me know when you get there?" The uncertainty in her voice stings, as does the knowledge that I caused her to sound that way.

"Yeah, I will."

She searches my face, and I wish I had more time to tell her everything that I've been thinking since last night. "Have a safe trip." She lifts up onto her toes and presses a soft kiss against my cheek. "I'm not sure what's changed between us all of a sudden, but I'm still willing if you are."

"Even if I'm just a rental?" I can barely meet her gaze now as my stomach twists.

Her face falls, the disappointment evident, and she takes a step back. "I see. And the gala? Your charity?"

"If I'm still here then, I will do everything we talked about." Now I'm forcing myself to look at her so she knows I'm serious. It's so hard to not let myself go to her, to break my resolve and give her more than I should without the solid foundation of time to support it all. "Everything."

She nods, giving me a half smile, but the sparkle in her eyes has dimmed. I could kick myself for doing that to her.

The speaker overhead sends out a tone before an electronic voice announces the bus pulling up to the platform, preventing us from saying more. "That's me."

"Have a safe trip."

"Thanks."

My shoulders fall as I turn away from her, and as soon as I'm on the bus, I pull my phone out to text her. To tell her I should have kissed her. To say that, despite my possibly limited time here, she's worth me risking my heart— that it might be too late because it's already well on its way to being hers.

But then I get the first notification. And then the next. And another. I read the first as yet another pops up.

Oh, no.

Chapter 21
Gale

It only takes Phoebe and Dinah one look when I get back to the office. They put the snowflakes they were cutting on the ground next to them.

"What happened?" Phoebe asks.

"Cold feet."

"Hey, that's okay," Dinah begins. "It's been a while. You're bound to get nervous when you're out of practice."

"Not me. Him."

Phoebe's jaw drops. "Him?" I nod. "After the way he couldn't take his eyes off you when he walked in? You rendered him speechless, and all you were doing was sitting here like I am."

"He called himself a rental." I sigh.

Phoebe's response is a single, flat. "Oh." Around here, we all know what that means.

I drop my head back and stare at the ceiling. "I get it. Really, I do. But ugh, why couldn't he have thought about that before my feelings got involved?"

"Would you really want to be with a rental?"

"What's a rental?" Dinah asks.

"It's a term they use for players who get traded to a team but don't last long because the contract they came with expires at the end of the season. Through no fault of their own, they attract a certain type of fan," I explain, pacing the floor.

"If you can call them that," Phoebe quips before adding, "cleat chasers."

We see them all the time. Girls who hang out as close to the dugout as they can once games are over, trying to get attention from the players. Getting as close to the player exit as they can for the same reason, all in hopes of hooking up. It happens more often during the late season call ups if we're close to the post season and are expected to make a run. The guys are usually younger, might not be as attached. It also happens at the visitor dugout, where women hope to hook up with someone just here for a few days. But if you stay here long enough, some of the faces you see multiple times. The girls want the possibility of the limelight, of being spotted with a famous player, hopes of being the new "it girl." Rental or not, only rarely does a player ever hit it off with a cleat chaser. Players don't want to be seen as a potential avenue for fame and fortune people. They want to be seen as people.

And that's how I see Finn. A really good person. Flipping and dancing on the field is only one part of him. He's thoughtful and dedicated. Someone I want to be around. Even if he is a baseball player.

"I don't care," I say after a moment, shaking my head. "If that's all he is, that doesn't make you any less right."

Phoebe arches a brow. "Come again? Did you just say I was right about something?" She picks her scissors back up but freezes with her hand on the half-done snowflake. "What am I right about?"

"Finn's a great guy, and worth my time, no matter how long he's here. And what if he's not a rental? What if he stays and we waste all of this time when we didn't need to? And if he is a rental, there are plenty of teams in the region. I could get to those games on weekends no matter who he's with. Wives are allowed to travel with the team, albeit separately, for one assignment too." I think back to the short warm-weather vacations my mom would go on to meet my dad on the West Coast or in Florida while the Snowhawks played teams there.

Dinah squeals excitedly. "Aww, you're thinking about marriage!"

I roll my eyes. "No, I'm not." I don't think so, anyway. "I'm just saying that there are ways to make this work if things got to the point where we were together but he was no longer on the team." The idea of him not being a part of the team already rankles me. Not least of which is because he seemed so invested in his charity of choice when we spoke. "He'd be a great asset for the foundation."

"Yeah, I remember what else you said about his assets this morning." Phoebe grins cheekily.

Dinah squeals again. "I think you have some explaining to do."

I stop pacing and lower myself to the floor where I had been earlier. "What? He looks really good in jeans." I grab a sparkly sheet of paper off the stack next to me and fold it into eight sections before cutting into it.

"Feeling better?" Phoebe asks as she unfolds her snowflake.

"Kinda." I sigh. "If only he wasn't going to be gone for the next couple of weeks."

The desk on Phoebe's phone rings, and she sets her snowflake onto a stack that keeps slipping sideways no matter how many times we fix it because of the type of paper it is. As she struggles to get to her feet, I stand without issue, both thanks to being on the floor for less time and a regular exercise routine that I've kept up with despite not dancing anymore.

"I got it." I hurry over to her desk before the call can go to voicemail. The ID on the phone says it's from here at the ballpark, our public relations department. Not uncommon given all of the events we do.

"Frost Foundation. Gale speaking."

A woman's voice responds, "Gale, just who I wanted to talk to," and I smile. Patty has been working with the team since my dad played. She's practically a bonus aunt.

"How are you, Patty?"

"Good, good. Hey, when you get a second, could you come down to my office so we can chat?"

"Sure. This about the gala?"

"No . . ." The waver in her voice puts me on edge, twisting my stomach into a knot. "But I'd rather not discuss it on the phone."

"Oh . . . okay. I'll be right there." Phoebe and Dinah both eye me quizzically. I shrug.

"Thanks, I'll see you in a few." Patty hangs up.

I put the phone back in its cradle.

"What's that all about?" Phoebe says as I walk back around her desk.

"No idea, but I have to go find out."

Dinah sets down the snowflake she just finished. "I should be heading out too." She stands.

I glance down at Phoebe. "Are you okay down there, or would you like some help up before I leave?"

She sticks her hand out, and together Dinah and I get her back on her feet. Phoebe shakes her left leg, then her right before hobbling back to her desk. "Ugh . . . pins and needles."

That's sort of how my stomach feels right now with not knowing what Patty wants to talk about, only that it has to be done in person.

Dinah says her goodbyes, then I head back to the office to stow my bag. But before I do, I dig my phone out and slide it into my back pocket.

"Okay, back whenever," I call over my shoulder as I leave the office.

Fortunately, the PR office isn't far. As another facet of the organization that regularly deals with those from the outside, it's also got a street-facing office as well. Outside, I feel a sense of déjà vu, only this time without Finn or french fries. I walk in the opposite direction of the staff lot, up a few dozen yards, then into the PR office.

It's not just Patty waiting for me once I'm inside. Someone from human resources is standing at Patty's desk, her eyes keenly focused on me. I steel myself and try to concentrate on Patty, who's giving me a warm smile. Her eyes, however, express concern.

"What's going on?" No sense tiptoeing around it.

"You've met Claudia from HR, right?"

I nod to the woman at Patty's desk. "Good to see you again, Claudia." But there's no smile in my voice. "Please. Tell me what's going on."

"We're hoping you could tell us," Claudia begins as she sits in one of the chairs across from Patty and motions for me to do the same.

I do, staying perfectly straight, my hands clasped in my lap, my knees off to the side, ankles crossed. The picture of perfect professionalism.

"What is your relationship with Finn Nixon?" Claudia

asks, and I'm suddenly wondering why we're in Patty's office instead of hers.

"No relationship." Dread churns in my stomach, but I keep my walls up and face passive. "I met him on the other day when he fell on me catching that foul ball during the game."

"And nothing is going on between you two?"

"Nothing." My tone is cool, clipped. "But even if there was, there isn't anything against that, is there?" Might as well get an official answer from the source. For Phoebe's sake.

"No," Claudia begins.

But Patty continues, "We do, however, ask to be kept up to date about these sorts of things, so we aren't surprised should something happen." That part is news to me, but this is not a preventative meeting. That's a phone call conversation. Even an email.

I press my feet hard into the floor, grounding myself in a way that's not noticeable. "And I take it something did if I'm sitting here now. What aren't you telling me?"

"Don't freak out," Patty warns as she turns her computer monitor so I can see it. At the top of the screen is the logo for a gossip blog that follows big league news from across the region. It's one that regularly posts dramatic and often made-up trade rumors or clubhouse fallouts. It's the type of site that loves a good scandal. A site that those sorts of fans only in it for the attention love to find themselves on when they attach themselves to ball players. It never lists its sources, making every piece of information dubious at best.

But there on the screen is a picture of me digging for a fry from the paper bag Finn's holding. Our arms pressed up against one another's as I'm mid laugh over something he's said, and he's gazing at me in a way that warms me just looking at it before remembering that he then failed to kiss me. I bite the inside of my cheek to keep from reacting as I read the headline.

Snowhawks' Newest Star Ditches Team During First Road Trip
The first baseman was spotted with a mystery woman outside Frost Field while team travels on Tuesday afternoon.

"That's me," I confirm. "But you obviously know that."

Patty nods. "We'd like to get ahead of this *news*." She says news with obvious sarcasm.

"Call it what it is, Patty. It's gossip. And not true."

"So he wasn't with you today?" Claudia asks.

"Okay, that part is true, yes." I explain the issue with the rental car and how I'd taken him to the bus station so he could rejoin the team in time for tonight's game. "In no way is he ditching the team, especially not for me."

"And are you sure there's nothing going on between the two of you?" Claudia presses. "You two look pretty chummy."

"No." I crack the tiniest bit. "I don't know. He's offered to help with the gala."

Patty claps once. "That's perfect."

"Perfect how?" She seems way too happy about this, whereas it's everything I've wanted to avoid. I'm amazed whoever posted this didn't identify me.

"That's what we go on record saying. A press release that Finn was here today to meet with you about foundation business and that he's already on his way back to the team."

My eyes widen. "You want to name me as the mystery woman? They're going to have a field day with that. Gale Frost's granddaughter and Dustin Frost's daughter striking up a relationship with a baseball player. I can picture the headlines already." I flash back to all of the tabloids during my parents' divorce. The distraction. The unwanted drama. The stress.

"I understand you have a complicated history with the media because of your upbringing. But at least this way we'll control the narrative. Get ahead of them. Put this out before those other headlines appear."

"I see your point."

"This isn't the first time we've had to put out a statement like this, even recently, for someone connected to the team. It's not like it used to be. Anyone can snap a picture nowadays and post it online to start rumors. Coming at it with facts and a united front, meaning having both you and Finn saying the same thing we will, is the best way to make it go away."

I take a deep breath and close my eyes. "Okay."

"Great," Claudia says. "Then it's settled."

Patty turns her monitor back toward herself. "Let me get cracking on this." She's not kidding as her fingers fly over her keyboard. "I'll send it to you before I post it publicly."

"Thank you." I get up from the chair. "I'm going to give Finn a head's up on what's going on. He's probably still on the bus. He might not know."

Claudia stands. "I guess my work here is done. But Gale"—I look up to meet her gaze—"I saw the way he's looking at you in the photo. If anything regarding your relationship status changes, please let me know." She gives me a kind smile, then nods at Patty before walking out of the office.

Patty smiles kindly at me. "And Gale?"

"Hmm?" I meet the woman's gaze.

"Good luck. With all of it. I saw how he was looking at you too. Don't let this get in the way of what could be a good thing. You deserve to be happy."

There's no point telling her nothing's going to happen

since Finn already put a stop to it. So I simply say, "Thank you." Then I give her a small nod and rush from the office, my hand already on my cell phone. This whole PR incident may be further proof of why I shouldn't date baseball players, but Finn deserves to know about what happened regardless.

I pull up Finn's number as I step outside, scanning the streetscape for anywhere that shot could have been taken from. Across the street somewhere based on the angle. One of the stores maybe? An apartment above them? Someone on the sidewalk we paid no attention to? I press *call* and wait half a ring for him to answer.

"Gale?" Finn's voice sounds conflicted as he says my name.

"Hey. Are you still on the bus?"

"Yeah. Fifteen minutes or so until we get to the station."

"Good. I wanted to give you a heads-up. There's a photo." I search the windows and open doorways across the street.

"I saw it."

"You did?"

"Yeah. I got tagged in it on socials." Of course he did. "I wanted to tell you but didn't think you'd want to hear from me. Especially not about this. I know you don't like being in the spotlight." He sighs, the sound almost sad. I don't like hearing him this way. "I'm sorry."

"It's not your fault." I pass the door to the foundation's office, not wanting to give whoever took that photo any more ammunition before Patty can post her press release.

"That's not all I'm sorry for."

"Oh." My stomach flops, and I wish I'd had more than one fry to weigh it down.

"I should have kissed you."

What am I supposed to say? Yes, he should have because I wanted him too—because I still want him to? Or no, because this would be way messier if he had and we really shouldn't be getting involved with one another? Wanting to stay on topic for the moment, I avoid his statement completely. "The PR team is going to issue a statement naming me as the mystery woman." I'll come back to his admission later.

"Now I'm even more sorry."

"Again, not your fault. But they're going to say you were here because you were helping the foundation. To paint you in a positive light as if this was planned on our end and to give some attention to the gala."

"Okay. I can work with that." He's sounding more like the Finn I knew prior to this afternoon's lack of a kiss.

"You don't actually have to do anything," I tell him as I pass the door leading to the staff lot. I'm not using this door either. Someone could still be out here, waiting for another photo. It's going to be awhile before I walk outside here again. At least on non-game days. There would have been too many people on the street if there was a home game today for anyone to get a good photo.

"But I want to. I've said that since yesterday when we talked about it."

"Gosh, was that only yesterday?" I scrub at my face with my free hand. I was not planning on being out in the sun like this today, and my SPF face lotion from this morning has long since lost its effectiveness. I need to get inside soon.

He lets out a puff of air in a half chuckle. "Yeah. A lot can happen in a day, huh?"

"Yeah." I round the corner of the stadium, and when I'm sure I'm out of sight from anyplace that could still get my photo from the street, I duck into the parking garage via the car's entrance, waving at the security guard on my way in. He nods in acknowledgment but eyes me quizzically, though he doesn't say anything.

"I think I may have an idea, but I'll need to see if I can get some stuff to pull it off."

"Okay." I stop walking and lean against a support pole so the phone doesn't cut out from me being too far into the garage. "But no worries if it doesn't happen. You actively being at the gala is fine enough."

"No. This is the least I could do. I'm going to make it up to you. For all of this. Hey, Gale?"

"Yeah?"

"I see the station now."

"Okay, I'll let you go. Keep me posted?"

"Of course. You do the same."

I want to continue this conversation. Agree with his earlier statement. That he should have kissed me. But there's not enough time for the rest of that conversation. Instead I say, "Keep your eye on the ball, but no falling on anyone else tonight, okay?" Hopefully he gets the hint.

"Deal." There's a hint of a chuckle in his voice.

"I'll be watching."

"I'm counting on it."

Chapter 22
Finn

I step off the bus and no more than twenty feet from the exit, I freeze at the sight of my ride. The team's traveling secretary had said someone would be waiting for me with a car, but I'd been expecting him to pick me up, or a team assistant, an equipment manager, even someone from the other team's game-day support staff as a courtesy.

Mack was the last person I'd expected to see, but there he is, arms crossed.

"Nixon," he greets me in a flat, authoritative tone.

"Sir." I nod sharply in return. "Usually I'd have some joke here to lighten the mood, maybe an *aww, is this for little old me* or something about rolling out the red carpet, but I'm pretty sure I know what this is about, and you deserve complete honesty and sincerity."

His face relaxes slightly, and he points to my duffel. "That it?"

"Yes, sir."

He turns, and I follow him toward a town car waiting a few rows back. No driver, so he came alone.

We stay silent until the car starts.

"So obviously you saw the gossip column," I start.

"Obviously. And obviously you had permission to leave the team, so those claims don't bother me. The whole team knew of the arrangement, and unfortunately too many know about being the focus of this gossip column. You're square with them. But what I'm trying to understand is how Gale got involved. This is from today, yes?"

"Yes, sir." I go on to explain what happened with the rental. "So the photo you see there is her stealing a french fry from the lunch that she had her friend Dinah pick up for me so I wouldn't be starving once I got here. I didn't take any extra time to be with her. There is nothing going on."

"I don't see this nothing you're claiming."

I whip my head toward him. "I can assure you, nothing's happened. The last thing I want to do is hurt her." Though I did exactly that by not kissing her.

"What I see is Gale happy. Finally."

"Sir?"

"Even before her father passed, Gale was, how should I put it . . ." He comes to a stop as the light turns red. "Serious. She's always been kind and had a good heart, but she's not freely giving of smiles. More like eye rolls, and we all certainly got plenty of those in the dugout as she got older. Sure, there were the polite, placating smiles, but real smiles, like the one I saw in that photo today? I think my girls would call those a unicorn."

"Girls? You have more than Macey?"

"Three daughters. And I like seeing my girls happy. All of them, honorary ones included."

"I like making Gale smile, sir."

The light turns green, and he accelerates. "I'm glad to hear it. I've already told you I'm watching you. Now here is my warning. Do not do anything to make that smile disappear. You're already proving to be an asset to the team in more ways than one. You could have a long career here. I would hate to have to get rid of you because you've messed this up with her."

I blink, momentarily stunned by that statement. "Are you saying I'm not just some rental for the second half of the year?"

He barks out a laugh. "A rental? You? After what we gave up to get you here? Hardly." He laughs some more. "You're funny, Nixon."

I have no idea how to answer that since I wasn't joking. And I'm still too busy processing the fact I'm not a rental.

Mack clears his throat. "Now, Gale won't like that she's being depicted as some mystery woman trying to divert your attention away from the team. It's only a matter of time before she's identified, and that won't be much better."

"Why *does* she avoid the spotlight?"

"Ah . . . that's a two-fold answer, and I'm not the one you should be talking to for some of it. But she knows how important the Frosts are to the team and the town. Really, the whole league. Plus the foundation, which wouldn't exist without her grandfather. She takes that seriously. Sometimes too much so. She'd rather let the foundation work shine through and focus the attention that follows her onto the charities she supports."

The stadium we're playing at comes into view. "So you're aware, Gale has seen the photo and the team is going to ID her as the mystery woman in the photo with me."

He raises a brow but says nothing.

"Something about taking back the narrative, so she says. And that I was with her on foundation business so they can mention the gala in the press release."

"Probably the only way she'd willingly agree to being named."

That fact stings, but I understand it. "Better now than leave people to speculate and spread rumors about her being a distraction."

"She'd never let that happen, you know. Be a distraction for you. Not when you're a master at it yourself. I see what you're doing with all of your videos, your antics. It's smart."

"Thank you, sir. What you see out there is me. But it's only a part of me. I've always had a plan."

"And does part of your plan involve Gale?" We pull up alongside the stadium, a section blocked off to all other traffic and anyone without a staff lanyard. There are few people here with hours still to go before the game. But within another couple of hours, this place will be bustling with activity.

I think about how just a few days ago I'd wanted to have one person come to the game for me. Not because they loved the team and I happened to be their favorite player. But for personal reasons. And how happy I was to see Gale there with the flower in her hair. That she'd done that just for me.

"In all honesty, sir, it does if she wants the same."

"Based on that picture, she does."

"Then can I ask for a favor sir?"

Turning off the engine, he eyes me critically.

"I need sparkly paper, scissors, and a permanent marker."

Chapter 23
Gale

A half hour before the game, Macey arrives at my house, Greek takeout in two bags hanging from her arm. Dinah is right behind her with two bottles of wine.

I'm in my pajamas, not expecting visitors in the slightest. We're supposed to meet up tomorrow for a pastry drop-off. "What are you doing here?"

"I brought food," Macey says as if that explains everything.

Phoebe comes running up the driveway, a grocery bag in hand. "And I have ice cream!"

"Well, come on in." I step aside to let them all in.

Macey sets the takeout on my kitchen table. "I got your favorite."

Phoebe hands me the ice cream. "Here. I got an assortment plus toppings." As a latter addition to our friend group, and one who doesn't hang out with us all the time, she's not as comfortable as the other girls with going through my things, even if it's just to put food away.

"Would you like something to drink?" I offer Phoebe. She's not a big drinker. "I've got seltzer water you can add flavor to."

She nods, and I scoot past Dinah, who's now digging through the drawer where I keep my wine bottle opener, so I can get Phoebe a glass. As I put away the ice cream and toppings, I pull out a bottle of seltzer water for her and place it next to the glass. "Flavors are next to my coffee pot. Help yourself."

Bottle opener acquired, Dinah moves to my cabinets to grab out wine glasses, and Macey's tearing into the bags and splitting everything into piles of containers. With four piles, meaning Phoebe has food too, this was clearly planned between the three of them.

Dinah pours a glass of wine and hands it to me. "We got an SOS about the photo and the press release."

My gaze darts to Phoebe, who shrugs. "They'd already seen it." She sips from her glass before adding in another squirt of flavor.

Macey turns, her takeout container in hand. "Shelby couldn't make it, but there should be texts on your phone from her. Cassie too. How are you holding up?"

I sigh. "Is it better or worse that nothing's happened between us?"

"Worse, definitely worse," Dinah says as she takes two glasses of wine to the couch. She hands one to Macey before putting the other on my coffee table. She returns to the kitchen table for her food. "At least there'd be some truth to what's going on."

I take my food and follow Dinah back to the living room, opting for my computer chair so I can use my desk as a table.

"What *is* going on, Gale?" Macey asks from my couch as she tucks her leg up under herself. "It seems like there's definitely *something*."

Phoebe takes the third spot on the couch, and all three stare expectantly, waiting for my answer.

I open my takeout container, avoiding their gaze as I admit, "I kissed him."

"What?" Dinah and Macey shriek in excitement, and Phoebe follows this with, "You did not tell me that."

"Relax. It was only on the cheek."

"And what did he do?"

"He walked away." I shrug. "The bus was there. He had to go."

Dinah groans. "No excuse. And that's even with knowing what he said."

Macey holds up her hand. "Why don't you start at the beginning so I can get the whole story."

So I do. By the time I finish, I'm done with my wine and the game is in the bottom of the first inning after a fast top half.

"I love those uniforms," Dinah says wistfully. The road uniforms for the Snowhawks are an icy, bright gray for both the pants and shirt with navy pin stripes on the pants. I've always found them to be classy, though they show grass stains more than the home uniforms do.

"Agreed." I lift my glass, disappointed when I remember it's empty.

"And Finn looks good in it," Macey teases, but she'll get no argument from me. "I wouldn't worry about the gossip column. The team obviously knows it's a bunch of baloney. And they didn't even know who you are? How reputable can this source be?"

She has a point. Any sports fan around here would have no doubt of who I am, even at that angle. It's not like I stayed that way for long. "Maybe they followed Finn from Saltair Shores? Or are just new to the area?"

"Always a possibility," Phoebe says, pulling out her phone. "He's got a large fan base."

"One of the biggest in baseball thanks to his viral videos," Dinah says, and Macey nods.

"Over a million followers." Phoebe holds up her phone and shows me her phone screen. "Why does he have a closeup of our arts and crafts session?"

I make a grabbing motion, and she passes me her phone. "It's similar, I'll give you that, but the paper's different. Those aren't either of our scissors either."

"So what's he doing?"

"Couldn't tell ya. There's no caption with it." I hand the phone back to her, and she pockets it as I dip a french fry into some tzatziki sauce. "Do you think I should talk to your dad, Macey? Tell him I'm not going to be some distraction?"

Thank goodness for Macey. That one fry of Finn's earlier today was not enough. I love potatoes. I do not love when they get to be room temperature like mine were once I felt like I could eat. Should have brought mine to the bus stop, though I thought I'd be occupied by something—someone—else.

Macey laughs. "You think you need to actually tell him that? He's known you for over half your life, remember? Give him some credit."

"I just don't want him to assume something that's not true because he saw the photo and for him to take it out on Finn."

"You know he's not like that. Besides, Finn wouldn't be on the field if he was."

I munch on another fry. "That's true. And it's not like he was doing anything wrong. He was just trying to get back to the team."

Phoebe takes a sip of her seltzer. "The only wrong he did was to not kiss you like he said he would." The other girls raise their glasses in agreement.

Macey laughs. "I can't believe how you told him that kissing is acceptable, no table needed."

I bury my face in my hands. "Ugh . . . don't remind me." I'm such a terrible flirt.

"Um, Gale? You just got tzatziki in your hair."

My shoulders drop. Of course I did. "Be right back."

We're in the top of the third inning when I'm done washing that bit of my hair in the bathroom sink. I might enjoy the spiced cucumber yogurt smell on food, but I did not want to wait until tomorrow morning's shower to get it off me.

"Hurry!" Macey calls from the living room. "Finn's coming up to bat!"

I quickly dry my hands but forgo blow drying that section of hair. It's not a lot, and the girls don't care how my hair looks. It's a me-thing that I do. Always aware of how I look from years of competitions and then the family reminding me how a Frost should look and act.

I shuffle-run back to my seat, tying my hair up with a scrunchie while I do so I can avoid any more accidents. I still have to make it through my ice cream.

But as I go to watch Finn, who's moved up a spot in the batting order, I'm greeted with the photograph of Finn and me on the television, text from a portion of the press release next to it on the screen as the broadcasters and analysts in the booth read the entire statement.

I already know what it says. I okayed it without edits when Patty sent it to me, but I don't like seeing it. "Anyone for another drink?"

Dinah hands me the bottle, and I drain the rest of it into my glass.

"She's grown up, hasn't she, Cliff?"

"You said it, Joe. I remember her coming up and visiting us in the booth when she was just a kid."

"We have some of that cued up, don't we?"

I groan. "Oh no. You have got to be kidding me."

"We do, and oh! Nixon draws a walk to get on base. That was a battle, wasn't it?"

"Sure was, now let's see that footage."

I'm confronted with a toothless me in a headset helping a much younger looking Cliff and Joe in the booth at Frost Field call plays while my dad was pitching.

The girls *aww* at the sight, Phoebe adding an "Oh my goodness, you were so cute!" at the end.

"Thank goodness they aren't pulling up any of my dancing in the stands footage." I knock on the wooden top of my coffee table. I'm not superstitious, especially not the way some ballplayers are, but I'm not taking any chances.

"Gale Frost is, of course, the daughter of Dustin Frost, legendary pitcher and former manager of the Snowhawks, and the granddaughter of the first Gale Frost, the founder and first owner of our beloved team."

Pictures of me with my dad and grandfather over the years dominate the screen as a picture-in-picture screen of Finn on first base appears at the bottom corner. I try focusing on him as the photos feel like a gut punch, many having been used at my dad's funeral last fall and at the on-field memorial for him before the season started. I breathe in long and deep in an attempt to keep my emotions in check. I will not cry. The tickle in my nose means nothing.

The last pictures are of me at foundation events, including

the last with my dad just a few months before he died, one of his last public appearances.

"Gale now runs the Frost Foundation, the official team charity of the Snowhawks, formed by her grandfather when he sold the team. For our viewers in the Snowhaven area, the foundation's Christmas in July Gala is coming up, and tickets are now available."

"You think these two will go to the gala together?"

"Now Cliff, you know how I don't like to speculate on personal matters."

"All I'm saying, Joe, is they look good together. They clearly are enjoying each other's company in this photo, and look! He's practicing his moves right now."

Cliff and Joe disappear from the screen as the network's producers bring the screen of Finn dancing on first base to full size.

"I hope he doesn't dance like that for real," Macey jokes. "What even is that?"

Phoebe laughs through her response. "Some sort of jig, I think."

"If he's not careful," Dinah begins, taking a sip of her wine, "They're going to tag him out."

I shake my head. "Footwork is too fast. Even for someone just goofing around. He's on top of the bag. Not worth the risk. He's a distraction if nothing else." I point at the screen? "See? Right there. The pitcher can't stop looking."

The pitcher brings his hands up, ready to start his windup, but Finn jumps off the base in a final attempt to break the pitcher's concentration. It works. The pitcher's foot pivots ever so slightly before he throws the ball toward home. He grimaces, realizing what he's done.

The umpire at the plate stands and points to the pitcher, yelling something we can't hear.

"What just happened?" Dinah asks.

"Pitcher balked," Macey says.

"Which is?"

Macey explains it while Finn finishes his jig of a jog, or is it a jog of a jig, to second base. Barely four days ago, I'd been horrified by Finn's on-field antics, worried about how he would impact such a storied team like the Snowhawks. That the Snowhawks were too serious of a team for such displays. But as Finn stands at second, watching the plate while Devon bats, I realize the goofiness he shows is not that at all. The sports psychology angle starts to make all the more sense.

"He's a genius."

The girls turn and look at me. "Who is?"

"Finn. He's not just some goofball. The dancing. It's a purposeful, serious distraction. He's read the situation." As I speak, Devon hits a single, but it's fielded too close to third for Finn to attempt running there. And as the top of the order comes up once again, Devon starts to dance on first base. Some sort of salsa variation that keeps a foot on the bag. "The pitcher's young. His first season in the majors. Finn's using that to his advantage. And he's got Devon following along."

A newfound feeling swells within me as the pitcher continues to be distracted, giving our leadoff man a golden opportunity to capitalize when he goes deep to right field. As Finn comes home and waits for Devon so they can do some special shake they've already worked out with one another, I recognize it as respect. And that is a highly attractive quality.

"So how do you explain that?" Macey asks as the game comes back from commercial at the bottom of the seventh.

"What is he doing?" Dinah asks.

"Is he? No . . ."

"He's making a snow angel in the grass."

"Who's he trying to distract now?"

"He's not." I shrug. "Our reliever is warming up on the mound. But he's maintaining appearances. Throwing people off and making everyone think he's just having fun. Plus, he's winning over the fans."

"And you." Macey wags her eyebrows at me.

I roll my eyes. "Fine. And me."

"Does this mean you're finally willing to give up your stupid rule," she asks, her eyebrow wagging having morphed into one raised in challenge.

Phoebe and Dinah both turn their gazes away from the TV.

"Stupid? You didn't think it was stupid when you made the same rule."

"Yeah, in high school. We're not kids anymore."

"We haven't been kids in a long time. Why only bring it up now?"

"Because there's a baseball player who might finally be worthy of you."

Phoebe holds up a hand. "Wait, I thought we sorted out this issue when I told you there was no rule in the handbook against dating within the organization. So your rule has nothing to do with dating Snowhawks?"

I shake my head. "It's always been all baseball players."

"And this began in high school?"

I nod. "Yeah. The baseball players were all over me, us." I wave a hand between me and Macey, who's texting on her phone. "They wanted access to our dads. To the team. Not actually us. It was easier to say we didn't date baseball players than to get involved. The same thing happened in college. I wouldn't even date fans. The rule kinda took on a life of its own."

Macey sets down her phone. "Cassie's in agreement. It's time."

"Did she have the same rule?" Dinah asks before taking a sip of her wine.

"Yeah," Meg begins. "Was the first one to break it too."

"Or at least try to," I amend, "since the whole promposal to Shane didn't work out."

"Not the point. The point is you deserve to be happy with someone, and a ten-plus-year-old rule shouldn't stop you from finding out if Finn could be that person when you are both clearly interested." I go to open my mouth, but Macey stops me. "And don't start in on the rental bit again. You've already argued against that reason yourself."

Dinah raises her glass. "All those in favor of Gale breaking her rule?"

"Aye!" Phoebe and Macey cheer loudly in unison, lifting their glasses into the air.

Feeling slightly ganged up on but very much loved by my friends, I too raise my wine glass. "Aye."

Unfortunately, despite the earlier home run and their opposing starter's early night due to a high pitch count, we don't come away with a win.

I see the girls to the door. "Thank you for all of this. All of you. I was totally planning a pity party for one tonight, and you've made it so much better."

Dinah flaps her hand at me. "No pity here, I assure you. If anything, it's him I pity for not making a move when he should have." I frown at the reminder, but she quickly recovers. "And he's already said he should have kissed you. So at least he's regretting that."

Macey hugs me. "And now that you're going to break your rule, let's make sure he kisses you the next time he sees you."

Chapter 24
Finn

I wake up early after a good night's sleep. This is one of the nicer hotels I've stayed in since I started playing, and the bed is worlds better than the couch I slept on the night before.

After a good workout and a hearty breakfast with several of the guys, I head back up to my room. The guys invited me to tour the city we're in this morning, but I took a rain check with the promise I'll meet up with them for lunch before we have to head to the stadium. Tomorrow I'll have to go out with them, though. Everyone on the team knows why I didn't travel with them to get here, but I don't want to feed into the rumors by not hanging out with them either. The press release helped, but social media is still buzzing with gossip.

And I plan to harness some of it right now.

I pull my small tripod out of my duffel and set it up so it can capture me sitting at the desk in my room along with what's on top of the desk. Satisfied with the resulting photo, I post it on my socials to entice my followers to come see what the stuff in front of me is all about. At the end of the caption, I tag the Frost Foundation, both as a clue and with the hope Gale will see what I'm doing.

Five minutes later, I stick the camera on selfie mode and lean in so viewers can only see my face at first.

"Hey there, Hawks fans! It's Finn. Not gonna lie, a lot has happened since I first popped on here to introduce myself to you all. First, thank you so much for the warm welcome you've been giving me out there on the field. You've all got great energy, and I love that. I hope to keep that going all season."

"Next, you may have seen a certain photo of myself and an unnamed individual outside Frost Field when the rest of my team was on the road. And although the team put out a press release, here it is straight to you from my lips. I was given permission to head to Saltair Shores to move my stuff up to Snowhaven. You might have seen a pic of me down there taken by my buddy and former Sailors teammate, Conner Malloy. There was a little snafu with the rental company, and I ended up having to borrow a car from a name you're probably all familiar with. Gale Frost."

I can't keep my lips from curving upward as I say her name.

"Gale runs the team's charitable foundation, the Frost Foundation, which her grandfather started. You might even have heard of the upcoming Christmas in July Gala."

I sit back in my chair and pick up my pair of scissors. "Now, what sort of Christmas would it be in Snowhaven if there wasn't any snow?" I pick up a paper that I've already folded how I needed to and make my first cut.

"The press release was not lying when it reported I'll be helping out a bit with the gala. Now, I have no idea how to run these sorts of events or anything like that, but when I got back to Snowhaven with my stuff, I saw the wonderful ladies who work at the foundation deep in piles of sparkly craft paper working on making decorations for the event. I've always been good with my hands, so this is one thing I know I can do." As I continue, I tell my viewers about the research being supported by the foundation, and how even Santa will make an appearance in a show of support.

"And of course, I'll be there too," I add, unfolding my finished snowflake, "in my gala best as will hundreds of these snowflakes, some of them with a bit of a personal touch." I grab the permanent marker that had been dropped off with the rest of the supplies to my hotel room sometime during last night's game and sign the snowflake.

I reach for another paper and begin the process over. When I'm not focused on making the right cuts, I look at comments coming in, hoping to see any signs of Gale or the foundation. It doesn't surprise me that Gale doesn't comment. She still hasn't accepted my request to follow her account, which is set to private, the only photo viewable featuring her leaning back against the railing separating her section in the stands from the field wearing a familiar T-shirt, a ballcap, and dark sunglasses. She's not smiling, not focused on the camera either, her face turned toward her right shoulder. Under those glasses, I can't tell where she's looking.

Are tickets still available? One commenter asks as I fold a new sheet of paper.

"Tickets are going fast, but some are still available through the Frost Foundation website. I hope to see you there!"

Another comment appears. How can we get a snowflake if we aren't going? I'm willing to buy!

"I'm going to field—ha ha, like that pun?—yes, I'm going to field that question over to the Frost Foundation to answer and see if we can figure something out for you and anyone else who is interested in getting one of these."

Finally, the comment I've been waiting for.

There will be a website later today where you can find out how to get your own Finn Flake.

I read the comment out loud. "See? There you go. Way to be on top of the ball, Frost Foundation. You catch that pun too? Though maybe we can work on the name a bit, huh? Finn Flake. Kinda sounds like I have a bad case of dandruff." I shoot the camera a cheesy grin. "I kid, I kid."

I keep cutting the snowflake, saying hello to viewers as I see their names pop up on the screen. There are a few hundred of them on here, so there's no way I'll get to them all, but it helps me connect with my fans, and people love the individual attention. That's winning me points with everyone even if I don't call a particular fan's name. Maybe it will be them next time.

Viewers start crowdsourcing suggestions.

Fan Flakes?

Foundation Flakes?

Jokingly they get called Frosted Flakes, but for obvious reasons, it won't be that one either. Pretty sure a certain cereal company would have something to say about that.

We'll work on it, comes the official word from the foundation's account. I wish I knew if it was Gale or Phoebe posting the comments.

I finish the second flake and sign that one on camera. "Oh, to up the intrigue here, I'm going to number the ones I do on these lives. That's right, lives. You'll be able to watch me make snowflakes a lot coming up. Check out this stack of paper!" I grab the camera, mini-tripod and all, and switch the view, my finger over the lens so no one gets a peek of my room, to show them the easily two-inch-tall stack of sparkly craft paper. I set the tripod back down, putting it back into selfie mode once again as I settle into my chair once more with my third snowflake. Okay, really it's probably my eighth. I had to practice before I went live. Those few won't be numbered, but I'll still sign them. "So tell me in the comments what you want me to talk about while I'm on here prepping these for the gala. I am going to have to get going once I finish this one, but remember what I said about getting your tickets. And as soon as I have the link for these limited-edition signed and numbered snowflakes, I will be sure to post it here for you all.

A minute or so later, more like three because these really aren't that easy to make despite my earlier claim that I'm good with my hands, I sign the snowflake and end my live video. I glance at the clock. There's enough time to make a few more before I need to head out to the stadium, so I keep working, hoping to hear something from Gale herself.

Chapter 25
Gale

Seven minutes earlier

Phoebe bursts into my office, her phone in her hand, the screen lit up.

I jump, scattering the proofs for the various gala sponsor thank you signs across my desk. My eyes are wide as my heart thuds against my ribcage. She's never done this before. "What happened?" I ask, my tone alarmed.

But her grin is wide, excited. "You have got to see this."

It's then I hear a familiar voice coming through her phone's speaker. "Is that Finn?"

I haven't talked to him since telling him what the press release was going to say. I feel better about that situation, especially after seeing last night's small jump in ticket sales, but I feel so removed from the me in the gossip blog's photo today. That me was expecting to be kissed a few minutes later, not dumped. Though I guess that's not the right word. Can't be dumped if we were never together. Rejected, maybe. But after hanging out with the girls last night, I'm not giving up. Just giving him space. Maybe as he settles in more, he'll stop seeing himself as a rental. Maybe next time he'll actually kiss me like he said he will.

"It is!" She shoves the phone in my face, and I'm met by Finn's face, blurry this close. I sit back a bit, and my eyes adjust and focus on Finn's boyish grin and hazel eyes as he mentions the foundation and our gala. Goodness, he's adorable that way.

"Bring it up on your computer," Phoebe tells me. "You'll see better."

She comes around to my side of the desk as I jiggle the mouse and head over to the foundation's social media account on the platform Finn's broadcasting on. He's sitting back as I maximize his live video, revealing his pile of paper, one already folded and him picking up a pair of scissors. My jaw drops, and I glance up at her, the excited grin still plastered to her face. "Is he?"

"Now, what sort of Christmas would it be in Snowhaven if there wasn't any snow?" Finn's says through the computer.

Phoebe squeals in delight. "Oh, he absolutely is."

Finn brings up the press release, not for the first time from the sound of it, and continues, "I've always been good with my hands, so this is one thing I know I can do."

"You hear that? He's good with his hands," Phoebe teases.

I shake my head and roll my eyes as I shush her so I can hear what Finn's saying.

"This year, the gala is supporting the work being done over at Barrett Hospital regarding skin cancer." I swallow hard as Finn mentions my dad and how he passed from the condition. I will not cry. Phoebe gently places a hand on my shoulder, reminding me she's here.

Finn continues, "The funds will be used to pay for additional screening events held at area beaches and several Snowhawks' games through the hospital's mobile skin cancer detection units. Did you know that one in five people here in the US will develop skin cancer before the age of seventy, but that if you catch it early, there's a ninety-nine percent chance of survival beyond five years?"

"He's done some research." My voice betrays the emotion I refuse to let show. It comes out in a hush. "I didn't tell him that when we were talking."

"It's why you'll see me at the front of the line at the first event held at Frost Field later this summer. You should join me there or at any of the other screening events. But back to the gala, if this fabulous cause is not enough of a draw for you, and it should be, Santa will be there too to show his support. And of course, I'll be there too"—Finn unfolds his finished snowflake—"in my gala best, as will hundreds of these snowflakes, some of them with a bit of a personal touch." Then he signs the snowflake with a permanent marker.

"There are so many comments on this. I can't even begin to read them all right now, but this is huge, Gale. Everyone wants tickets or wants snowflakes."

I don't have the comments showing on my computer screen, and when I look up at Phoebe, she's scrolling on her phone, her thumb rapidly swiping up and down on the screen. I pull up the comments so I can see them for myself.

"Tickets are going fast," Finn says to a follower of his, "but some are still available through the Frost Foundation website. I hope to see you there!"

I quickly type the foundation's website into the comments so at least some people will see it and click.

I don't think Finn sees it, though, and he answers another comment about how viewers can get the snowflakes that he's making. "I'm going to field—ha ha, like that pun?" Personally, I groan at it even if I do find it adorable that Finn uses them. "Yes, I'm going to field that question over to the foundation to answer and see if we can figure something out for you and anyone else who is interested in getting one of these."

I pull up the foundation's email program and drag it to one half of the screen so the other window with Finn's video resizes in the other half. "We need to get on this ASAP," I tell Phoebe, who confirms with an *mm-hmm* as I start an email to our website person, telling him what we need. I can add articles and update a few things, but no way do I have the technological ability to put something in place like what I'm hoping for. "Do you think outright sales or an online auction would be better for this?"

"Both. Low numbers get auctioned and higher ones can just be bought."

"Maybe save number one for the gala's silent auction."

"Makes sense."

"What should we call them?"

"I'm no good at naming things. We never keep the ones I come up with." She laughs. "But people like alliteration. Maybe Finn Flakes?"

"Good as anything I'm going to come up with right now."

I click send on my email, then hop over into the comments on Finn's video.

There will be a website later today where you can find out how to get your own Finn Flake.

Finn spots my comment this time and reads it out loud. "See? There you go. Way to be on top of the ball, Frost Foundation. You catch that pun too? Though maybe we can work on the name a bit, huh? Finn Flakes. Kinda sounds like I have a bad case of dandruff." He looks at the camera and smiles broadly. It's his public smile, not the one he's given me when we're together, not even that first meeting when I was little more than the public for all he knew.

Suggestions for new names come flying up in the comments. "We'll be able to see these again later, right?" I ask, glancing up at Phoebe.

She nods. "Maybe we should crowdsource ours from now on. Look at the sort of response it's getting."

We'll work on it, I type in to let him know we're open to the change. "Not Frosted Flakes. I don't care how much people like alliteration. That could be crossing a legal line, and anyway, this is Finn's doing. The credit should go to him."

"Oh, to up the intrigue here," Finn continues, "I'm going to number the ones that I do on these lives. That's right, lives. You'll be able to watch me make snowflakes a lot coming up. Check out this stack of paper!"

"That's a lot of paper." Even at $5 a flake, we'd get a good chunk of money. "This could be amazing for the foundation."

"I change my earlier opinion about an auction," Phoebe says.

"Agreed." I head back into my email and send the website developer a quick follow-up.

My heart warms as Finn keeps on talking. "So tell me in the comments what you want me to talk about while I'm on here getting these prepped for the gala. I am going to have to get going once I finish this one, but remember what I said about getting your tickets to the gala. And as soon as I have the link for these limited-edition signed and numbered snowflakes, I will be sure to post it here for you all."

"Look at you smiling again," Phoebe says.

"Hey, I smile," and my brow furrows in protest.

"Not like that, you don't. And that's not a bad thing. You're always polite to everyone and give them a kind smile, especially people we're serving through the foundation. But this one is different. A good different. It's nice to see."

Guess Finn's not the only one with a public smile.

"I'm just happy the foundation is getting such good buzz." I open a new browser window and drag it over my email, then pull up the event stats for the gala. The sales have climbed already since this morning. I highlight the number on the screen. "Look at this. He's doing this."

"And he's doing this for *you*."

"Nah. He's doing it for his charity. I told him he had to help out with stuff before I'll consider bringing his to the board." Even as I say it, I don't fully believe it.

"Yeah, and you've never made the guys do more than show up or donate before as their helping. I'm sure you said that to him." I nod, and she continues, "He saw what we were doing yesterday. He's being specific and direct to show you he's paying attention. And remember the snowflakes he was doing on the field last night? It's all part of it."

"He really does see the big picture and how to fit a bunch of little pieces into it, doesn't he?"

"And he wants you in the picture too."

I shake my head. "Not while he's a rental, he doesn't." Even if I am willing to break my rule for him.

"I don't know about that. He regrets not kissing you. Maybe he changed his mind about everything. This is big."

Hope starts to crawl out of the tight spot I'd packed it away in when Finn walked away, making it further than it did when he confessed that he should have kissed me. That he still wants to dance. "Maybe you're right."

"So I guess the question is, what are you going to do about it? Didn't we say last night that next time you were going to make sure he kissed you? Next move is yours. You said he was worth your time even if he is a rental. It's time to prove it."

Chapter 26
Finn

I almost miss the notification when it comes through, mid-scroll as I weed through the comments from my live video to make sure I didn't miss anything important, anything from Gale. I immediately click over to my texts.

GALE

Thank you. You've single-handedly sold thirty tickets to the gala just since your live began. I'm blown away.

My lips curl up into a full smile.

ME

You're welcome.

Seriously, you have no idea how huge this could be for the foundation.

I told you I wanted to do something hands on.

I never would have expected that, though.

> The moment I saw what you were doing, I knew it was something I could help out with. How did the rest of your snowflake making go?

> You only saw the beginning of it. Lots more to go. I'd be making them in my sleep if I could. I'll be making them every spare chance I get.

I glance at the stack next to me on the desk. I only finished one more after the live video.

> I hear that.

> Would you maybe want to make some together sometime?

My pulse picks up as the three dots tell me she's not done.

> I mean if you want to do it all on your lives, I understand, but I thought maybe we could video chat and do some or something.

I knew she'd like the snowflakes. That it would win me some points back after getting too into my head about possibly being a rental and failing to kiss her. This is better than I'd hoped.

> Like a virtual date?

The phone rings a moment later. It's Gale. Did she misclick when she was texting? I've done that before. I wait until the second ring, giving her a chance to hang up if she doesn't want to talk, before picking up. "Gale?"

"My answer is yes."

"Yes to what? That it's a virtual date?"

"Yes to that, and also I'm changing my answer about dancing with you at the gala. It's a yes. Not a maybe."

I pump my fist in celebration. "What made you change your mind? Is it my impressive footwork?"

She chuckles, which is a lot coming from her. "It's been a long time since I've done a jig, but I would hope your method of distraction would not be how you choose to dance all the time."

"You've also seen my arabesque," I tease, and her laughing grows stronger. I turn serious, however, so there's no question about my answer. "But no, when we dance together, there will be no distractions. Just you and me, your arms around my neck and mine around your waist as we slow dance across the floor."

"I like the sound of that. I know what you said about being a rental, and I get it, Finn. But even before all this, before the snowflakes and snow angel on the field last night, I knew you're worth the effort. Whether you're here or somewhere else come the end of the season, I want to see where this could go. No preventing something from happening because of the unknowns."

I want to tell her what Mack said. That I'm not a rental. But I want to see her face when I do. "Okay," I say finally, hoping that it doesn't seem like I took too long to answer.

"Just like that?"

"Yeah. Why?"

"I expected more pushback, that's all. After, you know, not kissing me."

"What can I say? You make a compelling case. And not kissing you is something I plan to rectify. Likely during our dancing if you'll let me."

"Before, I hope. You'll be back before then. I'm going to be wicked busy with last-minute prep, but I'm sure I could spare a few minutes for a quick peck."

"There's going to be nothing quick about it. I have a kiss to make up for, remember?"

"Two pecks, then." And now she's giggling. If I wasn't already thinking about kissing her, quick peck or not, this sound would have sent my thoughts right there.

"Two pecks." The answer comes out heavier than I intend, and I take a deep breath, needing to cool off.

There's no way she doesn't hear how affected I am by her in my voice. "So . . . maybe Friday? For our virtual date. I'm tied up in meetings tomorrow."

"Friday is perfect. Call me when you get to the office?"

"I will. I'm gonna let you go now. Keep your eye on the ball tonight."

"You bet I will. You'll be watching, right?"

"Always. Talk to you soon, Finn."

We hang up, and I toss my phone onto the bed. I need to finish this last snowflake (for now), clear my head, and get ready to meet the guys for lunch.

By the time I'm done eating, I receive the link to post for my fans. Curious, I check it out. The website is broken into three parts, one for ticket sales with a free snowflake upon arrival to the gala that I'll sign in person for them, another for snowflakes only for those who are not attending the gala or have a confirmation code for previous ticket purchase, and a third for an online auction of the snowflakes that I am numbering while I do my lives, except for the first one, which will be part of the gala's silent auction. I post a photo of myself in the locker room with one of the snowflakes I've made in here along with the link, crossing my fingers that it will be as benefi-cial to the foundation as Gale and I hope it will.

After the game, I find a text from Gale with the site's stats and a smiley face.

There's another update the next morning. And one before the game that afternoon with what's quickly becoming her signature sign-off to me. Keep your eye on the ball, but no falling on anyone else.

This continues into Friday morning, only instead of a text, it's the video call I've been looking forward to since we planned it.

"Good morning, Gale." As her face appears on my screen, I want to call her beautiful, gorgeous, sweets, some sort of cute nickname, but whatever this is, is still new, and she doesn't seem the pet name type. I don't want her to roll her eyes at something ridiculous I've chosen. Though it's cute when she does it, so maybe I do. Still, I default to the safe option of using her name only.

"Good morning, Finn, or should I say snowflake fundraiser extraordinaire?"

Okay, maybe she would go for a pet name. "Bit of a mouthful if you ask me." I grin. "I take it things are going well?"

"We might need to get you more paper."

"Only if dates like this are part of the deal."

She gently bites her lower lip to hide a smile. "I think we can arrange something."

We make small talk for a few minutes. It's clear she called me as soon as she arrived at the office—almost as if she couldn't wait to talk to me, the way I couldn't wait to talk to her. She flips on her light and starts her computer while we chat before she updates me on the ticket and sales totals. "See? Extraordinaire."

"I had some great inspiration, that's all." I level a heated gaze her way. Even in the harsh overhead lights, the pink tinge of her cheeks is evident.

"Sounds pretty special."

"Oh, she is. Worth every paper cut."

She throws her head back in a laugh, exposing her beautiful, slender neck, and I need to remind myself why we're on a call today. Because as much as Gale won't be a distraction at game time, right now, the knowledge that I can get this kind of a reaction from her is very distracting at the moment, especially when she looks like that on top of it.

I clear my throat, more from need than trying to get her attention. "What? It's true. Now how about we see if I can avoid getting any today."

"I keep Band-Aids at the ready when I do this sort of stuff." She holds up a finger with one of those tiny bandages across her fingerprint. "Occupational hazard."

"Good to know. I should do the same." I prop the phone on the hotel desk, keeping my face in the smaller picture at the corner of the screen so Gale can see me as I work. A moment later, she disappears off screen, and I get an eyeful of the ceiling and then the table in her office, her bouquet a bit smaller but still there, as she shifts to where she'll be cutting out snowflakes. Finally she sits, and her face reappears on my screen.

We make it through a dozen snowflakes for me and more than that for Gale as we get to know one another, playing the random question game because the answers don't require much effort to answer. Favorite foods, ice cream flavors, beverage choices. Things like that. It's nothing on a deep level, but it's giving me some great date ideas for when we're in the same place.

A call at her desk interrupts us, and she wheels back a foot or so before leaning back in her seat to reach for the handset, causing me to drop my scissors when I look up at the screen. Now that is a distracting view. I avert my eyes, eventually putting my hand up over my eyes to keep myself from ogling her unintentional show, as modest as a form-fitting team T-shirt is. I can't hear what she's saying, only she sounds composed, what I assume is her professional air back on.

"Um . . . What are you doing, Finn?" she asks after another moment, amusement lacing her voice.

I lower my hand and am greeted by her smiling face up close. "Giving you your privacy while you took your call. Your shirt fits you very well."

Heat flares in her cheeks as she sucks in her lips and squeezes her eyes shut. "Oh no, I'm so sorry. I didn't even think . . ."

"No apologies necessary. I won't lie and say I didn't enjoy what I saw, but I'm trying to be a gentleman."

"Why, Finn, are you trying to preserve my reputation?"

She's trying to flirt based on the singsong in her voice, but I answer her seriously. "I know what it and your name mean to you. I'm not going to take advantage, even when it's just the two of us."

Something passes over her gaze as it locks on mine, and she parts her mouth to speak but closes it before trying again. "Wow. Thank you."

I clear my throat again, breaking the hold we have on one another. "Everything okay with the phone call?"

She tilts her head for a second before understanding dawns.

"Oh, right. Yes. Everything's good there, but I'm sorry, I actually have to head out for a while, so I need to go."

"No worries, and hey, I only got one paper cut today." I hold my index finger toward the screen.

She shakes her head. "Band-Aids next time. Seriously." Then she breaks into a smile. "This was fun."

"Thanks. I enjoyed it too. Try for it again sometime? Maybe tomorrow?"

She nods, the lightest of pinks gracing her cheeks. "Already looking forward to it. I'll text you later."

But by the time warmups begin, her usual pregame text hasn't come.

Chapter 27
Gale

I hit resend again and again. "Ugh . . . Why can't I get a signal?"

"Dad says it's always weird out this way," Macey says, keeping her eyes on the road. "That something's always interfering with the cell tower."

I tilt my head back in frustration. "He's going to be on the field before this ever sends."

"At least you can surprise him later."

I smile at the thought. "Thanks again for coming with me."

"Of course! How many times have you been my wingwoman over the years? It's about time you do something like this in the name of love."

I drop my chin and level my gaze at her. "Love? It's been a week, Macey." There's no way, right? "We haven't even kissed."

"I call it like I see it. The Gale I thought I knew never would have stolen a fry from someone she wasn't totally into." Her tone shifts. "These last few years have been hard on you, and even if it took Finn crashing into them, it's great to see you shining through the loose chunks of mortar in the walls you've put up. But even before . . . everything, you were never like this."

"Like what?"

"Charged. Even in the way you're frustratedly hitting the send button on your phone. There's an energy about you that only comes out when it regards him. It's like your event day energy. Excitement, nervous, focused. But it's lacking the seriousness of an event. You're amped and ready to cut loose and have some fun."

I'm starting to see her point. I hit resend one more time, hoping the text will go through, before pressing the phone firmly against my leg in an effort to keep it from bouncing.

"And stop licking your lips. They're going to get all chapped before Finn has the chance to kiss you. And he is going to kiss you." She laughs. "Unless you kiss him first. I'm leaning toward the latter at this point."

"How much longer?" Now my other leg is bouncing. I shake them out, getting rid of the tension in them the way I used to before dance competitions. It doesn't last long.

The GPS answers me instead of Macey. "One more exit to go."

Once we've found a parking spot at the stadium, Macey and I don ballcaps and dark glasses before stepping out of the car. It's unlikely that anyone is looking for us, especially since Macey used the account tied to her pseudonym to get tickets for the game, but in case whoever took Finn's and my photo outside of Frost Field is here following Finn, they'll have less of a chance picking me out of the crowd.

Putting my hair into pigtail braids, something that hasn't happened since I needed to do it for a hip hop outfit back in college adds another layer to my disguise. It's so different from my usual high ponytail or half-up, half-down style. Macey's blond hair is swept into a low side pony. It's not a style she regularly wears, not as Macey anyway, but it looks good on her.

I'm wearing a Snowhawks jersey over a plain frosty-blue T-shirt. The jersey's unbuttoned and tied at the bottom. It also has Finn's name and number on the back. I asked the equipment manager at the field for one since merchandising hasn't started carrying anything bearing his name yet. Must not help him with the whole rental belief either. Macey's outfit is similar but reversed with a Snowhawks T-shirt and a white undone button-down over it, also tied like mine. She's wearing shorts, whereas I'm in fitted jeans, but she also didn't burn her butt on a hot metal bench seat in the outfield when she was five. I did, and ouch.

The only thing not different about my ensemble from what I usually have—though Finn's jersey is here to stay—is my sunscreen tube to reapply before the game starts. I'm also carrying a purse, something I don't enjoy at games, but carrying packages of sparkly paper on their own would have been a hassle and brought too many weird looks our way.

I scan the area outside the line to get in where people walk back and forth, hitting up the various stalls and vendor carts selling game-day programs, snacks, and souvenirs. "Do you see Cassie yet?"

Macey looks around, then shakes her head. "You don't think she bailed because of Shane, do you?"

"No way. She knows we were coming disguised." Macey doesn't know Cassie's seen every game Shane's played in Nevershade, disguising herself much like we're doing now. She probably already had a ticket for tonight.

"And there's no way I'd miss the chance to catch a game

with two of my best friends," Cassie says from behind us. Macey and I spin around to face her. "I almost didn't recognize you two!"

Macey wraps her in a hug, squealing with excitement, and I take in the sight of my two closest friends together. Cassie was my first friend. And when Macey came along in middle school, she and I clicked immediately thanks to our similar upbringing. But I wasn't sure these two would ever get along. It wasn't immediate, that's for sure. I was so glad when they got over their issues with one another and realized what good friends they could be. We haven't been together, the three of us, since my dad's memorial. Our visits are always too few and far between.

When Macey and Cassie step away, it's my turn for a hug, with less squealing. I'm excited to see her, no doubt, but that's never been us. We rock from one foot to the other as we hold tight, moving side to side. "It's so good to see you."

"Happy to be here for you." She lets me go and stands at arm's length. "The braids are cute." She laughs as she tugs at hers trailing over her shoulder.

"Tames those curls right up, huh?" Her hair's been one of her most noticeable features since childhood.

She nods, then pulls a ballcap from her back pocket and puts it on.

"Talk about barely recognizing you. Lookin' good, Cass," Macey says. "Shall we go in?"

Arm in arm, the three of us head for the line to get in. Macey hands over our tickets and we enter through the gate. After a spin through concessions, one of my favorite things about visiting other parks, we find our seats and split a loaded totchos flight while watching the Snowhawks take batting practice.

"You think you're ever going to make a move on Ian?" Cassie asks Macey as he jogs onto the field to stretch after both teams have finished batting practice. He's the first one back out. One of the longest running players on the Snowhawks, Ian's work ethic is admirable. He's got to be one of the best conditioned guys on the team. No one would guess he's in his mid-thirties.

Macey practically chokes on a salsa-covered tater tot. "Me? Make a first move? Yeah, no."

I can't help but chuckle at her reaction. "There's a first time for everything. I mean, look at me doing all this."

"Yes, let's look at you, shall we? Tonight is not about me." She's deflecting, but I'll allow it. "And look, there's Finn."

Finn trots over to Ian and drops down beside him, spreading his legs, then reaching over for his left foot. He says something to Ian as he switches to his right foot, and Ian laughs. There's nearly a ten-year age gap between them and only a week's familiarity, but the two laugh like old buddies. A minute later, Devon lobs a ball over their heads as he runs onto the field, followed by a couple of the other guys, including Shane.

Cassie noticeably sinks further into her seat, her gaze never leaving Shane's back. I pat her lower arm. "He's not going to be able to see you up here. It's okay."

We're further back from the field tonight and along the third-base side. It's where the visiting team's dugout is, and most importantly for Macey, it's where the third baseman is most of the time (obviously). At least tonight, given where our seats are, the likelihood of a baseball player stepping on my sunscreen is practically zero.

Finn and Ian stand, positioning themselves like at a starting line, and as the others reach them, they all start doing running lunges toward the ball Devon threw.

"They're racing!" Cassie shouts.

"That's new," Macey says with a laugh in her voice. "Can probably thank Finn for that."

Truthfully, they look ridiculous going at the speed they are. But it's cute. And even the Ravens fans are eating it up. "He's really bringing a new vibe to the team, isn't he?"

Macey nods. "I know you were worried about it before. About the culture of your dad's team changing. But look at them. This is a good thing. There's a levity that hasn't been there. Certainly not this season. Although your dad hadn't coached in a few years, his death still affected the team. You haven't seen it as much, avoiding games like you were." She lifts her hands up when I shoot her a look. "I'm not saying that wasn't understandable. I get it. I'd have a hard time, too, with the way I've grown up here since my dad joined the team. But it's been an off year for everyone. Somber. It's a wonder we're above five hundred with the way it's felt."

Even muted on my computer so I could check scores during the day—I didn't dare watch at home by myself at night —I could see that many had lost their spark. Part of me wondered if the loss of my dad had clouded my perception. Guess it wasn't just me.

"And now we've won all but the game we watched at your house. It's early, but we keep this up and playoffs are a given. We're not that far out of first."

I fight to speak through the tightness in my throat. "I'm sorry I disappeared." From more than just the games.

Macey reaches over and pulls me into an awkward hug over our shared armrest. "You're here now."

"I don't know how I'll make it up to all of you."

She shoots a look over my shoulder at Cassie, then lets go of me, a mischievous grin on her face. "I know how you can start."

"Name it."

"More totchos," she and Cassie say in unison.

Chapter 28

Finn

I rush back to the locker room after the game. When Gale's text didn't appear, I chalked it up to the wonky signal at this ballpark. It's always been like that. A few of the guys on the Sailors believe this park is haunted. I've not heard that from any of the Snowhawks, though. Probably some weird interference from crossed broadcasting wires or something. But now that the game's over, I hope to find a text waiting for me.

My shoulders drop in relief to see several.

GALE

Keep your eye on the ball, but no falling on anyone else.

Keep your eye on the ball, but no falling on anyone else.

Keep your eye on the ball, but no falling on anyone else.

Keep your eye on the ball, but no falling on anyone else.

Keep your eye on the ball, but no falling on anyone else.

Keep your eye on the ball, but no falling on anyone else.

I laugh at how many times it came through once it finally did.

Another comes in as I hold the phone.

Ugh, the reception here is wicked horrible. I'm sorry if you just got a zillion of the same texts.

ME

Any text from you is a good text. And it was only six times.

Oh, good. It felt like more when I kept hitting resend.

Wait, why is her reception horrible? I've never had a problem anywhere in Snowhaven.

You kept your eye on the ball tonight, and congrats on winning that lunge race.

That was in warmups. How'd she see that?

They play a clip of that during the broadcast?

No idea.

My pulse quickens.

Are you here?

I don't get an answer before Mack's barking my name. Worst timing ever. I pocket my phone as I walk toward the office, hoping this will be quick.

When I turn the corner, he's walking out of the office with Macey. She gives me a wink that's as playful as her father's gaze is stern.

"Remember what I said. And that I'm still watching you."

"Yes, sir."

Macey squints at me, her voice coming out lower than I remember it the one time I've seen her before. "And don't think that he's the only one who is." She uses her index and middle fingers to point to her eyes before flicking her wrist in my direction so that she's now pointing at me. "I'm watching you too. You hurt her and you have to answer to me."

Mack laughs openly. "And if you thought I was the scary one." He shakes his head. "Think again."

They turn down the hall, passing the open doorway to the locker room. Macey's head turns to peek inside, but her father quickly covers her eyes as they continue walking.

When I turn my head back toward the office, Gale's standing in the doorway. My heart leaps at the sight of her.

"They mean well." She rolls her eyes, but her lips are turned upward. Then her gaze locks on mine as I take two quick strides toward her, my heart now hammering with excitement.

"I'm going to kiss you now, if that's okay." I search her face, and nodding, she bites her lower lip.

I step into her space, wrapping one hand at the small of her back and cupping the back of her head with the other, tilting it up slightly and taking her mouth with mine. I'd planned for a sweet and simple first kiss, but that was before she showed up here, three hours away from Snowhaven. When her lips part, that's all the invitation I need to show her my dance moves on the field are not the only ones I have.

She takes one step back, then another, her hand clenching my jersey, urging me forward as she leads me into the room. The back of my legs bump into something cushioned, and I sit on the couch as she does the same, never breaking contact.

Had I known this was the type of kiss waiting for me, I never would have hesitated at the bus station, ultimately not kissing her. I should have kissed her then no matter the kiss now. Thank *everything* that she wasn't willing to give up on me.

I need to slow this down because I am not the type of guy to rush these sorts of things, and I am not jumping from first base to a home run on my first trip up to the plate. This isn't a game. Gale isn't some trophy to win. Slowly, the kisses becoming gentle pecks.

"Surprise!" she says quietly once our lips part, our gazes locked on one another. Gale's pupils are dilated, her eyes darkened like a winter storm. No doubt mine match hers.

I play with the loose strands of hair at the bottom of her braid, not wanting to fully let her go. "You're here."

"I'm here." She glances back toward the desk, and sitting on the chair in front of it is a large purse, more a tote than a handbag. I've not known Gale long, but it seems too casual for her. "I brought you something."

"Oh?" I raise an eyebrow.

She stands, and I drop my head onto the back of the couch, closing my eyes and already missing the feel of her in my arms.

"More supplies."

I crack one eye open as she pulls the sides of her bag her bag apart and she walks back toward me, revealing another two packs of sparkly paper.

"You mentioned how you were going to need more paper, and I figured I'd bring some to you."

"You drove three hours to bring me paper?"

Her eyes still crackle with heat from our hello, but there's a levity in them now that I've only seen one other time as she was stealing a french fry from me. She reaches into her bag and pulls out a small box. "And Band-Aids."

I repeat with a chuckle. "And Band-Aids."

She drops the box back into the bag before sliding the tote up onto her shoulder. The corner of one side of her mouth turns upward. "And someone to keep you company while you make more snowflakes."

"Ah, so that explains why Macey is here."

Gale blinks in surprise, then lets loose a laugh that is possibly the best sound I've ever heard because of how hard-won they are. "She does make a mean snowflake." She turns serious and reaches her hand out toward me. I take it and rise from the couch. She steps closer, walking the fingers of one hand up my chest before sliding that hand behind my neck and pulling me to her. "I meant me." She presses a soft kiss to my lips.

"I like the sound of that. How long are you here?" It's got to be past eleven thirty now, and now that she's here, snowflakes are the last thing on my mind. But if that's what she wants, I'll gladly oblige just to spend time with her.

"Macey and I grabbed a hotel room for the night. Cassie's apartment is too small for all three of us. I thought maybe you and I could do breakfast in the morning before starting in on the snowflakes."

Part of me aches at the thought of letting her go even for the night. But of course she got a room with Macey. They're best friends and they came here together. Gale's not the type to just leave her friend hanging. And I won't ask her to do otherwise. "What's Macey going to do while we're busy?"

"Breakfast with her dad, I assume. They usually do when we catch away games. Then trying to place herself in a strategic location to innocently run into Ian, I'm sure. Not while her dad's around, though."

"Oh, really?"

"She's got it bad, but do not tell anyone I told you."

"I wouldn't dare." Macey's got her work cut out for her. He's been the first one to the ballfield all week, reviewing tapes and doing yoga before warmups.

"Good. Because her dad was not kidding when he said she was the scarier one of the two."

I throw my head back and laugh. "Noted. So may I walk you back to your hotel?"

She kisses me again. "I was hoping you'd ask that."

Wanting more than a single kiss, I pull her toward me and take her mouth once more. I'm ready for a repeat of our hello.

"Um . . . Finn?" I pause but don't let her go. "Kissing you is great and all, more than great, but do you think we could get out of this office?"

"Right. Yeah." I step back and rub the back of my neck, letting out a hard breath. I sweep my arm toward the door. "Lead the way."

She exits the office, and I catch sight of her back for the first time. I'd seen she was in a Snowhawks jersey, kind of hard to miss when I'm wearing the same one, but the back of hers stops me in my tracks.

That's my number.

And my name.

It's my jersey.

It takes her a couple of steps before she realizes I'm not following. She turns and looks at me questioningly. "Finn? Are you okay?"

"Where did you get that jersey?"

"I asked for one since merchandising doesn't have shirts with your name on them for sale yet. The team's assistant equipment manager is a friend of mine from high school. Do you like it?"

My throat tightens, and I nod. "I do. You came for me."

She's my woman.

Mine.

"Of course I came for you. I told you I want to prove to you that something between us is possible no matter how long you're here. It's Fiddlefern Fjord. We have four ballparks within four hours of one another, not including the minor league stadiums, and another two outside the region within five hours. And that's just driving distance. It's faster by train, and although there's airport time to contend with, there are even more ballparks in major travel hubs that could see me leaving Snowhaven at noon and getting to the game that night."

Her tone changes to one laced with hesitation. "Why are you shaking your head at me? Are you still worried?"

I stop shaking my head, which I didn't realize I was doing, and the *no* that escapes me as I rush to close the few strides' distance between us, is hushed but heated. "I'm not a rental."

She wraps her arms behind my neck as I place mine at her waist. "I'm glad to hear you say that. I never viewed you that way, you know."

"No, I mean I'm here to stay. Mack said there's no way the team would get rid of me after what they traded away to bring me here. Unless I screw things up with you, that is."

Gale laughs. "You should have led with that. That is the best news."

My mouth comes crashing down to hers.

Chapter 29
Gale

This might be my favorite morning ever. First it's the morning after what might be the best night ever. Finally getting to kiss Finn was as amazing as I'd hoped it would be, and to hear that he's not some rental on top of it was more than I could have hoped for.

And now we're in this adorable café having breakfast together, holding hands, and enjoying our morning with one another before he has to head to the ballpark.

Tomorrow the team is traveling to the next stop on their road trip, and I'll have to buckle down getting everything ready for the gala. It's one of the busiest stretches of my work life each year, so I'm going to make the most of today. It was tempting to get tickets for tonight's game, but Macey and I are meeting up with Cassie for a late lunch before heading back to Snowhaven.

"Have you ever been to the baseball museum here?" I ask him after chasing down a bite of my stuffed French toast with a swig of orange juice.

He nods, swallowing the last bite of his second of two

breakfast wraps. "My first time up here with the Sailors. We all got a tour as part of the team donation of gear to commemorate the organization's first season. You said your friend works there?"

"Cassie." I smile at just the mention of her name. She was my first friend. One I'd made in kindergarten at the start of the school year. "She grew up in Snowhaven. She and her brother lived next door to Shane, actually."

He runs his thumb gently over my knuckles, back and forth, and goosebumps of the best sort erupt over my arm as jolts of electricity shoot up my arm and over into my chest with every caress. "It's neat how Shane gets to play for the hometown team. I always wondered what that would be like." He gives me a smile that's hard to interpret, but it doesn't reach his eyes.

"He didn't always. Got drafted to play up here, actually. Mostly stayed in the minors, though. I came up here to visit Cassie one time, and we caught a couple games." Not that I've ever been allowed to tell him that thanks to Cassie's ever-present crush on him.

"How long has he been with the Snowhawks?"

"Three seasons. You should have seen the party Shane's mom threw to welcome him home." Finn's smile takes on a faraway look again, and I squeeze his hand. "I'm glad you've become friends with him. Devon too."

"And I like that they're already your friends. So does this" —he gestures between the two of us with his free hand— "mean I get to find out how you came by the Frosty nickname?" He gives me his best puppy-dog impression.

I scrunch my nose as I contemplate this. "Not yet. That is not a story you earn after just a few kisses."

His mouth parts slightly, in jest or actual surprise, I'm not sure. "Doesn't quality count for something? Besides, I think there were more than a few kisses last night." He breaks into a wide grin, a real one, and it warms me all over.

It definitely does, but I'm not going to give in so easily. "They were great kisses. I'll give you that. You're getting there."

Finn raises an eyebrow. "Well, I love a challenge." He lifts the hand he's holding up and leans toward it, then kisses each knuckle softly before turning my hand over and kissing the inside of my wrist. If just his thumb across my knuckles sent jolts of electricity through my system, then his lips cause a full lightning storm, and whatever butterflies live in my stomach chassé and sauté to avoid the strikes.

As if realizing what he's doing to me, he flips my hand over once more, gently kisses the back of it, and places it down, though he doesn't let go, nor does he break eye contact.

"How about we get out of here?" Finn asks after the heated moment, his voice low and gravelly.

I nod, still transfixed by his gaze and unable to speak. I'm saved from responding more, when our waitress comes over to take our plates and Finn requests the check. She returns quickly, and we pay with cash using Finn's per diem so we don't waste another minute waiting for her to run a credit card.

Once we leave the café, I find my voice again. It probably helps I'm next to Finn and no longer looking at him. "Thank you for breakfast. You didn't have to."

He pulls me into his side as we walk down the sidewalk, kissing me on the temple as he wraps his arm behind me. "But I wanted to."

"It's not going to mess up the rest of your meals, is it? You'll have enough?"

"I rarely spend it all, so it will be fine. Promise. They feed us plenty before games."

I think back to the spreads my dad used to have available for him, both as a player and manager. "It's improved over the years."

"For a team like the Snowhawks, I would certainly imagine so. It's a step up from what the Sailors have."

"Do you miss it? Being on the Sailors?"

"I have my moments. This team is so different. But it's no more than I miss some of the guys who I played with in college. Those teams were a lot alike with the Sailors being so young. You develop a sort of kinship with whoever you play ball with. Well, maybe not Kyle."

"He won't be all sunshine like you, but he'll come around. Did you know he and Phoebe are best friends?"

That stops him in his tracks. "Phoebe, as in, works with you Phoebe?"

I turn to him and nod. "They went to school together. She was the mascot."

"Now that part I can see. How did they both end up here?"

We resume our walk, now holding hands, and I tell him how Kyle vouched for her when she was looking for a job. I'd agreed to interview her as a favor, grateful she had a resume to back it up, but once we hit it off within five minutes of meeting, hiring her was a no-brainer. And she fits in great with the girl group, even if she doesn't hang out with us every time we get together.

Finally we make it back to the team hotel. Finn's picked up the pace, and he's a whole stride ahead of me, still holding me by the hand as he leads me through the lobby.

"Where are you going in such a hurry?"

He presses the up button for the elevator repeatedly. What has gotten into him?

"That's not going to make it get here any faster," I say matter-of-factly.

He quirks a grin. "I'd like to think it does."

I shake my head. Can't argue with that logic. Not that I want to argue with him. That boyish grin makes me want to do anything but.

The elevator at the end of the row dings, and Finn pulls me toward it with enthusiasm. It's full, of course, and he bounces on his toes as everyone shuffles off, taking so long the doors start to close until he shoots his arm out to stop it.

"Careful," I warn him as he ushers me onto the elevator. "Don't go hurting yourself on an elevator of all things. Then where would the team be?"

Not looking at me, head down slightly, he presses the button for the doors to close, but the upward-turned corners of his lips tell me he's only pretending to be chastised. "I'll be more careful next time." He then faces me, his gaze warm and tender. "But I couldn't wait another moment to get you alone to do this."

Dropping my hand, he steps toward me and runs his hand along the length of my arm up to my shoulder. Then he follows the curve of my neck until he's caressing my cheek and tilting my face to look up at him.

He kisses my other cheek softly and proceeds to pepper me with gentle kisses along my cheek bone, my eyelids, my forehead. I shift for a better angle, glad I decided to leave our craft supplies in his room this morning before we left instead of taking it with us. No doubt the bag would be on the ground now, its contents spilling out as I place my arms over his shoulders and let my fingers play with the hairs at the nape of his neck. The Snowhawks have a personal appearance mandate that calls for clean faces and short hair. Any longer, and they might make him cut his, but there's just enough for me.

When the elevator door slides open all too soon, we reluctantly end our kiss, stepping back from one another. We stare at one another, a satisfied curl to his smile.

"I don't suppose there's any way to convince you to continue this once we get back to my room, is there?" Finn asks, his voice low.

Oh, how easy it would be to give in when his touch makes me feel so alive. "Tempting, tempting," I admit honestly while still keeping it flirtatious. "But these snowflakes aren't going to make themselves."

I give him a quick peck on the lips, then slide out from between him and the wall to exit the elevator. The cool air of the open hallway helps me regain my composure.

He whines, a puppy-dog look on his face, before following me to his room.

"That's only going to get you so far so often," I tell him, hoping it hides the truth of how efficient not the sound but the look could actually be.

He steps in front of me to swipe his key card in front of the lock, and he pushes the door open with his back to face me as he lets me in.

"Besides"—I step up close and kiss the corner of his mouth before skipping away—"I don't want to wear you out before tonight's game."

"Ugh . . . that is so not fair." His voice comes out raspy. "But a really good point."

The door falls heavy behind him, and as he follows me into the room, I pick up my bag from against the wall and pull out the craft paper. "That gossip piece may not have had all its facts straight—"

"Or any facts at all . . ."

My mouth quirks into a grin. "Or any facts beyond your name, but I'm not going to give it any life beyond that by letting it distract you or me from what we need to be doing right now. And that's snowflakes and a game later." I hand him a stack of paper. "So let's get cutting. Mind if I sit on your bed?" The hotel room's only seating is at the desk where Finn's supplies are.

"Be my guest," he answers without looking as he snaps a photo of it all.

I climb onto the bed, stretching one leg out and folding the other underneath me. I dump my supplies onto the bed, and a moment later, a notification sounds on my phone. Just in case it's Macey or Cassie, I check it, but like I assumed, Finn's tagged the foundation in a social media post. The caption under the photo he just took reads: *Reinforcements have arrived with new supplies. Get your snowflakes and gala tickets today!* Beneath that is the link for our site.

"Thanks for the shout-out. Our account has gotten five hundred new followers in the last week thanks to you." I open my package of paper. "Phoebe and I haven't checked them all, but the one's we have looked at all follow you."

He already folding a sheet of paper as he glances over his shoulder, saying, "I'm happy to do it." But as we make eye contact, he drops his paper, and it flutters to the desk. His mouth hangs open slightly.

"What?" There's a natural chuckle in my voice. I have a good idea exactly what caused his reaction.

He whips his head back toward the desk, picks his paper back up along with the rest of the stack and his scissors, then pushes off against the floor, sending his desk chair rolling back toward the bed. "I'll give that gossip piece one other nod toward accuracy."

I tuck a stray few hairs behind my ear, then tighten my ponytail, waiting for his answer.

"If anything was going to distract me, it would be you. You're beautiful, you know that?"

"Finn . . ." Maybe this was a bad idea, coming here on a game day.

He places his papers on the bed, then raises his hands in surrender. "Not saying I'll let it. We both have jobs to do, and I'm here to support yours in any way that I can, one hundred percent. But Gale, seeing you there . . ." He blows a steadying breath before grabbing his paper and scissors once more.

I bite back a grin, but the heat in my face has no doubt shown him his effect on me. "Thank you. And thank you for your help with these." I cut into my folded paper. A curve here, a line there. *Focus.* Truth is, he could be just as big a distraction to me if I let him be. If I let myself be distracted. And the fact he's not doing anything right now but cutting out a snowflake tells me all I need to know about him.

We fall into a steady rhythm of snowflake making, easy conversation, and furtive glances that we catch each other taking at least a few times during the quiet but comfortable moments between us when the loudest thing in the room is the snipping of our scissors.

We chat about our childhoods, about grade school and college, the things we enjoy now, and our hopes for the future. Every minute that passes, I fall further for Finn Nixon. Macey was right. Maybe it might be love.

All too soon, the alarm goes off on my phone.

I turn it off. "Unfortunately that means I need to get

going." I stretch my arms up over my head, the hem of my shirt rising above my navel.

"You set an alarm?" He raises an eyebrow, his voice teasing, but as he spots my bare midriff, his gaze darts away much like it did during our first videochat when I leaned backward.

I drop my arms. "Let's just say, you are not the only one who could have found themselves distracted in here this morning."

He swallows hard as his focus returns to my face.

"And I may have set a secondary alarm that I really need to leave by, so the faster we pack up, the more time we have."

As if he's racing to beat a play to the bag, Finn gathers the finished snowflakes, his signed, mine not, into one pile. He brings the remaining supplies back to his desk while I put the snowflakes and my scissors in my bag. Then I scoot to the edge of the bed and lower the bag gently to the floor.

The moment it's out of the way, Finn steps in front of me. I rest my arms on his shoulders, crossing them at the wrists. He pushes a loose strand of hair back behind my ears, gazing at me tenderly and then drops his hand down, placing it above my hip. "This was the best of surprises. Thank you for coming out here." He kisses my cheek. "For wearing my jersey." He kisses the other. "For cheering me on, even when I didn't know you were there."

I kiss him where his cheek gives way to jaw. "I'll always be cheering you on." Then the other side. "Even when I'm not in the stands."

"I've never had that one person there just for me. I get you have a long history with the team, that going to games is practically second nature for you, so what you did doesn't mean the same for you."

Sitting straighter and pulling away from him slightly, I

lower one of my arms and place a finger against his lips. "Once upon a time, that may have been the case. But Finn, the night we met was my first game of the season."

His brows furrow as he speaks against my finger. "But you work there."

"And the games, well, most of everything inside the stadium is really easy to avoid with the street-access door to my office. I'd not been to a game since my dad died."

"The baseball cards."

"What?"

"That explains the baseball cards. Why you didn't have a set."

"You remember that?" My heart melts from him remembering and making the connection.

"I remember a lot about that night. You also said how you'd missed being there with your friends."

"The girls had to trick me to get me to go that night. I thought I was there to support Dinah. Turns out, they were there for me."

"Gale . . ." He cups my cheek.

I shake my head. "Let me finish. Since then, I haven't missed a home game or an away game on TV. That night, whether sparked by the girls or you falling into my lap"—I chuckle at the memory—"something I'd lost was returned to me. And now I love it again. But my favorite part? It's seeing you out there. At first I thought you were some goof who was going to turn the Snowhawks into some mockery, but I was so wrong. I get what you're doing. You're not some jokester who doesn't take this seriously. You might be the most serious one out there in a way. It's brilliant the way you use fun to your advantage and ridiculously attractive. I can't wait to see what you do next, Finn. You. I go for you."

He's still, as if waiting for more.

I smile wide enough that I feel it into my ears. "I'm done now."

"Gale . . ." His hand on my cheek shifts so his fingers reach around toward the back of my head, and he tilts it slightly before capturing my mouth with his and pouring everything he has into this kiss.

But before it can become anything more, the second alarm on my phone goes off. Finn groans, and he drops his hand to the side of the bed as he slows our kiss. He lingers a moment longer, the alarm still sounding. Then he steps back, his head hanging in disappointment or frustration, and I cancel the alarm on my phone.

Finn takes a steadying breath, his gaze finding mine once more. Then he shakes his arms, followed by his legs one at a time. A slow, easy grin appears on his face. "Come on, let's get you out of here before I can't let you go." He holds out his hand, and I take it willingly.

We intertwine our fingers as we walk to the elevator, never breaking our hold as its doors open and we get on. We ride down in companionable silence, my head resting against his shoulder, a far cry from how we'd ridden up in it a few hours before.

Together we cross the lobby, and he walks me to the door. I lift onto my toes and kiss him softly on the cheek, knowing that if I kiss his lips, I might not be able to make it quick. The girls are probably waiting for me already at the little hole in the wall place Cassie wants to take us to for lunch.

"Keep your eye on the ball, but no falling on anyone else. I'll see you soon."

"Of course. I'm looking forward to it already." He brings my hand up to his lips and kisses my knuckles. Just like this morning at breakfast, each touch of his lips sends pulses of awareness up my arm.

When he lowers our hands, I take two steps away, me still holding on and him not letting go. On the third step, our hold breaks, and I cast him one final look before turning and walking away from the man I'm losing my heart to.

Chapter 30
Finn

It's in that moment I know, without a doubt, I love her. Watching her leave is one of the hardest things I've done. I'm kicking myself that I didn't make things official with her, ask her to be my girlfriend. It feels like we're together, that she's shed her worries about being with a baseball player, especially after wearing my jersey and what she admitted to me this morning, but until we have that specific conversation, I can't be sure.

Thank goodness I have games to keep me busy and my mind occupied.

Once I'm at the stadium, I get my head into the game like I should. Like how Gale expects me to.

And so the days flow from one to the next. Wake up, breakfast, video chat with Gale while I make snowflakes and she does whatever she needs to at work, head to the stadium or get on the bus to travel to the next city for the series there, warm up, play baseball, back to the hotel, a quick goodnight to Gale, and sleep. All the while posting to social media and going live and keeping up with my one summer class at the university down in Saltair Shores.

Cleat coloring aside, the trade to the Snowhawks has been smooth. And now that I'm not some rental, that the team sees me here into the future, the biggest unknown is school. That commute isn't doable during the season, and with Gale in Snowhaven, I don't plan on living elsewhere in the offseason.

The moment we get back to town after our road trip, the guys scatter. It's the All-Star Break, and we have a few days off. Actually off. At least most of us do. Shane's headed out of town to bash as many home runs as he can, and three of our position players and two pitchers are off to play in the game. I would have been there had I not been traded, but league officials deemed me ineligible because of the trade. It's a bummer, but I got there last year, and there's always next year. There are other things I want to do. Like see Gale. But I don't see her car in the parking lot.

ME

Hey, beautiful. Just got back to Frost Field. Gonna drop my stuff back at the dorm, then I'm all yours for whatever help you need for the gala.

GALE

I like the sound of that. All mine. You're the best. Heading to a meeting to lay the groundwork for the event after this one, but Phoebe's got a list to keep you busy. Can't wait to see you. Xx

The feeling is mutual. Xx

A hand claps me on the back. "You need a lift back to the dorms, or are you seeing Frosty first?"

I smile, remembering how annoyed I'd been when I

thought Devon was making fun of her with that name. "Dorms. You going?"

"Only for as long as it takes for me to pack up my bags so I can head out again. I'm taking my aunt to the All-Star Game to root on Shane."

"Ah. I was gonna see if you were interested in helping set up for the gala. But the game's going to be great."

"Yeah, man. I'm looking forward to it. Can't wait to play in it someday. But I'm bummed to be missing Santa's hospital visit. Kids love me."

Behind us, someone snorts. "That's because you are a big kid. You both are."

"Not wrong there, Kyle," Devon says as he sticks his arms out wide to his sides and spins. "Why do any of this if you aren't having fun?"

Kyle grunts in response, then directs his attention to me. "You mentioned needing help setting up the gala?"

I stop and turn around. "Yeah, why?"

"Figured I could help." He shrugs. "Got two hands and some time on them."

Devon *oohs* teasingly, and Kyle's hands in his pockets tighten into fists. "Shut up. I wasn't talking to you."

"I'm sure Gale and Phoebe will appreciate it." My mouth curves into a smile. Somewhere under that stony exterior is a good guy. I can't see Phoebe being best friends with him otherwise. It's still a little hard to believe.

He nods, his mouth set in a firm line. "You need a ride back here from the dorm?"

"That would be great, thanks." Then Devon can take off when he's ready.

He points at me in warning. "Don't make me wait for you."

"Wouldn't dream of it."

Once we get to the dorm, I hurry to get ready, then run to the registrar's office in the admin building. Hopefully I can get done what I need to before Kyle gets here.

"Hi, can I help you?" the woman sitting behind the long counter that runs the length of the room asks. She smiles politely. I wonder if she sees many people during the summer.

"Hi. I hope so. I'm Finn Nixon." She brightens, and I can only assume she recognizes my name. "I'm currently enrolled as a junior at SSU, majoring in psychology, and I'm looking to transfer here. Can you tell me what I'd need to do to make that happen?"

Her smile falters. "A junior, hmm?"

"That's correct. Almost a senior."

"Hmm . . . we don't usually accept students that far into their junior year. Too many university specific required courses, you see."

"I do." I already faced this problem once, leaving my first college when I joined the Sailors.

"You wouldn't graduate on time, I'm afraid." The woman frowns as if she's just given me terrible news. For some, it might be.

I, however, laugh good-naturedly. "Sorry. I mean no disrespect. I've been a junior for three years doing this part time. Graduating on time is the least of my worries. Would it help if I say I'm willing to take whatever gen-eds I'm required to?"

"That certainly helps. What are you hoping to do with your degree, Mr. Nixon?"

"Grad school." She seems surprised by this, though most people are given my current career. "And hopefully sports psychology long-term."

She brightens and types something into her computer.

"Oh, well, we don't have a proper sports psychology degree, but the master's program is built to allow students to self design based on research interests. And that happens to be a particular interest of one of our tenured faculty. You'll need to submit an application, and getting in isn't a guarantee, but why don't you send over your transcript and your course catalog, and we'll see what we might be able to come up with as far as transferring things over."

"I can absolutely do that. Thank you."

"You're welcome, and good luck." Hopefully, I won't need it.

Kyle pulls into the dorm's parking lot as I'm walking down the campus stairs from the tier above. The passenger door is locked when I try it, so I knock on the window. Kyle presses a button on his door, and this time when I grab the handle, the door opens.

I slide onto the seat. "Thanks again for picking me up. That was nice of you."

"Kind." The word comes out more like half a grunt as he pulls out of the parking space, and I'm not quite positive that's what he said.

"I'm sorry?"

"It was kind of me. I'm not nice," he says flatly.

"Noted."

"They're different."

"Okay."

He pulls out onto the street leading away from campus and toward the field. "I wasn't going to leave you without a way to get there when I'm heading that way too. It was the right thing to do."

"Thank you." I clear my throat, figuring out a way to move away from this strange topic. "You live out this way?"

"Close enough."

Okay, a non-starter. "Do you help out with the foundation stuff often?"

Kyle shakes his head. "I donate stuff when Phoebe asks and show up where she tells me to, but I'm not the camera-friendly type for a lot of these things. Manual labor I can do. Don't think any of us have helped like that before. When you mentioned doing it, figured maybe we should start. We don't always need to be where the cameras are to do good."

It's the most I've ever heard him speak at one time. "I take it you're not big into social media."

He snorts. "I'll leave that to you and Devon. I just want to do my job and do it well."

"That all this is to you?"

He nods, the movements abrupt, but he soon shakes his head. "Ball, I love. It's all the extra stuff."

"It's a lot sometimes," I admit to empathize with the guy, though I don't mind "the extra stuff" at all.

Feeling he needs another change of topic, I ask, "So you and Phoebe go back a ways?" Gale's told me as much, but I don't want him thinking we've talked about him. Seems the type who wouldn't like it.

"Since college. Lived on the same floor our freshman and sophomore years."

"Nice. You go to school around here?"

"Few hours away in Baycliff."

I nod, not expecting that. I'd assumed they were from around here with the way he helped her get the job. Not that she moved out here to be the foundation's administrative assistant job. "Cool, cool."

We pull into the staff garage at the field. Gale's not back yet. As we cross the lot, the door opens with a couple of bangs and a high-pitched *eep* that sends Kyle running to the door. I jog after him.

"What are you doing here?" Phoebe asks excitedly as Kyle grabs the door, freeing her and her push cart from the heavy door.

"Trying to take too much in one trip as usual, I see," he says in lieu of greeting.

"That doesn't answer my question." Phoebe tilts her head down to shoot him a look, but it's filled with amusement more than anything else.

I grab the door from Kyle, and he lifts the precariously perched top box off the cart. "Carrying this for you, obviously." It's the closest thing to a smile I've seen on him since his last homer.

It's then Phoebe finally notices me. "Oh, hey, Finn. Gale said to expect you. Where'd you pick him up at?"

"More like he picked me up at campus." I shrug. "Said he wanted to help. Figured more hands is a good thing. You still have stuff in the office to bring out?"

Phoebe blinks several times before her smile grows even brighter. She hits him playfully in the arm. "Look at you, you big softie." She turns toward me. "Yes. Lots more. Another cart too."

"Say no more." I dart through the doorway and disappear into the tunnels toward the foundation office.

Chapter 31
Gale

Christmas music plays through the speakers of the foundation's office as Finn, Phoebe, Kyle, Ian—Macey is going to be so upset she's not here, and Oliver load boxes of gala supplies and auction items onto push carts. There are now four, doubling the number we had when I left.

"Oh my goodness, everyone, look at you all. We'll be done in no time with all your help."

Finn places the box he's holding gently on the cart next to him, then carefully walks around the various piles of supplies still on the floor and makes his way to me. I hug him as he kisses me on the cheek. "You brought reinforcements. I'm impressed."

He steps out from the hug and moves to my side, keeping that arm around my waist. "That was all Kyle," he says quietly.

"Phoebe?" I whisper back, glancing up at him.

He shakes his head. "Came on his own. Even gave me a ride here. You did not tell me how much Phoebe likes him when you were telling me about their history."

"What? No. They're just friends." My gaze shoots over toward my assistant.

"Sure they are. Friends who happen to be way into one another."

"You think?" I keep watching her as Kyle takes a box out of her arms and puts it on the cart.

Finn chuckles softly as he answers. "I even saw him smile. I didn't think that was possible."

"Some would say that about me, you know."

He kisses my temple. "Rare but beautiful. Yours, not his."

"What are you two lovebirds whispering about?" Phoebe shouts from across the room.

Everyone turns to stare at us, and Finn kisses me once more before heading back to his cart.

Heat rushes to my cheeks as I walk over to her. "Just saying hello. Can you catch me up? I'll fill you in on the meeting while we drive to the event hall." I'm dying to talk to her about Kyle, but I'm not going to do that now.

"Sure. Here, take this." She pushes a cart my way, then takes a full one from Ian and Oliver. We head out toward the tunnels. At first, I think this is my chance to bring up her possible crush on Kyle, but we're no more than ten feet down the hallway when he comes lumbering out of the office holding one of our biggest boxes.

Last thing I want is for him to hurt himself lifting an awkwardly packed box. "Why don't you grab one of the other carts?"

"Too short. I have to bend over to push it."

"Alright, then." I'm not about to argue. "If you're sure."

He grunts.

"Words, big guy," Phoebe teases, biting her lip.

I'd never contemplate calling Kyle *big guy*, and I bet

Phoebe wouldn't do it if his teammates were around, but he doesn't sound annoyed as he says to me, "I'm sure." In a few short strides, he's caught up to Phoebe and me.

"Thank you for your help, Kyle. Finn tells me you're responsible for getting the other guys here too."

"Welcome. It's a good cause." Quieter, he adds, "My mom had cancer."

My chest tightens. "I'm sorry."

"She's good now. But I remember that time all too well."

I take a deep breath to steady myself. "I'm glad to hear that." Maybe someday it won't hurt so much to hear about other people having this awful disease.

"So does your helping out today mean you're going to come to the gala?" Phoebe asks, either sensing we need a change of topic or completely oblivious. Her sunny demeanor makes it hard to tell. "I've never seen you in a suit."

Despite carrying a box, Kyle walks past us to grab the door to the staff lot. "I'll think about it."

He's never come before. Always donates. Either monetarily or with used or signed gear. Though last year he was off hitting home runs so wasn't around to come even if he had wanted to.

Phoebe squints her eyes. "Do you even have a suit?"

"I have a suit."

She brightens. "Perfect! Then you have to come." She pats him once on the chest as she passes him and walks through the door he's holding for us. "I'm wearing silver."

She showed me a picture the day after it arrived in the mail. It's gorgeous. And a reminder that I still don't have a dress. Nothing like leaving it to the last minute, but the girls and I are going dress shopping tonight to look for one. I have to find one. I'm out of time.

Kyle closes his eyes in what I think is resignation until I spy the corners of his mouth. He does smile. In a so slight or you'll miss it sort of way. Interesting. I'll have to give what Finn said some more thought because her affections might not be one-sided. This is going to be a very interesting gala.

After another half hour of lugging boxes, we all head to the event hall. Although the hospital, baker, and Santa are all based in Heartwood Hollow, our neighboring town to the north is a little too small to hold large events like this. Many of the town's engaged couples end up booking somewhere down here if they're having even a semi-large wedding. But at least that means we don't have far to go with all of these decorations and auction goods. The decorations are going up today, and the auction goods are getting locked up until tomorrow when I'm here to finalize the setup while all the other key players, pun not intended, are at the hospital with Santa.

I love that Santa Paul, his elves, and some of our guys can give some holiday cheer to the kids there, but I also love that I'm a nobody in that respect. No one wants a visit from the daughter and granddaughter of a baseball player. Which means I don't have to go. Thank goodness because hospitals and I . . . well, I try to avoid them now if I can. Fortunately, Phoebe, Eva from Team Relations, and one of the team photographers have got it covered.

With the guys' help, the event hall quickly begins its transformation into a Christmas wonderland. Tables surround a large open space, a dance floor ready for a spotlight that will make it look like ice, no skates needed. The tables themselves have linen tablecloths in red, white, and green. Tomorrow the florist will drop off centerpieces for each table.

Off to the side, we decorate an area for Santa so anyone wanting pictures with him can get them. I picked up the staging from Paul the other night when I went to Heartwood Hollow to make the final payment to both him and the baker.

"I sent you a photo of the cupcake stands, right?" I ask Finn as he helps me string fairy lights about the windows near what will be the dessert table.

"You did. They look great. Are they here?" He glances behind him as if looking for a box he'd missed, and the chair he's standing on wobbles.

"Whoa, there." I grab the chair, chiding myself. Why am I letting one of our team's players risk himself like this? If I could reach, it would be me. Darn those last couple of inches. "No, they're not. Joanie from the bakery will bring them with the cupcakes. It was a really good idea you had."

"I do get them occasionally." He grins down at me, the barest hint of pink on his cheeks. "Thank you for letting me tag along that day."

"I'm really glad you did." Without that trip to the bakery, who knows where he and I would have ended up? Not putting up tiny lights that will hopefully make it look like twinkling snow falling softly to the ground, that's for sure. "You do have a suit for this, right?"

"Yes. Got one for a buddy's wedding two years ago. Made more sense to buy than rent. And it still fits. I checked. What are you wearing? I want to have a matching pocket square thingy."

"I, um . . ." I look away. "I don't know."

He blinks a few times. "But it's tomorrow." The surprise is evident in his voice.

I snort. "Well aware. I'm going tonight with the girls to pick something out. We were going to go before, but something came up, and this was the only other day I had time. There's been so much to do to get all of this ready." I wave my hand up in a circle as I look at the room. I don't tell him the something that came up was when Macey and I went to his game instead—which the girls encouraged, enough so that Dinah came up with her own excuse as to why she couldn't go either so I couldn't chicken out. If I have to, I can wear the dress I wore last year, but I'd rather not. It was the last public appearance my dad made. And it reminds me of him too much. Of that time just before. Yet I still can't get rid of it.

Finn's easy smile reappears on his face. "I'm sure whatever you find will be absolutely beautiful." He hops off the chair and then kisses the side of my head before sliding the chair over several feet so we can repeat the process.

As we continue to string lights, Phoebe sets up as much of the silent auction table as she can without placing the actual items. Table cloth, clipboards with paper at each spot where an item will go, and a pen attached to it so people can't steal the pens after bidding in an attempt to win an item. We had that happen once. Tomorrow, we'll have Bob stationed next to the table to prevent any sort of cheating or outright thievery. Kyle, Oliver, and Ian set up chairs around the finished tables. Whoever finishes next will start covering the chairs to match the esthetic.

That turns out to be me when the boys can't figure out how to cover the chairs without messing up the ties, leaving Oliver to help Finn with the lights and Ian and Kyle upstairs stringing paper snowflakes to hang down from the second-floor gallery space. These are the ones Phoebe and I made.

Aside from those set aside for ticket holders who purchased them, and the number one flake for the auction, which are all locked up in the storage area here, Finn's signed flakes are back in my office to deal with next week when we will send them to the online auction winners and those who only bought snowflakes but not gala tickets.

The online auction won't close until tomorrow, but we've already made over two thousand dollars on the signed and numbered snowflakes we listed, and nearly double that on the unnumbered ones that he signed.

Finn's social media following has made such a difference for the foundation. It continues to surprise me. That reminds me . . .

"Smile, you two!" I tell Finn and Oliver as I snap a picture of them. It turns into a mini photoshoot as the two begin hamming it up for the camera under the guise of "how about one like this" and "just one more."

"Go live!" Phoebe shouts at me.

My eyes widen. "What? No."

She levels me with a look. "You've seen how well it works for Finn. Try it."

My shoulders fall. She's right. I know she is. But ugh . . .

She gives me an encouraging smile, then lays it on thick with the one thing that she knows I'll do anything for. "Do it for the foundation. You never have to do it again if you don't like it."

"Fine." Before I can talk myself out of it further, and with my professional smile firmly in place, I press the button to go live with one of the foundation's social media accounts.

"Hi everyone, it's Gale Frost, executive director of the Frost Foundation, and I wanted to give you all a bit of a sneak peek into our prep for tomorrow's Christmas in July Gala. Let me turn this around so you can see what we have going on." And to get the camera off me.

I focus on Phoebe first, giving her a taste of the camera. But of course, she loves it. "First we have the foundation's administrative assistant working on setting up our auction. We have a great lineup of items, many donated by area businesses. Nights on the town, wine baskets, tickets to various events, all sorts of things. We also have a wonderful assortment of signed, game used gear from our players. Some of whom are also here setting up."

I pan up to Ian and Kyle. Ian waves, charming as ever, and it's easy to see why he's captured Macey's interest. He's been a fan favorite for years. Kyle is, well, Kyle and nods at the camera, and from this distance, if he is smiling, it's not visible from here. But I've seen something new in him today, and I wonder what's sparked the change.

"I'm sure you all recognize the snowflakes that they are hanging up. No, those are not the ones Finn"—I pivot, bringing the camera with me to focus on Finn and Oliver, who are now wrapping each other in fairy lights, earning the both of them a raised eyebrow because those strings are delicate—"signed or made during his lives. Phoebe and I made these. No one wants me to sign a snowflake for them."

"Don't be so sure about that," Finn calls teasingly, though the look in his eyes suggests he might be serious. It's hard to tell with all of the twinkling lights he's wrapped up in.

Either way, it makes me glad that I'm not on camera anymore, because that look does something to me every time that sends the butterflies stirring. "There was such a great response for signed snowflakes, but we do still have some available on our website for those of you who want to purchase one. I'll post that link again right after I end the live, which should be now. I don't want to ruin any surprises for those attending, and let's face it, there is still a lot to do." I sign off, post the ticket and snowflake website links like I said I would, then pocket my phone.

"Okay, everyone, I wasn't lying when I said there's still a lot left to get done, so let's keep up the good work."

Chapter 32

Finn

Ian picks me up from campus mid-morning. Our closer, Oliver, is already in the front, so I open the rear passenger door and slide in next to Josh, one of our relievers, then place my garment bag with my suit inside carefully on my lap.

"Morning, fellas," I greet them all and receive a variety of grunts and "mornings" in response.

It's a quick drive to the ballfield, where we meet up with a few more guys on the team. We'll be in two teams at the hospital, trying to cover as much ground as possible while Santa and his elves make the rounds as well.

I hang up my suit in my locker, grabbing the uniform that's waiting there for me. I quickly change, leaving my cleats behind. For this, I'll get to keep my street sneakers on. No one wants to see Finn, the regular guy in street clothes at the hospital. They want to see Finn, the ballplayer. And that's fine by me.

I take it back.

One person wants to see me out of the uniform.

Gale.

I think back to the day I surprised her with flowers and how she'd looked at me when I showed up to her office in jeans and a T-shirt. It was the same look she'd given me once I'd changed after the away game she surprised me at and again before breakfast. They say a uniform will do things to people, make them want whoever is wearing it. But Gale? She's almost immune. Maybe it's her personal and family history with the game, growing up surrounded by baseball players. But put on a pair of jeans? That's her eye candy.

I wonder what she'll be like when she sees me in my suit tonight, which now has a red pocket square to go with her dress. Thankfully Kyle needed to go to the mall and offered to bring me so I could get one. He wouldn't admit to what he needed, but considering I saw him in the big and tall section of the same store I was in, I will not be surprised if he shows up to the gala.

There's got to be something going on between him and Phoebe. If not, there will be. I'll eat my baseball glove if I'm wrong.

One thing I won't be wrong about is how beautiful Gale is going to be tonight. Red is a great color on her. But that's all I know about her dress. Long or short? Sleeves, straps, sleeveless? No idea. She wouldn't tell me. And since her shopping trip turned into a girls' night and an early bedtime, we didn't get a chance to hang out and I thus didn't get the chance to sneak a peek either.

She's been so busy prepping for tonight. Her dedication is amazing, and I hope she can let loose a bit at the gala so we can celebrate a few things together. A successful event, me not being a rental, the fact I love her. And I have every intention of telling her that tonight.

I slide my phone out from the back pocket of my jeans,

now folded in my locker, and pull up my text message window between Gale and me.

ME

> Getting ready to head out to the hospital. Hope your day goes smoothly.

GALE

> Thank you. *Fingers crossed* Phoebe will be meeting you all there with Santa. Have a good time. You're perfect for this. The kids are going to love you.

Thanks, beautiful. See you later. Xx

> Can't wait. Xx

"You coming, lover boy?" Oliver calls from the entrance to the locker room.

I slide my phone into my pocket as I stand, then jog to meet up with him and the others.

In the hospital lobby, Phoebe stands waiting with Eva from team relations and a guy I don't know who's got a fancy camera hanging around his neck and a bag slung over his shoulder that no doubt houses some other lenses. Next to them is a man holding a red bag that looks ready to burst with toys for the kids waiting for Santa. Given the man's bushy white beard, his stature, and cheeks reddened with makeup, I can only assume this is Santa Paul with only half the suit on. Can't say I blame him for not having a coat on. It is July.

"Well, at least *you're* all on time," Phoebe says in lieu of greeting, the tone unlike her.

"What's going on?" I ask her while the other guys spread out, saying their hellos to the nurses and staff working behind the desks here.

Santa Paul sighs. "My elves. Seems their sleigh was misfunctioning this morning, and now wherever they are, their phones aren't working either."

The offer easily tumbles from my mouth. "I can be an elf if you need one."

Phoebe's smile reappears, small at first, as she considers this. Eva seems less sure.

"The kids are going to recognize who you are, despite being an elf," Eva says. "We want to cheer them up, not reveal any truths we don't want them finding out before they're ready."

I shrug. "We can say I'm Santa's special helper for the day. It's July. The real elves are on vacation before the holiday season kicks into gear."

"He would fit in the elf suit," Santa Paul says. "And I do need someone to help me with this bag."

"Great!" I nod firmly once. "Where's the suit?"

Santa opens his bag and pulls out a red and green spandex-like outfit and then hands it to me. My eyes widen, and he chuckles just like an amused Santa Claus should. I can see why Gale hired him. He's perfect.

"There's this to go over that." He removes a much more forgiving cloth garment from the bag, also in red and green, and passes it over. Then a hat. "Can't forget that."

Eva eyes the pile in my hands. "Are you sure you want to do this?"

"Yeah, the kids are going to get a kick out of it." That's what matters. "I've got this."

"I have no doubt about that, actually." Phoebe's bright demeanor is fully back. "You're going to do great."

"Where can I go change?"

Phoebe points to a door several feet down the hall. "Bathroom's right there."

I take my costume and dart into the bathroom. Two stalls stand at the ready; the third, the largest occupied. I'd prefer to get changed in that one because there's more room, but I can't keep everyone waiting. I push into the first stall and lock it behind me. Carefully, I tuck my elf costume under arm. The last thing I need is to drop it in here. I push down on the back of one sneaker with the other, freeing my foot from it, then do the same with my now socked foot for the other sneaker. As I balance on my shoes, I undo my pants and let them fall. Next is my jersey, and I hang that over the door, which I should have done with this costume from the beginning. Would have been so much easier. I put the costume's outer layer over my jersey and let the spandex unravel.

After a few minutes, I manage to finagle myself into the lower half of the elf costume, giving myself a whole new respect for anyone who regularly has to put on tights, bathing suits, wetsuits, and the like. How did Gale do this for dance competitions? I looked it up. A competition isn't just one dance. It's multiple throughout the course of the day. I'd be tired from getting changed alone, and I'm in shape! Fortunately the top half goes on easier. More like a compression top, which I've worn under my jerseys before. They're just usually not attached to my pants.

Whoever was in the large stall has left since I started changing, and I'm tempted to shuffle over to it, but I don't want to be caught in a compromising position in the middle of the bathroom. When the outside door opens again, that seals it. I'm staying here. I finish getting into the bottom layer, then pull the second layer off the door, sending my jersey to the floor in the process. Gross. I open the door to grab it, then toss it back onto the door. Not sure I'll want to put that back on after.

Finally, I'm done changing. I bundle my jersey under my arms, then step off my pants so I can pick them up. But as I do, my phone slips out of the back pocket.

It would have been better had I not tried to grab it.

I can catch fly balls all day and make every grab, even when falling onto fans in the first row and squirting sunscreen all over them, but a phone in a tiny stall while holding my pants with one hand and my jersey held under my opposite arm? All I can do is bat it right into the toilet and send my pants leg in after it.

I curse.

"Daddy," a small voice says from several feet away, "that man said a bad word."

"He sure did, kiddo," an adult male answers.

"Sorry. Dropped my phone." Great. Now I'm stuck in here until they leave so they don't think that Santa's elves swear and so they don't think I do either. I mean, I do when the situation warrants it. And right now? Totally warranted. But they don't need to know that.

I yank my pants leg out of the toilet, grimacing. The bottom inch is soaked through and spreading three inches up the side that touched the water. I wring it out best I can. There's no use rushing for my phone. It's a goner. Submerged in the deepest part. I reach in for it with my thumb and index finger, then drop it onto my pants and pat it dry. Maybe someone can salvage the sim card. Thankfully I have everything else saved to the cloud.

Also thankfully, the man and his kid have left.

I throw open the stall door and plop my pants into the

sink. Then in what feels like the slowest way possible, thanks to the motion-sensing faucet, I rinse my pants leg because if it's going to be wet anyway, it might as well be with clean water, not toilet water. I also rinse off my phone since, why not? Can't ruin it any more than it already is.

I'm wringing out my pants once more when Ian pops his head into the bathroom. "Phoebe wanted me to . . . Do I want to know?"

I shake my head. "Had a bit of an accident." Then it dawns on me what I said. "Not that kind."

But Ian is already shaking with laughter.

Everyone is waiting for me once I make it out of the bathroom. "I decided I liked this outfit so much that I wanted to go home in it too. I hope that's okay." I look at Santa Paul, now in his full costume, his bag a little less full now. "My pants fell in the toilet."

Santa Paul's belly jiggles as he answers. "Oh, that is fine, yes. You can give them back to me at the gala."

I turn to Phoebe, who is biting back laughter of her own. "My phone also went for a swim. It went first. The pants were collateral damage. Can you tell Gale so she doesn't worry when I don't text her later?"

She nods before sputtering her way to a full laugh, unable to contain herself any longer. "I'm sorry, it's just so funny. And I was just not expecting this." She waves her arm up and down in front of me in a displaying motion. "But yes, I can let her know."

"I also need a bag to put this in," I say holding up my stuff.

"I can take care of that." Eva pulls a plastic bag with the team's logo on it from the tote bag she's carrying. "I always keep a few on me when we're doing team things. Never know when they might come in handy." She opens it for me, and I drop my things in. She takes the bag from me. "No need to be carrying it while you're going on your visits."

"Thanks." I shake out my arms.

Phoebe holds up her phone. "Gale wants a picture."

The camera guy brings his camera up as well. "As do I."

"Let's make it a good one, yeah?" I strike a pose, and we do a couple of photos of me alone, then me with Santa, and then me with Santa and the rest of the guys.

Finally when that's done, we do what we came here for. Bring smiles to the kids who are here and to their families too. And hopefully not have the kid and his dad realize I was in the bathroom at the same time as them.

Chapter 33
Gale

As busy as I am in the final hours leading up to the gala, I can't help but look repeatedly at the photo Phoebe sent me of Finn in his elf costume. It's adorable. She didn't tell me how it happened, so I can't wait until I hear it from Finn. Knowing him, he volunteered, but how did he destroy his phone? Did he forget his costume didn't have pockets?

My dress, on the other hand, does have pockets, so after staring at his photo for the fifth time, I drop my phone into one of those pockets and get back to work completing the last-minute tasks that need doing.

Yes, I'm in my dress since I will not have time to run home to change, and keeping my dress stored somewhere until I'm ready is an accident waiting to happen. Sure, I'm taking a risk wearing the dress now, too, but the Christmas apron I'm wearing over the front will hopefully protect it from whatever could happen. With the poofy white ruffles under the bright-red tea-length gown, I'm feeling a bit like a pinup girl turned housewife ready to pull cookies out of the oven. Given that this apron is the one I wear when I make Christmas cookies, it doesn't feel that far from reality.

An image of Christmas future flashes before me. The house is decked out for the holiday, and I'm in this dress making a last-minute batch of cookies before guests arrive. Finn's not in a suit, but slacks and an ugly sweater. Something baseball themed, of course. He's spreading plates full of appetizers on the table and making sure there are enough cups, little plates, and napkins for all of our closest friends. It's then I realize the house isn't just mine anymore. It's ours.

The thought that would have terrified me several weeks ago doesn't feel scary at all. It's welcome. That's saying something given how long I've been around a dugout even just as an adult. My adamant refusal to date ball players only lasted as long as it took for me to meet the right one. And that's Finn. I only wish my dad were still around. I'd love to know what he'd think about the professional-baseball-playing psychology major who uses fun as a way to psyche out his opponents and win over fans.

And somehow, win over me too.

"Hello? Is anyone here?"

I turn toward the familiar female voice and spot a woman in an apron, half obscured by a wooden cupcake tree.

"Joanie, hi!" I rush to the baker and help guide her to the tables where the cupcakes will go.

"Thank you," she says, putting the stand down, her bright smile making me feel instantly at ease. She gives me a quick once over. "Don't you look pretty! Like a nineteen-fifties Mrs. Claus with that apron. I should get my baking team some fun ones like that."

I thank her, then ask, "Is it just you doing the delivery?" She nods. "Do you want any help?"

"Oh, no. I'm good." She makes a show of looking around. "Is it *just you* doing the last-minute setup?"

"There will be others closer to the start time, but yes. Just me for now." I walk with her toward the door. The least I can do is make sure it stays open so she can come and go as needed.

"I would have thought Finn would be here."

"He's one of Santa's elves at the hospital today."

"And I bet he's wonderful at it. He's one of the good ones, Gale. And it's easy to see how much he cares for you. Don't let him get away."

Here she is, someone I know only on the periphery who could see how Finn feels in one short interaction with him, and yet I remained so uncertain, especially since the day after was the one where he didn't kiss me.

But I am certain now.

I smile politely at Joanie as I lock the door into the open position, and she hurries down the walkway toward her older station wagon. In the back, two more cupcake trees stand at the ready. I turn and walk away to let her do her thing so I can keep going with what I need to.

It doesn't take Joanie long to unload her vehicle and set up the entire dessert table. Cupcakes on the tree stands, plates of cookies as if they're set up for Santa sitting next to glasses full of peppermint candy canes, and squares of eggnog fudge and peppermint patties set on red and green cupcake liners, ready for the taking. We say our goodbyes, and I'm alone again for another couple hours before Phoebe shows up.

"Look at you!" she chimes, crossing the dance floor toward me as I place items up for bid on the auction table. Bob should be here soon to run security, so it's safe for everything to finally be out from the storage room. "That is such a cute look on you!"

I brighten and spin to face my administrative assistant and friend. She's gorgeous in a sparkly, floor-length silver dress with a side slit running up to her mid-thigh. Her hair's pulled up in a French twist that features a rhinestone-studded hair clip shaped like a snowflake. "No, I think we should look at you! Absolutely stunning!" What I don't say is that Kyle is not going to know what to do with himself when he sees her. I haven't talked to her yet to find out if he is her mysterious crush, and I don't want to make things weird between the best friends if he isn't. Especially not tonight.

A blush creeps up Phoebe's face as she tilts her head to the side and points at me. "We might need to rethink that apron, though."

I give her a good-natured eye roll. "It's not staying on. I didn't want anything to happen to the dress while I set up."

"Well, you should be all set since Finn already took the hit there. Outfit karma will keep you safe." *Outfit karma*, the idea that something will happen to only one person in a group's outfit. Like spilling food on a shirt while at dinner. Once it happens to someone, the rest of the people at the table are safe. It's something we joke about no matter if it's just Dinah visiting us in the foundation's office for lunch or if we're all together on a girl's night. Like when I got tzatziki in my hair. Everyone else made it through unscathed.

"So what happened?"

She's laughing before she even starts to tell me. "Like I told you via text, I'm going to leave the telling up to him. But oh my word, Gale, it's a doozy."

"He's okay, though, right?"

"Oh, he's fine. It's Finn. Took it all in stride. You should have seen him. I can think of no one better for the part. Don't be surprised if he gets an offseason gig with Santa Paul." She pulls out her phone and pulls up the foundation's social media page. "I already put these up, and Eva has a few more on the team's page, plus shared our post."

I take the phone from her and swipe through the several photos of the guys making the rounds in the hospital with Santa, Finn happily playing one of the elves. The way the kids' faces have lit up in each of them warm my heart. And I laugh upon seeing the final photo which shows Finn doing a flip in the hallway as a few kids poke their heads out of their rooms as Santa looks on with his index finger up to his mouth as if telling Finn to be quiet.

"Everyone loves him, don't they?" And as much I didn't want to fall for him, I love him too.

She nods. "And no doubt Finn will share these once he has a phone again. He mentioned getting a new one on his way here."

I let out a slightly disappointed sigh and hope he doesn't take forever at the store when he's supposed to be here. If the situation were reversed and it were me and my phone, I'd wait until tomorrow, wanting to get to Finn's event. But he wouldn't be him without his phone for videos and social media.

"Where is everyone, anyway?" I'd expected her to have at least some of the others in tow, not that we really need them at this point. We're almost done.

"Should be right behind me. Some of them, anyway."

As if on cue, Bob saunters in wearing a tuxedo. We never want to make why he's here too obvious, so instead of his security uniform, he blends in with the guests. Behind him are Ian and Oliver.

Bob hooks a thumb over his shoulder, a jovial expression on his face. "Found these two hooligans trying to gate crash."

They're quickly followed by Eva and two of the team's camera crew. She directs them to start taking photos of our setup inside and later to stage themselves outside to take pictures of the attendees as they arrive, using our outdoor Christmas decorations as a backdrop for the photos.

As the camera crew take off, Eva turns to me. "Okay, what do you need us to do?"

For the next hour, we finish up with all the little details: turning the twinkle lights on, adjusting centerpieces, and wiping fingerprints off our framed auction items (although by the end of the night, they'll have more on them). With forty-five minutes to go, our DJ shows up and begins his work. Ten minutes after that, Santa Paul shows up with an elf. My heart leaps at first sight, but it quickly calms when I realize it's not Finn. Where is he? I expected him to be here by now.

Every time the door opens, my gaze shoots toward the entrance, hoping it's him. Each time, a pang of disappointment hits when it's not, each building onto the last.

First, it's Macey and Dinah, ready to fix my hair. Then Shelby for my makeup. We *ooh* and *ahh* over each other's dresses, despite three of us getting them only last night.

With Phoebe here, our girl group is almost complete. We lack only Cassie, but between her living a few hours away and her reluctance to come to anything that Shane could be at, despite me telling her he's hours away at the All-Star events, she isn't coming. Now that her family's moved, I'm not sure she'll ever show up in Snowhaven again, save for a wedding or a funeral.

I ask Eva to take a group shot of us with my phone, and I send it to her.

ME

Miss you! Wish you were here!

CASSIE

You all look so good! I'm printing this out and framing it.

Aww . . .

Now I want one of you and that hot date of yours.

He's not here.

??? What do you mean?

I fill her in as best as I can with what I know.

What a day! But no worries, he'll be there.

But as the other players who had been at the hospital arrive without Finn, annoyance and doubt creep into my thoughts and wind through the knot in my stomach. And when Kyle walks in by himself, a single red rose with a silver ribbon tied around it, the lingering traces of doubt that I'd had about him, about us, that's been softly flurrying at the back of my mind blows in like a blizzard.

I rush toward the moody shortstop. "You haven't seen Finn, have you?"

He shakes his head as he looks around. "I texted and asked if he needed a ride, but he didn't respond. Figured he was here already. Shouldn't he have come with the guys from the hospital?"

"His phone broke. I don't have all the details. He's off getting a new one, but it's taking forever." Not said: on the most important night of my career and possibly our relationship, I'm coming in second to a phone.

Kyle puts his hand on my shoulder in an unexpected show of support. I don't think I've even shaken his hand before. "He'll be here. He's crazy about you, and after all he's done, he's not going to skip out on you or this." His words are to me, but his gaze is elsewhere. Finally it settles behind me, and the corner of his mouth quirks upward. "Now if you excuse me, there's someone I need to say hello to."

For a moment, my attention turns away from my missing date as Kyle approaches Phoebe. Her back is to him, and he places a hand just above the small of her back and then bends toward her to say something I can't hear.

She spins toward him, and her excitement shines bright. There's no missing the surprise in her loud "You came!" or the blush that blooms across her face when he holds out the rose he brought. What I only assumed before I now know for certain. Phoebe is totally into Kyle. And it's adorable.

"Phoebe and Kyle?" Macey says, coming up behind me.

"Uh-huh. They've been friends since college."

"That is so cute!" Dinah squeals from my other side, quiet enough so as not to draw Phoebe's attention as we watch her with the grumpiest guy on the team.

"I'm happy for her," Macey says.

"Me too," I add. "You haven't seen Finn, have you?" Maybe he snuck in somehow and hasn't found me yet. Though how you could miss me in the red dress and candy-cane-striped tights, I have no idea, so I doubt that's the case. He should have come straight here from Frost Field.

She shakes her head, and Dinah does the same. Both of their smiles do little to ease my worry. Macey's "He'll be here" is starting to sound like a strange echo of everyone else's assurances, though she agrees to ask the guys if they've heard anything from him.

I brush off their words and my thoughts as our first guests arrive. I have a job to do. This is my event. It's my night. My family's name attached to the gala, the foundation. My continuation of their legacy.

And as I greet those who have come to support tonight's charitable cause, one so close to my heart, I begin to pick up the pieces of the wall that once guarded it, wondering if I should rebuild.

Chapter 34
Finn

Two hours ago

The few cars arrive back at Frost Field, dropping off me and the guys, Eva, and the camera man. Phoebe drives away, a broad smile on her face as she tells us she'll see us all later. She's had a cheerful disposition since I met her, but this is bigger than that. No doubt it's Kyle related. I hope for her sake he actually shows up to the gala and doesn't chicken out. I try to picture the burly shortstop in a suit, but no matter what I do, the image doesn't come to me. And that's despite seeing him shopping for one. It seems that out of character for him.

I head into the locker room with the guys. They all need to get out of their uniforms and into street clothes. I'm going to need to wrestle myself out of this elf suit before getting into my suit. I figured I'd save time and head straight to the gala from here. Now if I can swing it, I'm going to try to get a new phone first.

As much as some might argue otherwise, I can live without

one, but I'd hoped to go live on my socials while I was there. Give fans who couldn't make it a taste of what it was like. Not to mention snap a few photos of me and Gale just for me. My only pictures of her are screenshots from our video chats and what she's posted on social media (now that she's granted my request to follow her), and it's time to change that.

Several of the guys hop into the shower once they're out of their uniforms, tossed haphazardly into the laundry cart. And although I toss my jersey in there, too, I hang my pants up in my locker. I don't want to think about leaving the damp pants leg in the middle of all the other uniforms until someone collects everything to wash. It's still break, so it might be another day or two, plenty of time to cause a stink.

I hurry to change out of my elf costume, hurry being a relative word with this spandex suit. Wearing it wasn't as bad as I first thought it would be. Once it was on, I could almost forget about it, and it didn't interfere with any of my moves.

Giving my fans a reason to smile is half of why I do what I do on the field. The flips, the dancing, the tricks with the ball, it's all unexpected and fun. And I'd be lying if I said those smiles didn't keep me going. Earning a hard-won smile powers me through.

But the smiles on those kids today? Being able to give them a few minutes reprieve from whatever is causing them to be in the hospital? Those smiles are easily among the top I've seen. The kids we visited lit up upon our entry to their rooms, and they stayed that way as we snapped photos, signed baseballs or hats for them, and they received presents from Santa. No wonder Santa Paul was so happy to don his suit in the middle of July for this.

Perhaps the only smile that's meant more to me recently is

the first real one Gale ever gave me. It almost appeared that first evening when I helped her cover up the sunscreen stain on her shirt. All that did was make me want to work for it more. But the first one was the day she showed up partway through the game with a flower in her hair. It wasn't big. And it didn't light up her face the way I've seen some do now. But the shy smile of acknowledgement when she pointed to the flower meant everything.

Too busy daydreaming about Gale's face, I nearly topple over in the locker room as I try to pull the leggings portion of the costume off my body. Thankfully, a wall catches me, the bang reverberating through the room.

"All good, Nixon?" Ian asks from several feet away.

"Yeah, fine. This was harder than I thought it would be."

"Might be easier if you sit down and work it off that way." He doesn't have to tell me twice. I plop onto the bench behind me. "I think the rest of us are done here. We gotta head out to change for tonight. You going to be okay by yourself?"

"Yeah, I brought my suit. I'll find my way there after the cell store." It's not that long of a walk.

"Alright, man. See you there."

The guys shuffle out of the locker room, and a few minutes later, a door slams in the distance, signaling I'm really alone.

Once I peel off the rest of my elf costume, which is a lot easier to do sitting down, I place the costume at the bottom of my locker, then head for the showers.

Within ten minutes, I'm clean, and my hair is tousled dry. I put on my suit, paying particular attention to folding the pocket square. I'd saved a video to show me how it's supposed to be done, but so much for that without my phone. Same for the bowtie. Maybe I'll look okay without it. I hope Gale doesn't mind. Or maybe she can tie it for me. I can't wait to see her. To dance with her and hold her. It's our "going public" moment. The sports gossip column may have tried to start something by posting that photo of us, but they jumped the gun. We were barely anything then. But now? The photos will be inescapable, even if they are just from our camera crew. And now? We're ready for them. They're on our terms.

I dig my shoes out of the pocket on the garment bag, swapping them for my dead phone. I'd mentioned to Phoebe and the guys I was going to try to replace it before the gala, but the later it gets, the more I'd rather just get there and see Gale. We can take pictures with her phone, and I'll post them later. Or I'll enjoy the moment while I'm there. How novel, though with Gale, it's been happening more and more. As long as my views don't nosedive, I should be okay. The lead up to the gala and all of my snowflake making has helped by providing steady content even if it's not my usual.

These aren't the best shoes for walking, but unable to call for a ride, I'm at an impasse on what else to do. I run into the bathroom and shove some toilet paper all the way down my sock above my heel as extra padding. I'd have a few days for any blisters to heal but rather not get them in the first place.

Finally, it's time for me to go. I grab the costume, toss it in my garment bag with my street clothes—I'll stash it all somewhere when I get to the gala—then head for the door. As long as I don't get lost in the tunnels, I should be golden.

Until I try the door.

And it's locked.

I jiggle the handle, but nothing. I pound against the door, but no one comes. I keep trying, hoping someone will hear me from wherever they are and will come to investigate. It's a big place, after all. If they're moving about, they're not always going to be somewhere they can hear me.

But two things are certain.

I am going to be so late.

And I've let Gale down.

Chapter 35
Gale

The girls all run up to me. Macey's got an uncertain smile on her face, the kind that an unsuspecting person wouldn't think anything of, but because it's directed at me, I'm instantly on alert. Behind her by several feet stands Bob, looking worried.

The knot in my stomach tightens. "What's wrong? Did something happen with one of the auction items?"

Macey shakes her head.

"Then why's Bob away from the table? Who's watching it?" Dinner is over now, and the dancing has started. Those not dancing are milling about and walking around, giving them plenty of time to bid on our silent auction items.

Phoebe raises and lowers her arms in a calm down motion. "Kyle's there with Oliver. Everything is in good hands."

"Then what?"

Bob steps up then. "It's Finn, Gale."

"Where?" I spin around, my traitorous heart leaping at the idea of him finally being here despite being so, so late.

"At the stadium." He can't meet my eyes. "I'm afraid I may have locked him inside."

"You what? Please explain."

He tells me how he was on security detail earlier today before coming to the gala, filling in for someone who called in. And how he secured the locker room area after seeing the others leave in their street clothes.

Macey takes over. "When I asked Ian earlier, he said Finn was there when everyone else left, still getting changed. But over dinner, he made an offhand comment about spotting Bob on their way out. So I asked Bob, and he told me what he told you."

I focus back in on Bob. "Are you sure?"

"I can't be positive. I was making my rounds, and when I saw all the cars were gone . . ."

"He doesn't have a car." I swallow hard, willing my heart to stop beating so fast. I pull out my cellphone. "The office number is still the same, yeah?"

Macey nods, and I scroll through my address book until I come to the entry for the manager's office adjoining the locker room. I haven't called this number on my cell since my dad was still managing the team.

My hands shake so badly, it takes a couple tries for my screen to register what I'm pressing, but finally I hit call.

After moments of dead air, the connection goes through, and the other end starts to ring.

And ring.

And ring.

Finally. "Hello? Help! I'm trapped in here."

"Finn!" My knees nearly give out with relief as the piles of rock wall around my heart turn to dust.

"Gale. Oh, I'm so glad to hear your voice. I'm locked in here."

"Sit tight. We're coming for you."

"I'll be here."

I almost say *I love you* right there and then, but he'll be here soon, and I'll tell him in person. I hang up and slide the phone back into my pocket, then look to Bob. "I need keys."

Macey places a hand on my arm. "We're already on it. Ian and my dad are on the way."

"I'm so sorry, Miss Gale," Bob says, wringing his hands with worry.

I let out a sigh. "It's okay, Bob." Me saying anything to the contrary isn't going to help the situation. He feels bad enough, and he's never going to let it happen again. One of those fluke things in a very long career with the team. Just unfortunately it happened tonight. With Finn.

He gives me a sad, tight-lipped smile before turning around, no doubt to head back to the auction table to relieve Kyle, who needs to get set up at the small table we have for players who are here to sign team posters for attendees who want them. Because he only decided to come last minute, he's a surprise for those who are here tonight.

Wrapping my arms around my middle, I take two steps toward the front door. "I need air." Phoebe moves to follow me, but I wave her and everyone off. "I need you here to take care of things. I'll only be a minute."

The humid July air does nothing to ease my emotions or clear my head. With the Christmas music playing, the decor, and the cooler temperatures inside, I'd almost forgotten we're a month into summer and not the start of winter.

Macey follows me outside, crossing her arms, a rebuttal already on her lips. "You're not getting rid of me that easily."

I nod. She'd never listen to me if I told her otherwise. I wipe my eyes. They're wet. I refuse to cry. But the steadying breath I try to take betrays me as it shudders instead.

Macey comes up behind me and gives me a side hug before rubbing my upper back.

"I'm an awful person, Macey. I thought he stood me up. After everything he's done for tonight, I almost believed he'd chosen getting a new phone over me."

"And how were you to know he wasn't doing just that? We all began to think it after a while. Don't beat yourself up about it."

"But how can I not? I should have known. I should have believed in him."

She squeezes me tighter. "It's a logical progression of thought. You're not the type to jump to thinking something's happened to him in a let's call the hospitals or let's call a search party sort of way. That's more a Dinah thing. Any one of us would have thought the same in your situation. Thank goodness Ian said something about seeing Bob so we could all put it together."

I take the change of topic that she's giving me, whether she realizes she is or not, and turn to her. "Speaking of Ian, you two seem to be getting cozy tonight."

"Well, some of that was your doing, you know, putting me right next to him at dinner instead of having me eat with my parents, so thank you." There's a hint of pink in her cheeks, and it's definitely not a reflection off my dress when the green of hers would combat it.

"Just distributing the players throughout the space so our guests can get special access. It is part of what they pay for after all." I wag my eyebrows at her.

"Hmm . . . and yet I end up with Ian, and Phoebe ends up with Kyle?"

"I swapped Phoebe and Kyle last minute with Finn's and my seats since Kyle hadn't originally been in my seating chart."

"And I see you trying to pair off the rest of us too."

"Oliver would be good for Dinah after the string of duds she's had, that's all."

She ponders this a moment. "Yeah, you might be right."

Fully in control of my emotions once more, I pull her in for a hug. "Thanks for looking out for me."

She wraps her arms around me. "Always. What are besties for?" I feel her shift, and then she taps me on the shoulder. "They're back."

Heart in my throat, I push out of her embrace and whirl around. The car's pulling into a spot halfway down the nearly full parking lot. Before the engine cuts off, I'm running toward the car, and one of its back doors is opening.

Finn rushes to the rear end of the car, and when he spots me, the smile that overtakes his face is breathtaking. He jogs forward to meet me, and I'm still several feet away when I trip over my high heels. I flail my arms trying to find purchase. Suddenly I'm in Finn's arms, and he lifts me up as I manage to wrap my arms around him. He spins me around before gently putting me back on the ground.

"You caught me."

"I'd never let you fall. About time I repay you for catching me the day we met." His eyes sparkle as he takes me in. He gently wipes his thumb across my cheek, catching a tear that's escaped. "Sh . . . beautiful, don't cry."

"I—" My voice hitches, and I try again. "I thought you weren't coming."

"I would never do that to you." He pulls me close, blocking me out from enough of the world that I'm only vaguely aware of people passing us in the parking lot. "I'm so sorry you thought that. That I made you think that. I am always going to be there for you, in your corner, supporting you any way that I can. Every event. Every setup for an event. Social media videos, appearances. Whatever you need. Nothing is going to stop me, not even locked locker room doors. They just might delay me for a while."

If I wasn't crying before that declaration—and I was, stupid emotions—I am now. Thank goodness he's hiding me and preventing anyone else from seeing.

"What happened?" I mumble into his shirt.

"Guess security thought no one was in there anymore."

I shake my head and look up at him. "They told me about that. Bob is very sorry by the way. I meant, what happened to your phone? Your clothes? Phoebe only said it was a doozy."

He releases a puff of air through his nostrils and raises his eyebrows. "It is that. Santa's elves never showed, so I volunteered. Then while changing into the costume, which is not easy to do in a bathroom stall"—I can already see where this is going—"my phone ended up in the toilet and so did my pants leg."

"Oh no . . ." And here I am getting tear stains all over his shirt. He's going from one wardrobe disaster to another.

He goes on to tell me about being trapped in the stall while a father and son came and went so he wouldn't ruin anything for the kid, either about Santa or him the baseball player.

And now I'm laughing. A full shoulder-shaking, can't get myself under control disaster. I don't know if this or the crying is worse.

Finn tightens his hold around me. "Sh . . . It's okay. Everything ended up okay. I'm here now." Great. He thinks I'm crying again.

I try to shake my head, but between the laughing and having just been crying, he probably can't tell. Lifting my arm up, I slide it between us and apply just a bit of pressure to his chest to get him to ease up. He does, and I take an awkward gasp of air, causing me to cough. I'm such a mess. Thankfully, my preferred mascara is waterproof, not that it's a feature I regularly need, though was definitely needed today. No doubt my other makeup did not hold up as well.

"Wasn't crying."

Finn gives me a look of adoration. "You don't have to hide what you're feeling from me." He wipes my cheek, this time with the heel of his palm.

"I know. I wasn't crying, though. At least not then. I'm sorry, but that is funny."

"Now that I'm here with you, yeah, it kind of is. But all the trouble it caused. I could have done without that."

"Well, you're here now. That's what matters." I take a step out of Finn's embrace and straighten the lapels on his suit jacket, pressing them down with my hand. "You clean up nice."

He holds out his arms at his sides. "Better than me in jeans?"

I scrunch my nose as I pretend to think. "Nothing will beat you in jeans."

"And how about you?" He whistles low. "You're stunning, Gale. Not just now in that beautiful dress, but always. Though nothing's going to beat you wearing my jersey." He raises an eyebrow, his gaze heating, stirring the butterflies in my stomach. They have absolutely no idea what to do with the whirlwind of emotions running through me, but they probably prefer it to the knot that's usually there.

I blow out a hard breath and fan my face. Must dry off. People are probably starting to wonder where I am. "Come on. Inside will cool you down. It's a real-life winter wonderland in there." I grab Finn's hand and pull him toward the gala entrance. I'll have to find one of the camera crew once I look respectable to get some photos of us out here.

Before reaching the door, Finn stops and tugs me back to him. He reaches for my face, and I step toward him so he can place it against my cheek. "Gale, I know being late put a rush to the evening's plans, but I haven't forgotten that I owe you a dance."

I lift onto my toes and gently press my lips against his. "I'm looking forward to it."

Chapter 36
Finn

Holding my hand, Gale leads me inside, and I'm struck by how magical everything looks put together. Yesterday's setup didn't do it justice, not under the fluorescent lights that were on at the time. But now I really see her vision. It's like a bright moonlit night, its light reflected on the snow. In addition to the twinkle lights surrounding the room, there are lights under blankets of fake snow at various points, helping people navigate throughout the darkened room.

Which has fallen silent as people turn and stare at us.

Beside me, Gale freezes, her grip on my hand tightening. She could own the moment if she wanted to, like she has countless times on stage and in the boardroom, but between this evening's unexpected events taking their toll and not liking this sort of attention, she's not her usual self. I squeeze her hand to remind her I'm right here.

Then as if a switch is flipped, everyone starts clapping, a chorus of "Finn, Finn, Finn" rising up among them. Oliver is standing up from the table he'd been sitting at a moment ago, his hands outstretched over his head in a victory pose as he shouts "Nixon!"

Oh, this is for me.

I raise my free hand up in a wave, smiling at the crowd. "Sorry, I'm late, everyone. You gotta try the new locker-room-themed escape room that Frost Field has."

Everybody laughs, and just like that, the cheering dies down and everyone resumes what they were doing before I walked in. With their attention elsewhere, Gale relaxes.

"That's not a half-bad idea," she says as we make our way through the room. "The escape room. Wonder if we can do something like that for Halloween. We typically do something around then to start raising funds for Thanksgiving turkeys that we'll donate with all the fixings to those who need it."

Once upon a time, it was me who needed it. "I like the way your brain works."

She smiles coyly at me. "It was your idea."

"But you're going to pull it off somehow." I kiss the side of her head.

"Speaking of food, you hungry?"

"Starved." I'd barely eaten lunch at the hospital out of fear that something else would go wrong and I didn't want to ruin the elf suit. Which I left in the car, and I really don't want to go back and grab it right now.

"I'll go grab you something. I'm sure there's plenty left in the kitchen."

"In a moment. I want to do something with you first." I lead her across the room, stopped every few feet as people ask for photos or to shake my hand. I oblige each time. Beyond coming together for a good cause, that's what these people are here for. And judging from the number of snowflakes I see at various table settings, with or without people at them, many are here to see me, at least in part.

Finally, we make it to Santa Paul and a single elf.

Gale stops a few feet away as an elf snaps a picture of Santa and another couple. "Finn, what are you doing?"

"Taking a picture with my girlfriend, of course." We've not discussed what exactly we are, but that's what she is. It's what I want her to be.

Her smile turns mischievous. "Girlfriend, huh?"

"If you'll do me the honor."

She pulls a face. "Maybe we should ask Santa to see if you're going to get what you want this year."

I blink at her, and now she's the one laughing. It does more for me than the whole room of laughter a few minutes ago did. I could live on this noise. Who needs food?

My growling stomach reminds me that *I* need food.

When the couple walks away, Gale pulls me toward Santa's lap. "Santa, I need to know if Finn's on the nice list this year. Me being his girlfriend is kind of riding on the answer."

I hold a hand up, chest high. "In total transparency, let me say I didn't forget your elf suit during the getting trapped in the locker room debacle. I did, however, leave it in the car. In case that affects your decision."

Santa Paul laughs, a few *ho-ho-ho*s thrown in for authenticity. Way better than any mall Santa I saw growing up. Not that I saw many up close. Or had my photos taken with them. Or if I did, my mom never bought them, my experience being enough . . . or rather, all she could afford. Things I'm going to rectify with my own kids someday. Hopefully with Gale.

"Never fear, Miss Frost. Finn has been a very good boy. He sure saved me today when my elves went missing." He turns to me. "One of your friends brought the costume to me before you walked in. I have it safely tucked in my sack."

"Oh, good. Glad to hear it."

"If you ever want to don the outfit again, you could have a fine career as an elf. Not everyone can pull it off. I'd say you could be Santa if you wanted, but I don't see you ever looking quite like this." He grabs his belly and laughs again.

"As long as I don't have to change in any more bathroom stalls, it might not be so bad. I'll have Gale give me your information. Maybe I can at least be a backup for you should any more elves wander off."

He holds out his hand to shake, and I take it.

"If you wouldn't mind, Santa," Gale says once we're done shaking, "could my boyfriend and I get a picture with you?" Her using the term boyfriend for me thrills me more than belting a game-winning walk-off home run, something I've only done once in my life.

"Ho-ho-ho, absolutely."

Gale hands her phone to the elf, while one of the camera crew walks over with his camera at the ready. Together we pose with Santa, taking a few photos in various positions. It's definitely different taking Santa photos as an adult. We don't quite fit the traditional way all grown up.

The elf hands Gale's phone back to her. We say our thank yous and goodbyes, and then Gale and I walk toward the back of the room, where wide stainless-steel doors stand closed with paper snowflakes taped all over them. The kitchen, no doubt. It's quieter here. The waitstaff are likely inside the kitchen or already gone for the evening, leaving whoever's responsible behind to do the cleanup. And there's no reason for any of tonight's attendees to be hanging out here. Unless, of course, they arrived late enough to miss dinner and now need food.

Gale kisses me softly before patting me on the chest. "Let me grab you something to eat. You must be really hungry by now."

She returns a few minutes later with a plate made-up for me.

"Okay, we have roasted chicken with a cranberry-orange glaze, a cranberry quinoa salad, maple glazed carrots, and cheesy mashed potatoes with a hint of rosemary. My favorite part of the meal." She tilts her head in a follow me motion. "Let me get you set up at one of the dining tables."

"Actually, set me up at the signing table."

"You're going to be constantly interrupted there."

"That's okay. I don't want any of the attendees to go home disappointed that they didn't get a chance to meet me due to my being late."

"Are you sure? We didn't make them any guarantees on who they'd get to see once they got up there. And Kyle stepped in to sign things too, so it's not like we had a window where no one was signing."

"Phoebe's rubbing off on him," I say with a chuckle. "But yes, I'm sure. I saw the snowflakes out there."

"You're the best, has anyone ever told you that?"

"Just you." I smile softly at my girlfriend. *Girlfriend.*

A hint of color appears on her cheeks as she looks up at me through her eyelashes. "Well, more people should." She leads me to the signing table at the side of the room, out of the way of the dance floor and the now-cleared dinner tables where people sit and mingle regardless of where they originally sat. I settle at an open chair at the end of the table, where Oliver and Josh are currently signing team posters and snowflakes.

Gale sets the plate down in front of me. "Enjoy while you can. I think you're going to be pretty busy." She lifts her head to survey the room. Already several people are standing or grabbing their signed items, readying to come back to the table to see me. Then she presses a kiss the top of my head. "I have to go have a quick chat with Claudia from HR, but I'll come rescue you a little later for that dance."

"I'm looking forward to it."

An hour later, I've eaten about three quarters of my dinner, mostly scarfed between people coming up to have things signed, some purposefully holding up the line so I can finish chewing or swallowing the bite in my mouth. I've been managing two lines. One on my right coming at me from getting things signed by my team mates and the other on my left for those who already have the others' signatures and just need mine.

A few minutes later, Gale comes over and tells us all that they're closing the line in a few minutes. A moment later, the DJ's announcement echoes the same, telling anyone who still needed signatures to get in line now. Only a handful stand and make their way over. Finally, fifteen minutes later, I'm signing the last snowflake of the night.

"You are a star for doing all that. I thought your lines would never end," Gale says, walking over to me once the last fan is out of earshot. She holds out her hand, and I hand her my left.

I flex my right to stretch it out some after all that writing. "I regularly sign for the kids before games, but nothing like that."

"You're okay, though, right?" she asks, genuinely concerned. "I didn't cause you some weird tendonitis or something, did I?"

"No more than cutting all of those snowflakes did," I tease, shooting her a cheesy grin so she knows I'm not serious. "It's all good now. No worries come game day. There's probably one thing that could help it out, though."

"Name it."

"Holding you in my arms on the dance floor." I gently tug her in the direction of the dance floor in the middle of the room.

She follows readily. "Now that is something I can do. Been looking forward to this all evening."

"Only all evening?" I look at her and wink. I've been wanting to do this for weeks, though now that it's here, I have to admit, to myself anyway, that I'm a little nervous. I may have some moves, but Gale's danced almost all her life. Hopefully I don't step on her toes.

"Okay, you got me there. Longer than that."

We make it to the dance floor right as a new slow song comes on, and I hold my right hand up for her to take. As she does, we break hold with our other hands, and I place mine at the small of her back, pulling her in close. She puts her hand on the back of my neck, her fingers sending electrical pulses through my system as she plays with my hair. I'm due for a cut per team rules, but I'm so glad I haven't gotten it done already.

We start to sway, and I lift her left hand to my mouth and feather kisses across each knuckle. She lets out a small gasp as I turn her hand to place one on the pulse point at her inner wrist. Keeping my lips there, I lift an eyebrow to acknowledge the reaction. After another moment, I finish my kiss and flip her hand back over. As much as this is Gale and me, girlfriend and boyfriend, together on the dance floor, it's still a work event for her, and I can't get carried away.

"You liked that, hmm?"

She nods, her tongue peeking out to wet her lips. "I like a lot of things when it comes to you."

"I like a lot of things when it comes to you too. Might say I even love them. I'm not sure if it's too soon, and I know we just became official, so it's okay if you don't feel the same right now, but Gale, I love you."

The grin on Gale's face widens into a brilliant smile before she stops playing with my hair and pulls my head down toward hers instead, our lips meeting, then deepening into their own dance together. I feel her own restraint, holding this back from being something more, and I wonder if she's trying to keep things appropriate, as well, and if she's as affected by me as I am by her.

She breaks our kiss but doesn't release my head, our foreheads pressed together. Is this the moment she'll say it back? Surely, she wouldn't still be smiling if she wasn't.

"Finn, I—"

"Excuse me, Miss Frost?" a male voice interrupts as the song ends.

I squeeze my eyes tight. Just a moment longer and I would have known what she was going to say. I suppress a groan, knowing that it wouldn't be appreciated given I have no idea who this guy is.

Gale pulls away from me and faces the older gentleman. So not a romantic rival I don't think. I give him a short, and what I hope is polite, nod, though I want to be anything but. Did he really have to interrupt right then?

The man holds his hand out for Gale to shake, and her guarded demeanor suggests she doesn't know him either. So not a teammate of her father's or anyone else associated with the team either.

"I'm Mark Anderson with the Major League Charitable Organization. We've spoken on the phone."

Recognition flashes in her eyes, and she smiles. Warm, but

professional. "Mark, hi. Oh, thank you so much for coming, especially during such a busy time for the league. Must not be easy to get away during the All-Star festivities."

His smile mirrors hers. "I have a great team behind me taking care of it."

"That's good. Have you met Finn Nixon, our newest Snowhawk?" She places a hand between my shoulder blades, centering me.

He turns to me, hand extended, and we shake, exchanging greetings, before he turns back to Gale.

"I'm sorry to interrupt, but I need to go catch my flight back to New York, and I was hoping to talk to you. Privately."

Gale stiffens so slightly that if my hand wasn't at the small of her back, I might have missed it. "Oh, yeah, sure. Follow me." She turns to me. "I'll be right back."

Then she leads Mr. Anderson away, leaving me on the dance floor. Alone.

Chapter 37
Gale

I bring Mr. Anderson upstairs to the gallery area, where the sounds from the main floor are muted slightly. Although it's been fully open to gala attendees all evening, only a handful of people have made their way up here to the space overlooking the dance floor. Had I come up here with Finn, Mr. Anderson likely never would have found me.

He motions to one of the small tables up here, and I clear away a napkin and small dessert plate left by an earlier guest before taking a seat across from him.

He folds his hands on the table. "Congratulations on a wonderful event. I have no doubt that if your father were still here, he'd be very proud of what you're doing to raise money for this cause."

My throat immediately tightens with emotion. On a regular day, hearing those words from a relative stranger wouldn't make me choke up, but between the event high and knowing I can breathe for a while once it's over, plus all the stress and emotions from Finn's late arrival is just too much. And that's not even tackling the fact he said he loved me. I now understand the phrase a roller coaster of emotions. Today has had so many highs and lows.

"Thank you. Did you know my father?"

"Not during his playing years. But we met a few times during the set up of the Frost Foundation. Traveled out to meet the original board of directors. Before your involvement."

"I didn't know."

Mr. Anderson leans in slightly. "Why I'm here tonight is to see how one of the bright young minds in the sports foundation sector runs an event. Forgive the pun, but you've really stepped up your game for this one, on the social media side especially. Getting Mr. Nixon involved—"

"He volunteered all on his own. It wasn't something I asked or told him to do." I feel the upward pull at the corners of my mouth as I talk about him, unable to hide my opinion of him. Though given what Mr. Anderson interrupted, I'm sure he knows.

"He's a charismatic individual. A benefit to the team and foundation, I'm sure."

"That he is," and I'd like to get back to him, "but you're not here to talk about him."

"Correct. I'm not. As I was saying, we in the Major League's Charitable Organization have been very impressed by what we've been seeing from the Frost Foundation. You've done a fine job, and correct me if I'm wrong, but you and your assistant are the only full-time staff?"

I nod. I started a proposal to increase the staff size last year, but it took a back seat after my father's death and I buried myself in work. But now? It's time to revisit that. I can't have work be the only thing in my life anymore. I don't want it to be.

"Even more impressive. The MLCO recently took a look at

its mission, core values, and vision plan, and we're striving to achieve a bit more diversity within our organization, bring in a younger generation, women, minorities. You get the picture. We would like you to consider applying for a position within the organization."

This is not where I saw this going. "The MLCO wants me?"

"You have the skill and background that we're looking for."

"But I'd have to move, wouldn't I? To New York." He confirms, and I continue. "The Frost Foundation is my family's legacy. That's not something I can just walk away from."

He nods understandingly. "Nor would we expect you to. I'm sure you could retain a position on the board. Many of our employees sit on various boards both locally and nationally. Plus, you would get a chance to bring your causes to us and put them on a bigger playing field."

"That's a lot of mobile skin cancer detection units," I say quietly, more to myself than to Mr. Anderson.

"It certainly could be if you come work for us," Mr. Anderson says encouragingly. Then he sits back. "I'm not telling you that you have to decide right now to take the job. I'm saying to think about applying, that's all."

But if he's come all this way to tell me to apply, I assume my chances of getting the job are pretty good.

"No decisions have to be made tonight."

I nod, not really knowing what to say.

He must see it as an agreement. "Great. I look forward to seeing it come across my desk." Mr. Anderson stands. "I'll let you get back to your gala. Congratulations on a wonderfully run event. I hope it raises what you hope it will."

I don't tell him it already has. We're well beyond our original goal, much of that thanks to Finn's snowflakes and the extra tickets he's surely responsible for selling as a result. It will do so much good for the hospital's skin cancer research. "Thank you, Mr. Anderson."

"Please, call me Mark. We're colleagues."

I nod yet again, but don't make the name correction verbally. Mr. Anderson suits me. We're not colleagues. At least not yet. Maybe never if I decide not to apply to the position. "Thank you for coming all this way. Have a safe flight back to New York."

We shake hands, and he heads back downstairs. I could follow, but our conversation is over. I don't want to stay awkwardly silent behind him. Instead, I remain upstairs, collecting my thoughts, which are now even more all over the place. The roller coaster that my emotions are riding now includes a few loops I didn't expect, and I for one prefer to be in control when my feet go over my head.

As I pace next beside gallery railing, overlooking the floor below, watching the gala attendees dancing, chatting, or enjoying their evenings, I get lost in my thoughts. Could I actually leave the Frost Foundation, leave Snowhaven? Finn?

"Gale?" Finn asks hesitantly from behind me.

"Hey." I spin toward him and put on my best smile. Which must stink because he sees right through me.

"When Mr. Anderson came back down and you didn't, I started to worry. Are you okay?" I shake my head, and Finn's eyes go hard as he rushes toward me and then tucks a lock of hair behind my ear as he assesses me. "He didn't hurt you, did he?"

"No, nothing like that." I place my hand on his chest. Even through the suit coat, I can feel it pounding. "I'm sorry I worried you."

His hand caresses my cheek, and I lean into it. "What happened?"

"He was headhunting for a position with the Major League's Charitable Organization."

"He'd be stupid not to try." I gaze up at Finn, and there's no ounce of joking in his eyes as he stares back at me. "You're amazing at what you do. Look at all of this." He spins me around, wrapping his arms around my middle as he rests the side of his head against mine. "You did this."

I stare out at everything I'd just been looking at, trying to see it through his eyes. It's been a great event. A successful event. I should be proud. Maybe if other things had been different tonight, I could be. "Tonight is only as successful as it is because of your help."

"But you are the reason I wanted to help. No you, no me." He kisses the side of my head. "That's the way it goes."

"You alone raised so much money thanks to your snowflakes."

"Which I only had the idea for because I saw you making them with Phoebe and Dinah first. I just leveraged my following, that's all."

I sigh. "What am I supposed to do, Finn?"

He turns me back around to face him. "You apply. You find out what it's all about. There's no saying they're going to offer it to you."

"They don't send people by plane to talk to people they're barely interested in. If I apply, I'm probably getting the job."

"And you can decide then if you'll take it."

"Why do you make so much sense?" I try to smile and bring back some of the lightness I should be feeling.

"Because I'm looking at it from the outside."

"You're very much on the inside. What does this mean for us?"

"Gale, this changes nothing. I'm going to love you whether you're here or there. If this is something you want, don't let me stop you. I'm gone half the time. And I can live anywhere during the offseason. I'll request a trade to one of the teams in New York if I have to."

"But not this season. The Snowhawks need you. And no matter where I am, this team is important to me. They're part of my family legacy. So is the Foundation. It's why I'm not sure I can leave it, even if I could bring my causes to a national stage."

"Don't you know? You are your family's biggest legacy. Even if there was no team. No foundation. There would still be you. Gale Frost. You will always be the one thing that meant the most to them. Of that I have no doubt. And so if your legacy, *yours*, not theirs, means expanding upon your work here by taking it to New York, so be it. They'd be so proud."

I'm crying now. Again. Tears streak down my cheeks openly, too many for Finn to try to catch no matter how many times he wipes my cheeks with his thumbs as he cradles my face.

"I'm sorry. I usually don't cry like this."

"You never have to apologize to me for that. Thank you for letting me see it."

It's then I realize he's positioned his back toward the other tables scattered across the gallery, shielding me from anyone who might be looking, knowing that I wouldn't want anyone else to see me this way. It's this that actually helps me regain my composure, this act of love. I take a steadying breath, picking up my wobbly emotions after they've exited the roller coaster, tripping from all the loops and dips and turns they just experienced, some of it in the dark. And once they're all on their feet, they walk out of the ride and out into the sun. And I smile. Really smile at Finn.

He smiles back, the concern etched into his face washing away. "Feeling better?"

"Yeah," I say on a semi-contented sigh. "I think I am."

His eyes twinkle, and earlier thoughts about him being Santa replay in my mind. He could totally pull it off with a look like that. "Good, then let's get back down there. It's getting late, and I'd like to dance with you a little more." He steps backward, taking me by the hand to lead me to the stairs.

"Finn, wait." I pull him back to me. "There's something else I want to tell you, but not now. Maybe later tonight. At my place?"

"I'm all yours."

Chapter 38
Finn

Gale unlocks her side door, casting me a look over her shoulder. This will be my first time inside her house in person. I never made it beyond the driveway my first time here, and I've only seen bits of her walls as backgrounds to our video chats when I've been on the road.

She pushes the door open and then steps inside, holding it for me to do the same. As I close it behind me, my backpack over one shoulder, Gale flicks on the light, illuminating the kitchen.

After the gala and a race to clean up what the foundation was obligated to, Gale drove me to my dorm so I could get out of my suit. I dressed comfortably in light sweatpants and a T-shirt, not far off from how I sometimes dress when I'm heading directly home after a game. Something comfortable, nothing more, nothing less.

Given the hour, I packed a change of clothes, my toothbrush, and because I won't presume that anything will happen tonight, one of my assigned books for my summer class.

"Feel free to have whatever is in my fridge if you're hungry.

I noticed you didn't get to finish your dinner. If you don't mind leftovers, there's cold pizza and some falafel." She turns to me, sheepish. "There's been a lot of takeout these last few days. Too busy getting ready for the gala to stop and make something."

"I'm good right now." I'm being polite. I could probably eat the rest of her leftovers without blinking, but I don't want to leave her without anything.

"You sure? I'm thinking pizza, myself." She walks over to her fridge and pulls out the pizza box. She opens it up, revealing bacon, onions, and—

"Is that potato?"

"I realize we've never talked favorite pizza toppings during any of our chats, but don't knock it until you've tried it."

"It's perfect. You're perfect."

"Oh, so your pro potato on pizza." I nod. "Good to know. Cold or hot?"

"Cold."

She breaks two slices off from her leftovers and then splits them before handing me one. "Oh, sorry. You can put your bag down wherever."

I drop it onto a chair at her kitchen table, then take a bite of my pizza slice. I moan as the salty and savory flavors hit my tongue.

Gale stares at me, a slow grin growing across her face even as she chews. "Good, right?"

"Amazing. Devon has been holding out on me when it comes to pizza places."

"He probably goes to the place closest to campus. This one's a bit farther away. They don't deliver, but it's so worth it."

We make eyes at one another as we continue to eat,

standing in her kitchen between the counter and the table, the intensity inside the room growing the more our gazes linger. She's still in her dress from the gala, all dolled up and eating cold pizza out of the box. If I didn't already love her, I'd be done for with this alone. Her letting her guard down, not being so prim and proper, is one of the most attractive things I've ever seen.

I finish my slice first, and she motions to the box, but I shake my head.

Gale grabs the pizza box, and places it back into the fridge, her other hand holding the last of her slice. She closes the fridge door before popping the bite into her mouth. She closes her eyes, savoring the flavor.

When she's done, we wash our hands at the sink, side by side, tossing glances at one another.

"Join me for a movie?" Gale asks before grabbing the hand towel hanging from the drawer next to her. "I'll be waiting for you in the other room."

She sashays out of the kitchen through the open arched doorway, me close behind as we enter the living room.

Overall, the room is clean and well put together. Proper. Like Gale. A decent-sized television sits on a tv stand, books and framed photographs lining the shelves underneath. A gray couch sits across from the TV, a coffee table between them. Off to the side is her computer desk, a full desktop situated under it in a cubby. A recliner sits opposite that.

"I barely use them, especially during the season, but I have all the streaming services, so I'm sure we'll find something." She tosses me the remote with perfect aim. Unsurprising given her father's storied career with the Snowhawks as a starting pitcher before he ever became a manager. "I'm going to change. I'll be right back. Put on whatever. I like a range of stuff."

When she comes back a few minutes later, I'm scrolling through pages of movies, trying to decide. But the moment I lay eyes on Gale, I drop the remote, and it falls to the ground in front of me.

She's barefoot, her candy cane leggings gone, revealing long, toned legs that disappear under navy satin sleep shorts. And paired with it is a familiar shirt, the stain faded but still visible.

She tugs on her ponytail, tightening it, lifting her shirt up slightly and showing off a thin line of skin where shorts and shirt separate, drawing my focus. As she lowers her arms, she glances down at her shirt because I'm still staring. "It's been relegated to pajama duty now, but I couldn't get rid of it."

"I'm glad I didn't ruin it completely."

She walks over to the couch and sits, one leg tucked under her as she faces me, her gaze warm. "On the contrary. It might be my favorite now."

"I think it's my favorite too." I reach up and stroke her cheek.

She raises an eyebrow. "Not your jersey?"

"That's my favorite *jersey*, of course. But this"—I let my hand glide down her neck to her shoulder, and I grip the shirt sleeve—"is my favorite shirt."

"What other favorites do you have?"

"After tonight? Candy canes. I don't think I'll ever be able to look at another one ever again without thinking about you in those stockings."

"I could go put them back on if you'd like." She wags her eyebrows, her tone teasing.

I chuckle, the sound more like a rumble from the heat she's making me feel. "Maybe some other time. I'm rather fond of what you have on now too."

"I admit to this being how I usually sleep, but I'm usually under blankets once I change, so I'm actually kind of cold."

"Well, come here then." I lift my arm up onto the back of the couch, and she shifts to sit next to me instead of facing me. She snuggles in as I wrap my arm around her, and I kiss the top of her head.

"I love you."

She's quiet a moment, and I almost think she's somehow drifted off to sleep when she begins speaking.

"Winters here can be long, sometimes starting before the end of the season, though that's rare, and lasting into the start of the next season, a little less rare. The town's called Snowhaven for a reason. But we're a hardy stock up here. Chains on tires if needed, extra pieces to give better traction to our boots, and recipes for all sorts of snow related foods. We're used to it. And as kids, we didn't care that it was snowing for the fifth day in a row. We just wanted to play outside."

She chuckles. "Even me. Even if it meant only getting fifteen minutes of playtime before I had to head out to a dance rehearsal, I wasn't going to miss any of that time in the snow. I loved it. Still do, though I wish people could drive better in it.

"I already told you how my best friend Cassie lived next door to Shane growing up. We all went to the same school, though Shane is older, but because he was friends with Cassie's older brother, we all ended up playing together outside. This must have been a school break near the holidays—Thanksgiving or Christmas, I don't remember— because Devon was there too. He fit right in between being our age and Shane's cousin. He was kind of a bridge that way.

"Anyway, it had snowed overnight, enough that it made sense to go on foot everywhere instead of by car throughout the neighborhood. So when Cassie called, I eagerly trudged over the few blocks in the snow to go play.

"Everything was a competition back then between her and her brother, between her brother and Shane, and that naturally extended to Devon and me. That day, it was snowmen. The snow was of perfect packing consistency. Cassie and them were already building by the time I got there, so of course, I had to think quick in an effort to catch up."

"Of course," I say, kissing her head to urge her to continue. I've been looking forward to hearing this story since I first heard the nickname, and I can't wait to find out where this is going.

"So I build a snowman's head first, and by the time I'm done with that, I'm getting pretty warm because of how bundled up I am. So I shed the puffier outer layer of my coat. Well, the layer under that was warm, and it melted the initial bits of snow that got on me. But more clung to that. Much like how snow gets caked onto gloves. I used this to my advantage, rubbing a thin layer of snow up and down my body, arms and all.

"Then I flopped into the snow and rolled. And rolled. And eventually I started to accumulate quite a bit around me. It's what I'd wanted, but I hadn't thought it all the way through. One, the snow didn't stick to my snow pants the same way as it did to my jacket, ruining the whole snowman effect. And two, I froze my arms to my sides."

"Were you okay?"

"Yeah, my arms didn't get frostbite or anything like that, but my sleeves were stuck good to my jacket. I couldn't move them at all. But of course, I wasn't going to freak out and let them all know something had gone wrong. I kept going, rolling around even more.

"It was only after everyone else was done and wanted to go inside that I had to come clean because I was even more stuck and couldn't get up. They actually had to chip away at the snow with sticks and rocks . . . but not before they stood me up and decorated me. Stick arms, buttons down my front, even a scarf and hat Cassie had been using for her real snowman.

"So yeah, I turned myself into a snowman that day. Frosty the snowman. Because of my name but like the song. That is why Shane and Devon call me Frosty. And now you know."

Biting back a chuckle, I turn toward her. "Thank you for telling me."

She studies me, a slightly skeptical air taking over. "You may laugh now. I can see you holding back."

I let it out slowly, the chuckle coming out rumbly at first but building until it's full laughter. Gale lets me get most of it out of my system, but eventually she presses a kiss to my lips to quiet me.

"I'm sorry for laughing."

She shakes her head. "I told you to. And it is funny. Now."

"You have no idea how it means to me to be trusted with that story."

"I'm not sure even Macey knows. That was before her dad was on the team, and Cassie's never called me Frosty."

"Well, it's safe with me."

"I know." She kisses me again. "And that's just one reason why I love you. I love you, Finn."

She loves me. *Me.* Hearing her say it is akin to getting signed by the Sailors in a way. A life-changing moment that marks the before and after. From now on, I'm Finn, the one who Gale loves and who loves her back. And I can't wait to see where life takes us from here.

Chapter 39
Gale

I wake up in my own bed the next morning, the haze of waking up clouding the fact I don't remember coming to bed last night. The last thing I remember was watching a movie with Finn, telling him how I got the nickname Frosty, telling him I loved him. The kissing. Oh goodness, the kissing. I'm not sure I'll ever be able to get enough of that or the feeling of his arm wrapped around me as we cuddle, his head resting softly against mine as my head rested on his shoulder.

I slide out from under the covers, my feet hitting the bare wood floor. I glance down, double checking, my pajamas seemingly in place. Not that I expected anything less. Finn's been nothing but a gentleman, never pushing to go beyond my lines of comfort. But already he has me wanting to redraw them. Because I've never been so comfortable with any other guy. He could easily be the one. I love him. Of course he could be. I want him to be.

I tiptoe into the bathroom and brush my teeth. If I didn't get to my room on my own, I definitely didn't brush my teeth, and that's not how I want to greet Finn this morning.

Assuming he's still here. He wouldn't just leave, right? Not at that hour. He brought a bag. I fix my ponytail, and deeming myself good enough, I walk down the short hallway toward the living room.

Finn's stretched out on the sofa, my computer chair pulled next to him and locked in place, his left leg across the seat. Next to me, he doesn't seem so large, but my couch is on the smaller side. Lying down, he takes up all of the available space. He's still sleeping, his sculpted chest rising and falling evenly, so I use the time to study him. In sleep, his face is soft, serene, and yes, beautiful. The morning sun highlights a thin, pale scar on his chin. I've been up close and personal with this face several times recently in a variety of lightings, and this is the first time I've noticed it.

"I can feel you staring," Finn murmurs.

I jump, not realizing he'd woken up, and he cracks open one eye as he flashes me a smile.

"Sorry for startling you."

"Sorry for waking you."

"Don't apologize. You are the best thing I've ever woken up to. What time is it?"

"A little after seven."

"Do you have to work today?"

I nod. "Later. We always go in late the day after an event. Gives us a bit of time to recover after a busy night." Mine busier than usual for several reasons this time.

"Good because I'm not ready to get up yet." He pushes himself into a sitting position, and I move my computer chair to reclaim the room in front of the couch. Then I sit next to him, pulling my legs up onto the couch as I cuddle into his side.

"Good morning, beautiful." He kisses the side of my head.

"Good morning yourself. What time did I fall asleep?"

"Maybe halfway into the movie. I carried you to bed once it was over."

"I can't believe you did that. You should have taken the bed. I fit better out here."

"I wasn't going to take your bed and leave you out here, especially not without asking or being told first." He stretches his arms up over his head. "Besides, this couch isn't so bad. I've slept on worse."

"Well, thank you." I tilt my head up to face him and reach my hand toward his face, kissing the scar I'd seen a few moments ago.

"Got it diving for a ball when I was ten. Had to get stitches."

I kiss my way to his mouth, turning and pulling myself up onto his leg, then wrapping my arms around his shoulders. "I love you." It feels so good to say that, and watching how his eyes sparkle as he reacts to the statement causes me to melt even more for this wonderful man.

"Love you too." He slides me further up his lap, setting one hand against the small of my back as the other plays with the hair in my ponytail, kissing me the whole time. With his fingers tangled up in my hair, he's in control, tilting my head to the side and blazing a trail of kisses along my jawbone and down my neck.

I let my arms fall, and I grip the front of his shirt with one hand, his heart pounding hard enough for me to feel it as I explore his chest and abs through his shirt.

When he moves to the other side of my neck, he moves his hand from my back up my side, delicately running his fingers along my shirt. Unfortunately, it's my one major ticklish spot, and try as I might, I'm unsuccessful in fully biting back my laugh as I reflexively jerk to the side.

Finn's eyes fly open as he straightens, his other hand getting caught in my hair as he pulls back instead of down like he should have.

"Ouch!"

Finally he frees his hand. "Oh my gosh, are you okay?"

I rub the back of my scalp. "Yeah. I should be."

"What was that?" His eyes are still wide as he stares at me.

I pull a face, squinting my eyes in embarrassment. "I'm ticklish there. Like, really ticklish." I peek one eye open.

His face warms instantly, gaze twinkling with delight. "I will have to remember that for next time." He leans toward me and kisses me on the cheek. "But for now, how about breakfast?"

"We ate my original plan for breakfast last night, but I'm sure I can whip up something." I slide off his lap and head into the kitchen.

He follows me a moment later, and together we cook up cheesy scrambled eggs, sausage patties, and toast English muffins for breakfast sandwiches. All the while we exchange stolen glances and find excuses to touch one another, be it a simple graze of the hand or leaning around the other to get something we need. The latter probably needlessly complicates half of what we're trying to do, but it sure is fun. And then we sit across from each other at my kitchen table, my feet rubbing against his.

A girl could get used to this.

And over the next few weeks, I do. If the team is home, Finn stays over at my place. We cook breakfast in the morning before I head into work, either dropping him off on campus or bringing him to Frost Field depending on when he needs to report for game-day activities. Then after catching the game, usually with one of the girls, I wait for Finn to be done and drive him back to my place.

The routine is welcome, and I miss it—and him—when he's on the road, though thankfully none of the road trips are as long as the one prior to the gala. And thank goodness for video chats to help fill in the gaps of his presence when he's away. Definitely not the same, but better than nothing.

The girls help too. Our once-regular girls' nights and dinners resume, filling in holes left by more than just Finn being gone. They'd become infrequent during my dad's illness. Nearly non-existent after his death until they tricked me into going to that fateful game. The one where I first met Finn. Would we be what we are now had that foul ball not sent him on a collision course toward me? Truthfully, probably not, though I'd like to think he'd have still helped out with the gala in some way, putting us on a path to being something more on a slower timeframe, but I'm so glad it's worked out the way it has. He's become a fixture in my life, one I want to stay forever, so our lives can involve breakfast together in the mornings, winding down together after games, and eventually throwing kids into the mix and letting them be tiny dancers or ball players or whatever their hearts desire to do.

My mom threw me into dance the moment I was old enough to do the toddler class, pageants too. Fortunately for her, I loved the dancing. I'd like to think that she would have let me stop if I hadn't enjoyed it, but given how long I did pageants, I doubt she would have. She liked the camera's eye too much, and she tried to make me like it too. So much so, it did the opposite. Though her behavior contributed the most to that. The moment they divorced, my dad seeking sole custody and getting it without a fight, I stopped the pageants but kept the dance. Probably the best thing she ever did for me.

Work keeps me busy, too, the times while Finn's away. Our next event is coming up in September. A youth skills clinic and fitness initiative. Local yoga and dance studios will be leading classes inside the grand concourse, while outside on the field, the Snowhawks players will teach kids to run the bases, throw baseballs, and catch. That's in the infield. The outfield will have various field day activities. Part of the parking lot will be sectioned off for an inflatable obstacle course and a rock wall. Another part will be dedicated to area food trucks.

Tied to the event is a sports equipment and shoe drive, taking community donations. The research I did during my senior capstone project showed that waiting until just after the new school year and sports season started yielded more donations as adults realized the kids in their lives had outgrown their gear only after trying to put it on at the start of the season.

And new this year, we'll be hosting a live auction to benefit Finn's charity the night of the clinic and supply drive. I can't wait to tell him.

My work computer dings with a new email in my inbox. My heart lurches into my throat at the sender's name in the notification window. Mark Anderson.

At Finn's insistence and assurance we'd be fine, plus added encouragement from the girls, primarily Macey and Phoebe, I applied for the position with the Major League Charitable Organization two days after the gala.

Then I heard nothing.

Until now.

It's been five weeks. I'd started to think maybe there had been wider search for someone to fill this position. Surely something I was headhunted for in person would have moved faster. But as I read, that begins to seem unlikely.

Dear Ms. Frost,

Hello, Gale, it was so nice to connect with you at the Frost Foundation's Christmas in July Gala. I was thrilled to receive your application shortly thereafter. You have an impressive resume and a vast history of working with a wide range of charities.

We would like to proceed with the process, and so we at MLCO would like to invite you to New York to tour our offices and meet with our team face to face. This, of course, would be of no cost to you as it is an extension of our interest in you.

If you find this agreeable, please contact Ginny, the administrative assistant here at the MLCO, and she can assist you with your travel plans.

I look forward to discussing further.

Best,
Mark Anderson

I forward the email to Phoebe, who bursts into my office moments later. "He sounds awfully confident that you're going to New York. I mean, you are, of course, going, but still, presumptuous much?"

"Am I going? Should I go?" All my doubts from weeks ago come rushing back in.

"Yes. Yes, you are. We talked about this already. At least suss it out. If it doesn't seem like the place for you, don't take it. But don't let what's going on here stop you. The foundation will be fine. I'll be fine. You're not going to leave me with some terrible boss when it comes time to finding your replacement." She quirks a grin at me, then scrunches up her face in an attempt to get me to laugh.

I don't, but I appreciate her effort. It gets me out of my head enough to push some of my worries away.

"You are a wonderful administrative assistant, you know that? And a fabulous friend. Thank you."

"Then my job here is done." She pivots on her heels, but spins right back around. "And you should probably get ready to greet the bus. It should be here soon."

I glance at the clock on my computer screen. "Right, thank you."

"Didn't want you to forget because of the email." She leaves my office and returns to her desk, calling over her shoulder, "Gotta make the most of your twenty minutes."

With the team traveling back to the stadium today and a game tonight, Finn might be back in town, but we won't see much of each other until after the game. I've been looking forward to some quality time together since he left. And as I lock my computer, the email from Mark Anderson still maximized on the screen, I need it more than ever.

Chapter 40
Finn

One of the perks of Gale working for the team is when the bus arrives, she's there waiting for me. The guys rib me about it every travel day home. None of them have significant others who can wait for them like this, not that many of the guys have significant others to begin with. I take the teasing in stride. I've been looking forward to this even more than normal for the last three days.

Snowhaven State University emailed me to say they're setting up an interview with the chair and a few of the professors in the psychology department for a possible spring acceptance into the program. It's unfortunately not for fall, but at least the class I'm currently registered for down in Saltair Shores is all online. I can't wait to tell Gale. I'm doing all I can to remove any obstacle to being with her. School's the biggest one.

"There's something wrong with your girl," Kyle says from the seat in front of me as we turn into the garage.

Instantly I'm alert and standing. Devon and Shane, long-time friends of Gale also stand, craning their necks.

"Yeah, she looks off," Shane adds.

They're not wrong. She stands shoulders slumping, a contrast to her usual perfect posture drilled into her from years of dance and pageants. And as we draw closer, her hair is mussed on one side, a clear sign she's been running her fingers through it, pulling strands loose from her ponytail in the process.

I'm off the bus seconds after it comes to a stop and the doors open, rushing toward her. I drop my duffel at her feet and sweep her into my arms, lifting her off the ground.

She wraps her arms over my shoulders and locks them together, hands under forearms, clutching me to her.

"What's wrong, beautiful?" I stroke her hair, heart pained at seeing her like this.

"I'm so glad you're home."

My heart swells. *Home.* That's exactly what she is to me. My home. And hearing her use that term to describe where I am sends warmth flooding through my system. But, "That doesn't answer my question." I set her back down on her feet and cup her cheek as I stare into her eyes.

Her shoulders fall a tiny bit more. "Do you want the good news or the bad news first?"

"The bad news. But let's get out of here for a few while you tell me." I hoist my duffel up onto my shoulder and take Gale's hand. We start walking to the tunnels as the guys whistle and holler behind us. Most of them anyway. I doubt Devon, Shane, and Kyle are. Not when they saw how Gale's acting.

She pulls me down a side hallway, and I follow. I honestly have no clue where it leads. Not to her office, not to the team area, but on days like this when we don't have much time, this hallway has been empty, giving us privacy and an opportunity to catch up.

I plop down my duffel, and we both sit on it, still hand in hand. She lays her head against my shoulder, and I rest my head on hers.

"The bad news," I say again.

"Mark Anderson's invited me to New York to discuss the position. Email came this morning."

I squeeze her hand. "I'm still waiting for the bad news."

She eyes me. "That *is* the bad news."

"It's not. As I told you that night, they'd be stupid to not want you."

"After five weeks, I thought they'd forgotten about me." She sighs. "But now they're paying for the trip. It feels like they're pretty committed to the idea of me."

"So go. Learn about it. And if you decide the job is what's best for you, take it. I support you no matter what." Although I want to factor into the considerations, she needs to make this decision for herself because of herself. I'm not going to add more to her plate by telling her about school right now. "I already told you I'll go wherever you are." So maybe it's a good thing transferring schools wouldn't be until spring. Gives me time to figure out somewhere else to go if need be.

She nods firmly, her shoulders picking up as her resolve settles.

"So now that we've determined that wasn't bad news, what's the good news?"

"Shoes Soles for Souls is officially this year's beneficiary of our Snowhawks Skills and Sports Clinic auction."

"What? That's amazing. How?" Happiness over the surprise swells in my chest.

Her eyes beam as she explains, "I presented it to the rest of the board, explaining how we could tie in a live auction to the event we're running. That it makes sense for it to be your charity because part of our efforts that day is the collection of gently used gear and clothing, everything from cleats to ballet shoes and balls to nets. When I pointed out how much you brought to the gala, everyone was happy to approve the motion. So it's happening. I'm not sure how big the auction will be since we tapped a lot of places and people for donations for the silent auction, but that just means we'll have room to grow next year."

The next words tumble from my mouth in a rush, but I mean them wholeheartedly. "You can have my cleats. For the auction."

"Your cleats?" Nodding at her, I raise an eyebrow, and understanding dawns across her face. "Those cleats?"

"Of course those cleats. I can't think of anything more fitting than for me to donate them for my preferred charity. They're one of a kind."

"They're going to be the highlight of the auction is what they are." She presses a lingering kiss to my cheek. "Thank you."

I shake my head. "The thanks is all mine. You're the one making it possible, getting Shoe Soles for Souls the support, running the event in the first place." I pull her in close and tilt her face to meet mine in a soft, sweet kiss. "You're amazing."

I prevent any reply when I take Gale's mouth with mine, more passionately this time. We only have a few minutes left, and I'm going to make good use of them after days on the road away from her. Our video chats are great. I love being able to see her and hear her voice, but nothing beats holding her in my arms, where she's meant to be. I pour everything I have into my kisses, hoping to fill her with the confidence she needs to go rock her interview, the knowledge that I'm supporting her no matter what even if I want her to stay here, and the love I have for her, will always have for her.

All too soon, the alarm on my phone goes off, signaling it's time to get going. I fumble for my phone in my back pocket to turn it off while we slow our kisses. I stare into her eyes as our lips part and our foreheads rest against the other. Although it wasn't our most intense make-out session, even in this hallway, our breathing is faster, heavier. Probably my favorite pregame workout to get the blood pumping.

"I love you. See you at the game?"

"I'll be cheering from the stands. Keep your eye on the ball tonight."

"Always do." I kiss her softly one last time. "That's how I found you."

The smile, the one she only uses for me, comes easily to her face. Hopefully this means our talk has eased some of her concern over the interview.

We'll see how that goes, and then I'll tell her about school.

I rise and hold out my hand for her, not that she needs my help to stand. She may not have danced in a few years, but she keeps up an exercise routine to stay in shape. Even if I hadn't seen it regularly in our mornings together over the last few weeks, it's easy to see in how she moves. How effortlessly and fluidly she stands. She could teach the team a thing or two.

Gale's interview today comes while I'm in the middle of a road trip two weeks later, so I'm not there to see her off at the airport this morning, to kiss her goodbye, or tell her it will all be fine, no matter what happens.

My phone pings endlessly with notifications as I wait for word from Gale to tell me she's landed in New York. I'm used to it happening regularly thanks to post-game highlights and social media notifications, but this is too many, too fast. My stomach clenches at my immediate thought. Something's happened to Gale or with the plane. But it's all social media or alerts of my name being posted online and retrieved by search engines.

More photos of us have hit the sports gossip site.

I pull up the first result.

Doomed to Fale?

Oh, that's original, combining Finn and Gale like that. Not. I'd roll my eyes, but I'm too concerned over these photos taken weeks ago and now posted way out of context. Gale pulling out of my grasp as she walks away from the team hotel in Nevershade the day after she surprised me on the road. Me looking longingly, which could easily be construed for sadness. Her head down and not looking at me. The caption talking of some incident at the hotel that never happened. All we did was make snowflakes that day. And kiss. Several times. We stayed firmly on first base. But there was hardly an incident unless that's what one calls making out in an elevator, but had the hotel had an issue with that, the team would have brought it up ages ago.

That's not the worst photo, however. That one's from the gala before I ever arrived. Gale's waiting outside for me in front of the snowy Christmas backdrop they used for the red-carpet entrance. It's clear she's holding back tears, her arms wrapped around her middle as if holding herself together. Macey must be just out of the frame. They were together hugging when I got there. The post goes on to talk about some blow up we had that caused me to almost be a no-show. Although that's a load of bologna, seeing her so broken like this kills me. And the fact I didn't have my phone means there's no social proof on my accounts from that night. Sure, I was tagged dozens of times in pictures with fans as I signed things for them, but that doesn't prove anything other than I eventually showed up.

But the last photo doesn't have me at all. It's only Gale. At the airport this morning. The concluding paragraph of the post spewing lies that things are so bad between us she's looking to leave the team her family built in order to get away rather than demand the team trade me so that it retains its hopes of a playoff bid.

If phones weren't so expensive and this one so new, I'd throw it across the room. How dare they post this. Lies, all of it.

The biggest? That we're doomed to fail.

Chapter 41
Gale

I'm so convinced I'm going to get this job I spend the time waiting to board and the entire two-hour flight researching other professional team's charitable foundations. Seeing who runs them. Who supports those at the top of those organizations. Who their boards are. Finding who I would want to work with if I wasn't trying to find my replacement. Phoebe is fabulous at what she does, but nonprofits are not where her background lies. She's only learned on the job, and while that absolutely counts a whole lot in my book, it doesn't make her qualified to replace me. It does qualify her for a promotion away from an assistant title, though, and I've already put that into motion. She deserves that whether I leave or not.

Giving her the title of Office Administrator is only one of several things I've pitched to the board lately. They don't know I might be leaving. And some things I've brought up have nothing to do with that possibility but are things I started last year before my dad's death. I'd also like to get more staff in overall, separate the foundation from the team's operating staff a bit, free them up and allow us to do more things. And if I can't get staff, at least get some interns. My internships helped me immensely during school. We're close enough to a few colleges to make it happen during the year and can open our search more widely during the summer.

I fall down a research rabbit hole as I investigate what programs the other foundations spearhead, curious to see what we might be able to emulate in Snowhaven. I'll put a binder together. Leave it for my replacement. They'll bring their own ideas, of course, but a little inspiration never hurts.

When the pilot announces for us to prepare for landing, I stow my laptop in my messenger bag. It's just this and my carry-on. I fly out from here tonight to surprise Finn on the road. When I talked to Ginny in the office, she said they were willing to fly me anywhere as long as it was cheaper than the ticket back to Snowhaven. With Saltair Shores having a bigger airport, the price came in less. It's a slightly shorter flight too, and with Finn back in Saltair Shores for his first series against his former team, I want to be there to support him. Continue to show him that I'll be there for him even if Snowhaven stops being home base for me.

The moment I'm allowed, I turn my phone off airplane mode and send Finn a text to say I've landed. As I disembark, my phone dings. And dings. And dings. Finn must be chatty, but I'm in no position to answer until I make it to baggage claim. I only have my carry-on, but Ginny from the MLCO is waiting for me there, and I don't want to keep her.

The sign makes her easy enough to spot, and after exchanging pleasantries, I follow her to the short-term lot where she's parked. Finally once I'm sitting, I check my phone.

"Sorry. It's just that it kept dinging while I was getting off the plane," I tell her. "I'm all yours after this."

"No apologies necessary. I get how it is."

Two of the messages are from Finn.

FINN

Glad you made it safe. I love you. Xx

And good luck. Not that you need it.

ME

Thanks, I love you too. Xx

I click over to the next message, which is from Phoebe.

PHOEBE

Have you landed yet?

ME

Yeah, heading to MLCO office now.

Her reply is immediate.

Good. Ignore everything else until after the interviews. You'll do great!

I do as Phoebe says after letting the rest of the girls know I've landed safely in New York via our group text. They reply with a chorus of *good luck*s and *we love you*s. I'll miss them all terribly if I get this job. Cassie's the only one with any idea of what it's like to leave the group and probably the one I'd still have a chance at seeing semi-regularly despite the distance because of how our jobs are. Occasionally things won at auctions are immediately donated to the museum where she works. I imagine the MLCO has that happen sometimes too.

One of the things in the folder for whoever replaces me is the idea of a team museum. Our own Hall of Fame. We retire numbers of past players who've been with the Snowhawks for a significant amount of time and have contributed to the team in a large way, quickly becoming fan favorites and staying a favorite for their tenure, but we don't have our own space to celebrate those individuals within the stadium at Frost Field. We should. It's a bit out of my purview, but the suggestion has to come from somewhere. Hopefully my replacement agrees. Not that she would, but it was always my hope that if a museum did open at Frost Field, Cassie would come back to run it.

"Have you ever been to New York before?" Ginny asks me once I've slipped my phone back into my messenger bag.

"Oh, yes, several times. This was one of my favorite places to travel to and watch my dad play. There was always so much we could do when he didn't have game-day-related stuff going on."

"I'm sure it will be quite the adjustment if you move here. It was for me."

"Small-town girl?"

She nods. "You do get used to it after a while."

We make small talk the rest of the drive to the MLCO offices located within a tall skyscraper with curved glass sides. It's not the same skyscraper that houses the operations of baseball's national major league organization, but it's within a few blocks. Ginny pulls into a large underground garage, then ushers me through security before leading me to the elevator. Several floors later, the door slides open to a small waiting area with two desks. One empty. I follow her there, and she grabs the phone on the desk.

"Miss Frost is here," she says a moment after she presses a button on the receiver. "Will do." Then she motions toward a row of chairs, and I take a seat.

A few minutes later, Mark Anderson struts through the door. "Good to see you again, Gale, how are you?"

"I'm well, thank you, Mr. Anderson. Good to see you too."

"Please, call me Mark." I nod. "Come on, let me show you around."

I stand and follow Mr. Anderson—Mark—for a grand tour. Beyond the doors of the waiting area, the majority of the office features an open plan, work stations set in triangular groupings, a large oval table in the center of the room. The room is airy with plenty of natural light. And compared to the Frost Foundation office, it's huge. Easily triple the size. Maybe four time the size. Toward the other end of the floor are closed-off offices, one of them being Mark's, and two more for other directors within the organization.

"How many people do you have working within the organization on any given day?" I ask in between introductions with various staff. Individuals dedicated to single facets of foundation work: communications, marketing, sponsorships, partnerships, educational programs, youth programming. Run so differently than our tiny foundation where Phoebe and I wear multiple hats each day. "I saw on the website that you list more people than there are desks."

"We think that assigned seating stifles creative thinking and collaboration between departments." He points to a row of filing cabinets underneath one of the wall-to-wall windows overlooking the street below. "Everyone has their own cabinet to keep their stuff handy no matter the desk they're at. So today there's eight staff in the office out of twelve. Internships and fellowships often bring us to twenty. Whoever isn't here right now is off doing remote work somewhere."

"Remote work?" Could I work for the MLCO without leaving Snowhaven?

"Yes. Off-site. Either at events, meetings with donors, the occasional work from home day." Oh, occasional. Guess staying in Snowhaven wouldn't be a possible.

We continue the tour of the office, which turns into a tour of the mini-museum on the floor below the offices. Cassie would love it. All the while, Mark speaks of how the MLCO fits within the major league umbrella. It reminds me of how the Frost Foundation operates within the overall Snowhawks organization.

When the tour ends, Mark takes me several blocks away to lunch at a little hole in the wall, where we're joined by the other directors. Mark asks for a corner booth, and although the atmosphere in here feels casual, enough so that Mark has ditched his tie, I'm aware this is still very much a part of the interview, even when the conversation takes a more personal tone.

"What's it like dating one of the hottest players in baseball?" the director of development asks as she sets down her fork.

I nearly choke on my water, betrayed by my attempt to drink something every time they ask a question so that I can answer with the hope there isn't food in my teeth. Although I chose a safe meal in order to minimize the risk, one can never be too careful.

I dab at my mouth with my napkin, wiping away water that tried to escape. "Excuse me?"

"Oh my gosh, that probably sounds so bad," she says, eyes widening and her cheeks reddening. "Sorry. He's handsome, but I meant media wise. He's among the top ten most-followed major league players."

"He's hot at the plate too," Mark adds. "His average is up since joining the Snowhawks. And it was already All-Star material."

I appreciate the extra buffer he provides, giving me another moment to compose myself. "He would have been on the All-

Star team had it not been for the trade. It is okay, though, right? There's no conflict of interest or rule against dating a player if employed by the MLCO, is there?"

The director of communications shakes his head. "No. Our rules involving any players is one of mutual respect. They are individuals doing charitable works, just like any non-player is who donates their time, talent, or treasure, with the organization. Therefore, we ask that no one on staff or volunteering goes begging for photos and autographs. We do not prevent it from happening if they offer, however. Our offices are full of signed things that have been gifted to us over the years, and I'm happy to count many players, past and present, as friends." He leans in as he studies me. "But related to my colleague's question, how do you handle the unique pressures that come from both being famous and being with someone famous, the gossip and whatnot. How does it affect *you* in *your* job?"

After a sip of water that does not result in me nearly spraying everyone with my drink, I set down my glass. I'm not sure how I feel about this man, and the question seems strangely personal.

"I would like to think that it doesn't. Growing up the way I did, the press—of all sorts—was around constantly, and I experienced the sensational side of it with my parents' divorce. My mother was particularly fond of it. Both for herself and for trotting me out in it. I'm sure she still enjoys it. I took after my dad as far as gossip and paparazzi go, trying to not give them material to work with and avoiding it as best as I can. I'm a consummate professional in my job and expect nothing but professionalism back from those I work with, no matter the project or person. While gossip is bound to happen given the nature of a ball player's celebrity, especially one of Finn's fame, we're just two normal people who enjoy each other's company.

We're living normal lives. If anything, I think it makes me more empathetic to what some of the players deal with regularly." Finn and I haven't been the only target of gossip on the team, just the latest, helping to put the whole thing into perspective.

"This last incident, however, has some grain of truth to it, though."

"That was fully rectified through the team's press release. I think Finn's more than proven that correct with his help at the gala and his performance on the field. Although his methods are at times a bit unconventional, you won't find many players more dedicated."

"That's not what I'm talking about."

"I'm sorry?" What is he getting at?

"I mean, you are here in New York. Even if the reasoning behind it is not what they say it is—"

"And we know it's not since we asked you to come here today," Mark cuts in, "just as we know what they said about the gala isn't true since I was there."

The director of communications sends a look Mark's way. "Yes, now. As I was saying, how is your current job handling the news that you're exploring other opportunities?"

My whole body tenses at his statement. "I'm not sure I follow."

"So you don't know?" he asks. Is that concern or disappointment on his face?

Mark levels him with a look, the tension thick between them. Not sure I want to work with that sort of office dynamic. "She was on a plane this morning. She probably doesn't."

Yet as he says that, I have a pretty good idea.

Mark looks at me with sympathy. "I wasn't going to bring it up so directly. But yes, there was something released this morning with various allegations resulting in you looking for other work."

I draw a deep breath as I draw my phone from my bag. "Forgive me for doing this, but it's probably best if I just read it for myself."

Mark nods, and I click on my screen, unlocking it with my face. I run a search for my name, and several hits from today appear at the top of the results. The first is from the site that published the picture of Finn and me weeks ago. I click into the "article," if you can even call it that. The piece is full of nothing but untruths except for one. I did get on a plane this morning. And it was to find out more information about a potential job.

"These photos aren't even from the same time. That's this morning. But the gala was weeks ago, and the first photo was two weeks before that."

"As we already stated, we have no doubt that everything written within is untrue," Mark says. "We're sorry to have sprung it on you." He might be, same with the development director, but I doubt the director of communications is.

"No, it's all right. I'm just surprised this is the first I'm hearing of it. This came out while I was in the air, but I texted several people when I landed, and no one mentioned this." I think back on my text exchanges. The girls don't follow this sort of thing, and at the time I was texting, they were all getting ready for work if not already there. But Finn? No way. His notifications are always alerting him to something or another. And Phoebe. Even though I can access the accounts from my phone, she's the one who handles the social media for the foundation. How had she not spotted this? Her words come back to me. *Ignore everything else until after the interviews.* She knew.

I take another sip of my water, composing myself before

saying something I shouldn't. When I set it down my glass, I smile politely and stand. "I'm sorry, but I should really check in with my team about this."

Mark nods, as does the development director. The communications director makes no reaction whatsoever as if he's used to dropping bombs on people over lunch interviews. He must be a joy to work with. And who's to say I have to? An idea sparks in my brain, but first things first.

"I promise to make it quick." I scurry over to the restrooms, praying that it's empty. Fortunately for me, at least one thing is going right at the moment, and the ladies' bathroom is a single with a very heavy door separating it from the little hallway its sits off the side of.

I dial Phoebe's office number. As much as I want to talk to Finn and hear his voice, he's getting ready to report for game-day activities if he's not already there. Being a road trip, they're probably providing lunch before the pregame meetings.

Phoebe's sunny hello two rings later barely makes a dent in my attitude.

"When you told me to ignore everything else, did that happen to include yet another sports tabloid piece on me and Finn—mostly me?"

She lets out an audible breath. "Yes. Yes, it did. It wasn't something you needed to worry about before your interview. Is it over?"

"Nope." I wrap an arm around my stomach hoping to ease the knot that's doubled in size from this morning. "And while I appreciate the sentiment, it came up during lunch, Phoebe. They all knew about it. I was totally blindsided."

"Oh. Well, they know it's a bunch of bologna, right? I mean, you're there because they headhunted you. You're not fleeing Finn and Snowhaven."

"Sure, they know that, but does the team know that?" The last thing I want is awkwardness between me and the rest of the organization while I'm trying to do my job. The job I still want to do. The relief of that realization washes over me, unfurling the knot in my stomach, albeit slightly. It won't be fully gone until I'm back in Snowhaven.

"It will be okay. I've already talked with Patty. Stop pacing and take a deep breath."

"I'm not pacing," I say as I come to a stop. Okay, so I was.

"Uh-huh," she says skeptically. "I know you."

"Yes, you got me there. So what's the PR spin on this? Are they putting out another press release? Are we if they aren't?"

"Beyond correcting the tabloid's accusation about why Finn was late, their statement this time is basically that they are respecting the lives of those within the Snowhawks organization and thus are not commenting further. See? Not so bad. And unless our paparazzo got on the plane to follow you to New York, there's not going to be photo proof of where you are. You can say you had a layover there if you had to."

"A layover in New York on my way to Saltair Shores? I'd have gotten there faster by bus, maybe even a bicycle."

"Stranger things have happened. Look at you falling for Finn after your self-imposed ban on dating baseball players."

"Okay." I sigh. "You're right."

"Oh, I like the sound of that," she teases. "I'm right."

"Ha . . . ha. Thanks for the update. I should probably get back out there." I can't stand them up like a bad blind date. The baseball world is too small. No matter what happens, they'll still be connections that I may need.

"I'm sorry I didn't just tell you."

"It's okay. I get why you didn't. But, please, do tell me next time." Not that I want there to be a next time, but seems we're the it couple of the baseball world right now. "Being surprised like that isn't fun."

"I will. Now go knock 'em dead," she says, chipper demeanor firmly back in place.

"Actually, I don't want to do that."

"What are you saying?" She doesn't sound confused. Excited is more like it.

"I think you know what I'm saying."

"Oh thank goodness."

"Even if it means more work?"

"Absolutely."

We hang up, and I quickly check myself in the mirror to make sure I'm good. Then I shake out my arms and legs like I used to do before going on stage at pageants and dance competitions, readying myself to put on a show. Shoulders back and head held high, I walk back out to finish this interview on my terms and end a high note.

And I do.

By the time lunch is over and I'm back in Mark's office, he's ready to make an offer.

But I don't accept.

I counter offer.

Chapter 42
Finn

The visiting side of Saltair Stadium is smaller than the home team's, but there's an odd sense of familiar but different for all of it. Same mirror orientation, same colors, same bench material, though those are narrower. The showerheads aren't top of the line with the ability to be used as a handheld. It has a different smell too.

When I tell the guys that, they all laugh, but the Sailors' side smells like a refreshing sea breeze as if there are windows that open right out onto the bay to get that smell naturally. This smells like a locker room.

But they've all only played on this side before. Of course they don't how different the other side is. It's the same way I know the visiting side at Frost Field is just a bit colder in addition to being a little smaller. And how its walls are a bright but icy gray, the way our road uniforms are. I prefer this to the white of the Sailors' road uniforms, but I wouldn't tell them that.

The home side has a wide hallway for stunts and group line dancing too. Built that way so the Sailors could prove they were different from other teams right from the start. It was one of the reasons they wanted me to be on the team when they first scouted me and offered me a contract as an undrafted free agent. I was already going viral by then with my videos.

But now that I'm on the other side of the stadium, I wonder how different it will be. I know their tricks, their routines. After all, I taught some of them.

It's weird knowing that the guys are filming a warmup video right now as I stare at the clock, wondering how many notifications my phone will get between now and when I can check it. Between the coverage of me being back in Saltair Shores for the first time as a Snowhawk and the ridiculous article about Gale and me being doomed to fail, it's more than I think I've ever gotten, and that's saying something given my shocking trade.

Shane nudges me under the table with his leg.

I shoot him a what was that for look.

But it's Mack who answers. "I said, you know this team the best. What should we expect on their turf?" He levels me with a look that orders me to get my head in the game. I'm grateful he's not yelling. We've already chatted about today's tabloids. I've already assured him things between Gale and me are fine, better than fine, actually. And he's already warned me what will happen if they're not. So now that we've moved past that, he expects me to be on my game.

To prove I've got this, I slap on a smile. "Well, you've seen how I am, obviously."

On the other side of me, Kyle snorts. "Obviously." He might not fully appreciate everything I can do, but he's come around big time. He never would have willingly sat next to me a couple months ago. But something shifted the day he volunteered to help set up for the gala, to give me a ride there. I wouldn't say we're bros, not the way Devon and I are. Or even Shane and I. But maybe, just maybe, we're friends. Devon's probably still internally grumbling about Kyle taking his usual spot next to me.

I glance at the shortstop of few words. "What you see on the highlight reels and the tapes are all accurate. Expect the whole team to be like that. Dancing. Tricks. Singing." With the Sailors and Snowhawks being in the NL and the AL, respectively, the two teams didn't meet up often until recent rule changes about interleague matchups. Last season, the Sailors went to Snowhaven. This year, it's the opposite. Some guys on the team have never played the Sailors at home to know how different they can be from their road games.

Kyle groans. "Singing? You don't sing." Elbows on the table, he brings his hands up to his face.

"That's because you don't want to hear me sing. I don't want to hear me sing either." I laugh. "What you saw when they came up to Snowhaven last season is tame. It's not their turf. They don't have the same space for their pregame rituals on the road. Don't let them fool you with their dancing around the bases. It's all a distraction. They're a solid team. They're always aware of where the ball is and can instantly snap out of their act to take advantage if you let your guard down. And they coordinate. It's rarely one act on the field." I look at the guys around the table, making sure they all acknowledge me.

When my gaze connects with Mack, he claps once. "All right, thanks, Nixon. You heard it, men. Now, go finish what you need to. It's almost time to hit the field for batting practice. You know what you should be doing." Everyone rises to stand, but Mack tells me to wait up a moment. "Got something for ya."

He motions me to follow him once every one else is out of

the room. They all saw what got published today. No sense keeping them in the dark. Over the years, several of the guys have been the focus of similar tabloid ridiculousness. Someone is focused on this team, more so than some others. The Sailors don't have this problem. So needless to say, the guys get it. No one bats an eye when Mack keeps me behind despite us already having hashed things out.

He leads me to his office but does no more than poke his head inside it before pointing at me to go through the doorway. "Ten minutes," he says a bit loudly as I brush past him. Then he pulls the door closed, leaving me alone.

But then the desk chair spins, revealing Gale's smiling face.

She stands, and I rush over to her, immediately pulling her into my embrace, my hands at her waist. Relief floods through me, and I let out a breathy, "You're here."

Gale reaches up and wraps her arms behind my neck. "You knew I was coming." She leans up and kisses my jawline, just next to my chin, on top of the scar I got as a kid. It's become one of her favorite spots.

I tilt my head to kiss her properly. "Yes, but I wasn't expecting to see you until after the game." I let my fingers play with the end of her ponytail.

"I've got some connections. What sort of girlfriend would I be if I didn't use them every once in a while?" She shrugs out of her jersey, the one with my name on it, letting the material fall off her shoulders. She spins so her back is to me, revealing my number and last name on her shirt. "I didn't have to use any connections for this, though. They make them now. You like?"

"I do." More so because she's wearing it. I lean forward and kiss her neck from behind. She tilts her head to the side to give me more access. I leave a trail of kisses on my way to her ear. "The jersey's still my favorite. Though that may be tied with your candy cane stockings from the gala." I wag my eyebrows at her, eliciting an amused eye roll.

"I'll keep that in mind." She glances at her cell phone. "Six minutes."

Time to get serious. "How was your interview?"

"It went well. Would have been nicer had they not sprung that gossip rag on me, though."

I reach for her hand and take it in mine. "I should have told you."

"I get why you didn't." A coy smile creeps onto her face. "We really need to work on our couple name."

I chuckle. "I'll say. Fale, really?"

"Terrible." She shakes her head in mock disappointment, the motion accompanied by another eye roll.

"Agreed. Especially since this is one thing I never intend to fail at. I love you, Gale. You're it for me." It's the closest I've come to telling her my intentions.

"Good. Because I don't fail at anything. Ever." She gazes at me, expressing more in that one look than her words do, then kisses me softly. "I love you too."

"So does that mean you got the job?" I should have led with this question, but so much is riding on this answer that I haven't asked until now, almost afraid of what she'll say as much as I'll accept whatever it is.

"I did."

I didn't expect the pang of discontent at her admission, just two little words, but it's there all the same. Still, I promised to support her no matter what. "That's great, congratulations! I knew you would."

"I didn't take it."

I swallow the gasp that tries to escape, nearly choking on it. "You didn't?"

She shakes her head. "I countered their offer with one of my own. One that will keep me here."

My heart leaps with joy. "So you're not leaving?"

"No. I couldn't. Snowhaven, with you, is my home." Home. Me. I'm a part of her home. If I had a ring on me, I'd drop to one knee right here in the place I thought would be my home until the trade that changed it all and brought me to her.

Since I can't propose, I do the next sensible thing and follow up with, "What did they say?"

"They're thinking about it."

Mack knocks on the door before opening it, his index finger tapping at his opposite wrist.

Gale rises onto her toes and pecks me on the cheek. "I'll tell you more later. Keep your eye on the ball tonight."

"Always."

She looks away from me, toward the door. "Thanks, Mack."

He nods. "Your stuff's fine here for the evening."

It's only then I notice the carry-on suitcase and messenger bag against the wall. I kiss her forehead. "See you later."

After trailing early, we pull off a win, thanks to Shane coming up clutch in the cleanup spot late in the game. Gale and I head back to the hotel together, separate from the rest of the team. Let the paparazzi catch us if they're around. We'll show the world we're not doomed to fail. More like the opposite.

I don't have a ring yet, but I will. Soon if I swing it.

That night, Gale fills me in on her counter offer. Not a job but the formation of a national commission consisting of other baseball teams' charitable foundation staff. Directors, assistant directors, whoever wants to be on it. One reason the MLCO had wanted Gale was because she was female, but in her search to find her possible replacement, she saw a lot more diversity. And as she studied the programs the other teams run and the charities they support, she noticed a lot of similarities and, therefore, a lot of opportunity for collaboration. She saw even bigger opportunities than what the MLCO was offering, not only for her family's legacy but for the causes that meant so much to her and others.

"And it keeps me here," she adds as we curl up together on the hotel room's couch. "But would allow me to travel across the country to meet with other commission members and see how they run their foundations. Both for meetings with the rest of the commission, and smaller informational meetings between collaboration partners depending on the project. And if some of those meetings happen to take place where you also happen to be for a game? All the better."

"I love the way your mind works." I kiss the top of her forehead. "I have some news too."

She stiffens. "What is it? Is it Dave? Does he have a timeline for his return?"

"Last I heard, he's just starting his rehab assignment. They expect him down there for a few weeks. It's already September. I don't think he'll factor into this season. Maybe for a playoff push as backup."

Gale eases back into my side. "Especially if you keep doing as well as you have been."

"I have some serious motivation to keep me going."

"So what's your news, then, if it isn't Dave related?"

"I have an interview with the Psychology department head here at Snowhaven State to join their program in the spring."

"You're transferring?" Her cheek rises against the side of my chest as she smiles before turning to look up at me.

"Mm-hmm . . . No need to go head back to Saltair Shores for classes during the offseason. Just me"—I kiss her cheek—"staying here"—and then again softly on the lips—"in Snowhaven."

"That's great! Oh my goodness, I'm so glad. I wasn't looking forward to you having to be away in the offseason." She reaches up and wraps her arms around my neck. "You know you can stay with me when the season's over, right? You practically do now."

"Are you sure? I wouldn't want to impose." Though it's everything I hoped. Especially once I propose. "I could see if one of the guys needs a roommate."

She shakes her head. "I'm sure. When's the interview?"

"The day after the foundation's next event."

"Wow. It's going to be a busy two weeks." And that's an understatement, since she has no idea I've got ring shopping on my list.

Chapter 43

A selection of text messages between Gale and Finn over the next two weeks.

FINN

What about Ginn?

ME

I'm not a big fan of the drink. Plus, it sounds like it could be the nickname for someone named Virginia.

Frixon?

How do you even pronounce that?

Like friction. Though I'm not sure if that's a good thing.

Galegan?

Gale-gan?

Gal-eh-gan.

It has potential.

It's better than Fale, at least.

Fran? FR from Frost and AN from Finnegan?

No. Just no.

What about Galen?

Like gallon?

No. Gale-N. Or I guess Ga-Lain. Short for Galenus who was a Roman physician for the emperor Marcus Aurelius. I looked it up.

I mean, maybe? But then everyone's going to be fighting over how to say it. It will be the great gif debate all over again.

It's gif.

With a G or a J sound?

I see your point. Not Galen.

It doesn't fit the format for couple names perfectly, but what about Finagle?

That's cute. But the definition of the actual word isn't us.

Why is this so hard?

We'll figure something out.

Dare I say we'll finagle something?

Did you just make a joke? I thought I was supposed to be the funny one in this relationship.

What can I say? You're rubbing off on me.

Chapter 44
Gale

"I can't believe someone bid that much on my cleats," Finn states as we walk toward the foundation office together on Monday morning. It's been just over two days since the first ever live auction held at the end of the skills clinic and sports supply drive. Both things were a wonderful success.

"They're kind of an obscure item," he continues. "Whoever won them must be quite the baseball fan."

"Or just a fan of yours." I bump into his side, smooshing our joined hands between us. "You know how baseball fanatics can be. But it's exciting, isn't it?" He has no idea the anonymous bidder is his biggest fan ever. Me.

"Yeah. It's going to allow Shoe Soles for Souls to distribute so many shoes to kids throughout the region."

We reach the office door, and I slip my free hand into my purse to retrieve my keys. "And now they're heading off to a museum." Really, what was I going to do with them except donate them? Sure, I could have kept them for him. Or eventually donated them back to the foundation for a future event, but I couldn't keep bidding on them anonymously forever if I did that. Someone would eventually outbid me and then they'd be gone. They deserve to be at the museum. Now they'll be preserved for the public good into perpetuity.

As I unlock the door, he asks, "Think they'll let me visit them from time to time?"

"If they're not on display, I'm sure you can arrange something. Cassie's always telling me about players she's met while giving private tours. But why would you want to visit your old cleats?"

I lead him into the office, and he closes the door behind us as I open the blinds to show people we're open. We still have several items from the auction that need to be picked up, so it's promising to be a busy day. And I'm still waiting to hear from Cassie about the cleats.

Since she started at the museum, she's been the one to process all my donations. I assumed she would have made arrangements with me by now regarding their pickup or telling me if I should come drop them off, but she's been silent since I told her I won them.

"They're lucky, that's why," Finn says after a moment.

I turn toward him, one eyebrow raised. "Why are they lucky?" I already know the answer, but I want to hear him tell me again.

He sets his heated gaze on me, lighting my insides, and he closes the space between us in three short strides. "I last wore them on the day I met you." He lifts a hand to my cheek, tracing the ridge of my cheekbone with his thumb, before pressing a kiss to my lips. It's gentle and soft with the promise of more if I want it. And I do. Oh, how I want this man. Now and forever.

My purse strap slides from my shoulder, and the bag lands on the floor next to me with a soft thud before I wrap my arms around his back, one hand between his shoulders and the other at the back of his head so my fingers can play with his hair. It's time for a trim, per team rules. Besides, it's still warm enough that it gets too hot for him under his helmet when it's on for too long. But I'm already looking forward to the offseason when he promises to let his hair get shaggy for at least a little while.

I pull his head closer to me, deepening our kiss, wishing I hadn't already raised the blinds because one kiss will never be enough for me. Not from him. Forget the paparazzi. Let them take their photos. They aren't going to go away, but they can't hurt us. This is their last chance to get pictures here anyway. Come next week, we'll be getting privacy films applied to the windows.

A banging on the window next to us breaks the moment, and I jump. Finn pulls me in tighter as we turn toward the glass where Devon and Shane stand waving like the goofballs they are, making kissy faces at us.

"Friends of yours?" I jokingly ask Finn.

"Yeah, they're good guys, but their timing stinks." He kisses my forehead, then steps away and waves off the guys, who continue down the sidewalk heading toward the staff entrance through the parking garage.

I pick my purse off the floor. "We're lucky it was just the two of them." And I'm not talking about the paparazzi. I can only imagine my embarrassment had it been one of the foundation's big donors. "Busy around here for an off day."

Finn follows me into my office. "A lot of the guys are here for extra practice today."

"Really?" I stow my purse in my desk drawer. "Do you need to be there?"

"Eventually, but they know why I'll be late. You're sure you're okay with me using your office for a bit?"

As if I'd tell him he couldn't use my office for his interview with Snowhaven State University. "Of course I am. You have my support, one hundred percent."

He lowers himself into my chair. "And that support is just one reason why I love you." The words still thrill me every time I hear them.

"Love you too." I kiss the top of his head as I reach around him to type in the password to my computer for him. "I'd wish you luck on your interview today, but you don't need it. The university would be stupid to not let you transfer." And not going to lie, I'd be devastated for him to have to head back to Saltair Shores for school.

"Thanks, Gale." Finn pulls a USB drive from his pocket and puts it into my computer tower. A backup for all the online backups of talking points he made for his interview.

"I'll leave you to it, then. I'll be right outside packing auction items." I close the office door behind me, and Finn disappears from sight. Sadly, my office doesn't have a window looking into the larger space, so I can't peek in and see how things might be going.

The foundation reminds me a bit of Santa's workshop with bags and boxes everywhere, waiting for me to resume my sorting, packing, and transferring items to winning bidders. It's a mess, but a good mess.

I'm in the middle of posting to the foundation's social media account about what I'm doing today—I've been better about doing social media myself lately and not letting it all fall to Phoebe—when my phone vibrates in my hands.

CASSIE

Sorry for the days of no response. I'm coming home today.

About time she gets back to me, and with good news too. Any time I get to see my long-distance bestie is a good time.

ME

Yes! Do you have enough time for lunch before you go back with the shoes?

Loads. I'm home for two weeks.

Wait, what? She doesn't even stay more than a few days for Christmas, not since she still lived in dorms that closed for winter break.

I need details, but I. CAN'T. WAIT. TO. SEE. YOU!

See you soon!

There's got to be a story there, but I'll have to get it from her in person because she doesn't reply.

Auction winners come and go throughout the morning. Usually that would make the time race by, but between Finn being in the other room interviewing and being excited by Cassie's impending visit, I can't stop looking at the clock. The morning crawls instead. But finally lunchtime arrives, and the foundation's office looks almost back to normal. I'm only waiting on Cassie to come pick up the cleats, and hopefully she'll be here soon.

Finn emerges from my office while I'm sprawled on the

office couch, a chapter into my latest ebook, with a beaming smile on his face.

I click the screen off on my phone and slide my feet to the floor so that I'm in a sitting position. "I take it things went well?"

"You're looking at the newest student of Snowhaven State University."

"Yes!" I spring up from the couch and throw my arms around him. He lifts me into the air and spins me around before setting me back down. I kiss him, breathing "I knew you'd do it," when I come up for air, then place my forehead against his.

"They've already approved my thesis topic, too. And get this. I'm allowed to take up to six credits before matriculating into the program. That means I don't have to take the course I've signed up for in Saltair Shores for the second half of this semester. I can take one up here. Two if I can do an independent study. The chair seemed interested by my suggestion for one, but I have to write the curriculum for it with a reading list. But if I do that, I'll finally be a senior after this semester." His eyes twinkle with excitement.

"I'm so proud of you. Everything's really coming together." Between yesterday's successful event, Finn getting into school here in Snowhaven, and the MLCO deciding to help spearhead my idea for a commission consisting of baseball charity foundation staff, we have a lot to celebrate and be thankful for. And that's not even the biggest thing.

First baseman Dave Mossen isn't coming back to the team. His rehab assignment with the Snowshoes and the Snowcaps has made him realize how much he likes working with the younger players from our farm system. He plans to retire after this season with the promise of being hired on as a member of either the coaching staff for one of our minor league teams or as player development personnel.

Although Finn was told he wasn't a rental long ago, he's now the official first baseman of the Snowhawks.

"Thanks. It really is." He smiles warmly at me, eyes staring into me as if he's memorizing this moment. "I should probably get headed to practice."

"Right. As much as I want to keep you, I should probably let you get to it. Come find me after? I'll still be here, hopefully wrapping up for the day, not still waiting for Cassie."

"Of course." He has to find me later anyway since we rode here together like we do most days, but I don't say that.

Instead, I ask, "Do you want to say goodbye to your shoes before you go?"

I'm teasing, so I'm taken slightly by surprise when he says, "Yeah, that sounds good. Can you grab them for me?"

Well, I did offer, so I head into my office and reach for the box on the table. "Okay . . ."

"Can you make sure the shoes are tied before you bring them out?" Finn calls, stopping me.

"Really?" I raise an eyebrow and glance toward the ceiling. Is he serious?

"I know it's silly and you're probably rolling your eyes right now, but I'd like to see them looking their best before they go."

"Well, when you put it that way . . ." I joke. I lift the flaps on the box to reveal the shoes and my breath catches. There, tied in a shoelace's bow, is a diamond ring.

"I hope you realize that the diamond is not part of the auction winnings," Finn whispers, his voice husky, from right behind me. "Though I would be the biggest winner if you would do me the honor of putting that on and agreeing to be my wife."

I am not a crier, but happy tears have a way of leaking out sometimes, and right now is one such instance. When I turn around, he's on one knee, ready to take my hands in his own and his eyes glistening with happiness.

There's no thinking necessary as I gaze at this amazing man. "Finn, I . . . Yes. Yes, I will marry you."

He stands as he continues at a normal volume now, "I fell on you hard the first time we met, but I fell for you harder." A rogue tear slides down the side of my nose, and he captures it with his thumb before running it over my cheekbone. He presses his lips to mine, and I'm grateful we're in my office for this moment. "I know this is fast, but I know what I want, so why draw it out to what some people say is an acceptable amount of time before proposing?"

He squeezes my hand, the one about to declare to the world that I'm his and he's mine. "I thought about a grand proposal, a team flash mob or something on the Jumbotron even, maybe vaulting over the wall and proposing to you where our lives first collided, but when it came down to it," he carefully unties the lace and slips the ring free, "this is a moment for the two of us. The world can find out when we want them to. Though I'm not sure I'm going to be able to keep myself from telling the guys at practice."

He slips the ring on my finger before kissing my knuckles, then my wrist, up toward the inner curve of my elbow before he takes my mouth once more.

Once when I was a kid, a batter my dad was pitching to hit a long fly ball that struck a spotlight on a pole where the right-field corner meets the stands. The glass shattered into tiny pieces that fell down like glittery stardust, illuminated by the remaining lights. It was magical to watch. Right now I'm like that stardust, illuminated by Finn's beaming smile as we move together until I bump up against the table where the shoes are.

He pulls away and rests his forehead against mine. "I finally figured out our couple name."

I chuckle softly. We've been hashing it out for days. Joking mostly. "What is it?"

"Finale. Because you and me—there's nothing after that. Just us. Forever."

"I love it." So much better than Fale.

"So what are your thoughts on a Christmas wedding?"

I tilt my head up to meet his lips once more and kiss him softly as I twirl my finger in the hairs at the nape of his neck. "That sounds perfect. Think we could go all out and get you in that elf costume again?" I waggle my eyebrows at him as his gaze goes wide, and I laugh. "I'm kidding. About that last part, anyway. Not about the Christmas wedding being perfect."

Finn breathes an audible sigh of relief. "I wouldn't have said no if that's what you really wanted, but I'm very glad you weren't serious. But maybe you could wear those candy cane stockings?"

"I think that can be arranged. I know candy canes are your favorite." I lean my head against where his chest meets his upper arm and shoulder, pulling him in for a hug. "And maybe you'd like to take some dance classes with me to prepare for our first dance?"

"My moves at the gala not good enough for you?" he asks teasingly, holding back a laugh. "But seriously, I would love that."

"It's just as much for me as it would be for you. I'm rusty. It's been years since I've danced."

He steps back to look me head on. "You were dancing in the kitchen while we made breakfast this morning."

I raise my eyebrow. "That is not the same, and you know it."

"I do."

"You're supposed to save that for Christmas."

He shakes his head. "I could say it today and mean everything behind it just as much as I will then. As much as I will every day for the rest of our lives. I do love you. I do choose us." Then he sighs. "I do have to go to practice."

"Do you really have to? Surely they'd understand." I promised to never be a distraction, but this has got to qualify as a special case.

The corner of his mouth ticks upward. "We have the rest of our lives to celebrate being together. Let's start tonight. Dinner with our friends later?"

Our friends. I like that and nod.

"Besides," his look becomes sheepish as he glances down, and a light pink tinges his cheeks, "I may have been the one to call this extra practice in the first place."

"You did?" I study him. "Just how close were you to proposing via team flash mob?"

He laughs and pulls me closer once more. "This wasn't for that, I promise. Devon, Shane, and some of the other guys want some lessons in trick moves."

"Acro practice? This I got to see."

"Well, hopefully Cassie will get here soon for my shoes, and then you can come down and watch part of it. But I do have to go now." He kisses me again, this time quickly on the lips. "But if this goes well, there will be plenty of other practices you can watch."

I try to imagine the team out on the field, large mats rolled across it, trying forward rolls, backbends, and cartwheels. Maybe I can convince Cassie to come watch with me. It might be a tall order with Shane here, but if I can rewrite my rule about dating and falling for a baseball player, then anything is possible.

I walk Finn to the office door that will lead him to the concourse. The kiss this time promises more later. A whole lot more. A future together. Forever.

Epilogue
Cassie

Friday night during the auction

GALE

Finn's cleats are up next. I'll text you if I win so we can set up the donation.

ME

When you win, you mean.

Even from a few hours away, I can feel my best friend's nervousness. She shouldn't be worried, though. Gale Frost doesn't let herself lose.

Is an anonymous donation any different than a public one?

Given who she is and who her family is, this isn't Gale's first donation to the museum's collection, but there's never been a reason for her donation to be anonymous before.

Not so much. There's an extra form to acknowledge that your name won't go on the exhibit label and that you forfeit the benefits you'd be granted by a public donation.

How many lifetime memberships to the museum do I really need? Wait, can those be transferred? We could give it to Finn.

I search the donor database for his name, unsurprised to see it already listed.

He's got one. Besides, you won't be getting one as an anonymous donor anyway.

Good. It all works out, then. Thanks again for taking care of the paperwork for this!

Good luck!

Not that she'll need it.

Twenty minutes later, she nearly fools me into thinking she hadn't won the cleats after all.

Finn's shoes have been won by one Cordelia Smithson.

Wait, what? How in the world did someone outbid you?

Relax, it's just the name I'm putting in our system. Of course I won.

Where in the world did you come up with that name?

> It's one Macey uses for her secret season tickets on the third-base line. I thought we told you when we came up to see the game.

> You totally forgot to mention that part. Oh, the lengths she'll go to because of her crush on Ian.

We've all had our own crushes on guys on the team over the years. Macey's crush on the several years older than her third baseman is the second-longest one still standing. Only mine is longer. No one can really top a crush that began in childhood.

I've had a thing for Shane Montclair, the Snowhawks' catcher since I was seven years old. He was nine at the time and had just moved next door. He soon became best friends with my older brother. They played ball together all the way through school. It was a big deal when Shane got drafted out of high school. An even bigger deal when he signed a contract with the Snowhawks after playing elsewhere for a few years. A hometown sports hero returning to where he grew up.

Of course, by the time he returned, I'd moved away. First for college and then grad school and now work.

> Okay, I'm going to let my boss know and get the process started.

> Thanks for staying late for this!

> Of course! Be sure to thank "Cordelia" for her donation.

> Are you coming home soon? It's been way too long.

I don't answer her. Truth is, I have no idea. Now that my

brother lives out of state with his wife and three kids and our parents moved to be closer to the grandkids—seems they gave up on the idea of me ever having kids, thanks, Mom and Dad —there's not a whole lot to go home for. Sure, my friends are still there, the house, too, though my parents use that as a vacation home now. I'm free to use it whenever I'm in town. It saves on a hotel bill and keeps me off friends' couches, but last I knew, Shane's next door again. So the house is not as appealing as it might have been.

Someone might think that getting to stay next door to one's crush is the perfect opportunity to make a move. But me? I can't bear to face him. But that's what I get for humiliating myself when I revealed to him my feelings for him. Note: grand gestures are not for me, the doing portion of them at least. I've never been on the receiving end. But since my senior year of high school, I haven't been able to face Shane in person beyond a fast wave as I dart back inside my parents' house or to my car.

Seeing him from far away in the stands, however, now that's a different story.

I've been to every game he's ever played in the stadium neighboring the regional baseball museum where I work. Is a perk of my job getting free tickets? Yes. Yes, it is. Have I gone to many games outside of those he's been in? No. No, I have not. Do I see this trend continuing at least until some other guy sweeps me off my feet and makes me forget all about Shane? You bet.

It doesn't take me long to initiate the paperwork for "Cordelia's" donation, but I'll have to wait for my boss, Sue, to sign off on it Monday morning. It's a done deal in my mind, no way will anyone not want this for the museum's collections, but the collections committee still needs to okay it.

We meet bimonthly as a rule, but if a record is close to

being hit, we'll meet for a few minutes to discuss what we'd be willing to accept into the collection to commemorate the feat. Same thing happens if someone wants to donate a big-ticket item to us. We tend to not want those donors to have to wait.

Although I'm on said committee, as a junior member, I'm not allowed to call impromptu meetings. Sue, the chairperson, can.

ME

> Got a fun donation coming in, and I think the committee should meet so we can jump on this ASAP.

SUE-BOSS

> What are you still doing at work at this hour?

> Also, tell me more.

Yeah, it's a Friday night and nearly nine p.m. I should have gone home three hours ago, but Gale called in a favor. With nothing else to do but go back to my apartment, why say no? My social life here isn't the greatest, and I don't even have a cat waiting for me.

> An anonymous donation of Finn Nixon's shoes, the ones he colored in when he was traded to the Snowhawks. They were just auctioned off for charity, and the winning bidder wants to donate them to us.

> Would this donor happen to be a friend of yours?

Even before Gale donated a lot of her dad's and grandfather's personal baseball effects, my boss knew all about my ties to one of baseball's most storied families. Did it help me get the job? Maybe. I've never asked.

> The donor wishes to remain anonymous.

> I see. Well, I like it. I'll send out a meeting request Monday morning so we can formalize everything and get ready to acquisition them for the collection. Good work on this one.

> Thank you.

> Now go do something. Go see a movie. Go out to dinner. Go home. Just leave the office. I'll see you Monday.

> Leaving!

I do not tell her that option three on her list is my go-to. And she certainly does not need to know that tonight I have a date with Ben and Jerry, a bunch of rom-com movies, and the attempt to push Shane Montclair out of my head.

Monday morning

Sue opens her binder and sets it on the large oak table in the museum library that we use for meetings. Yes, an actual binder with paper in it. As much as the world is pushing us digital, we museum people still love our paper records for a lot of things. "Okay, I called this meeting today because we have an opportunity to acquire a unique item through an anonymous donation, and I think we should do what we can to get them right away for our Today's Game exhibit."

The exhibit is one of our more fluid as it showcases those objects being donated by players, teams, or individuals that have current playing connections. Someone have a perfect game? A ball or cap or glove from that pitcher goes in the case. Someone hits for the cycle? A bat or batting glove used in the game gets added. We've had bloody socks, busted balls, broken bats, bird poop caps, you name it.

The chief curator sits up straighter. "Are you going to tell us what it is?"

"Yes." Sue pulls a photograph from the binder, doing her best to bite her tongue and not say something snarky back based on the tightness of her cheek. Obviously she was going to tell them what the object is. Whole point of the meeting.

She slides the photo across the table toward him. "Finn Nixon's colored-in sneakers used the day he was traded to the Snowhawks from the Sailors. I believe it was you who came running to the office to show us the video of him coloring them with permanent marker on his bus ride to Snowhaven, shouting, 'We need to get these for the collection.' Well, now we can get them. Finn donated them to a charity auction, and the winning bidder is donating them to us."

"How much did they go for?" the curator asks.

Sue turns to me, and I fight a shrug. "I don't have the exact figure as the paperwork hasn't been completed, pending the approval of acquisition." Although the figure could help us with insuring the shoes as part of our collection, this is purely because he wants to know. He doesn't handle insurance. Sue does.

"So are we in agreement?" Sue presses, shooting a glance

my way. "I'd like to move forward with this so we can get it from our donor. Officially, I say yes."

"Seconded," I quickly add.

The two librarians and archivist tie for thirding the approval. The other curators follow suit, with the last affirmative nod coming from the chief curator. But considering I was in the office the day he came running in wanting the shoes, I know he isn't going to say no. He just wants to have the last word, like always.

All in all, the meeting takes less than twenty minutes. Obvious acquisitions never take long.

Sue stops me at the door to the library on our way back to the collections office. "Cassie, I want you to go home and pack your bags. I'm sending you to go get this one. Solo."

"Me? Solo?"

She resumes walking and leads me down the back stairwell that connects the library to the basement via two flights of stairs that prevents us from having to wind our way through two and a half floors of massive exhibit space. "You are from Snowhaven where the shoes are, correct?"

"Well, yes, but I've never gone by myself to get things."

"Are you telling me you can't handle it?" By the tone of her voice, I can tell she's teasing, but I'm on high alert. Snowhaven and back is no more than a long day trip. They're the sorts of things she and I usually do together so we can write off our coffee for the road and lunch before the return home.

"I can handle it, but why?"

She sighs. "I also want you to take a few days off while you're at it. Stay at home in Snowhaven for a bit. Reconnect with your friends. Catch a game. Have some fun."

My throat constricts at the thought. "Take a few days? Am I in trouble?"

"No, nothing like that. You've been here for nearly two years, and you've hardly taken any time off. You can only carry over so much PTO from year to year, and with the start of your third year coming up, you're looking at losing two weeks that are rightfully yours."

My foot catches on nothing but surprise, and I nearly stumble into the door jamb for our office. "You want me to stay in Snowhaven for two weeks?"

"A few days, two weeks . . ." She shrugs. "Will I know if you spend all of that time in Snowhaven? No, but Nevershade is a small town, so I'll probably find out if you come back early."

"But don't you want Finn's shoes for the exhibit?"

"Sure we do. But what's another two weeks? Sometimes we wait months for a batter to feel ready to give up a bat after he feels it's cooled off from whatever record he hit with it. I, however, do not want you to lose time off that's rightfully yours."

"But—"

"Cassie, you are in your twenties. It's okay to act like it sometimes. There's more to life than your work here."

"I do more than work."

"Sitting at home reading doesn't count. When you interviewed here, you used to talk about all the games you'd go to with your friends. You did that when you first got here, but I know you've only been to the one homestand against the Snowhawks because I have to put in the request for your tickets."

"What if I'm paying for my tickets so I can have better seats?"

She eyes me. "The seats we get aren't terrible. And you're too smart to pay for what you can get for free. Why did you stop going? It's not because you don't like baseball."

I'm certainly not going to tell her I requested all those games back then because Shane was bouncing between the Nevershade Ravens and its farm team. So I shrug instead. "It's more fun with friends."

"Then it sounds like you should make some plans with them once your home."

"I'm not going to get out of this, am I." It's not a question.

"Nope." She smiles, way too satisfied with herself, while my heart beats out of my chest. The Snowhawks have a lengthy homestand right now, and if I have to go home, I'm not sure I'll be able to avoid running into Shane. Not without help, anyway. I'm going to need the girls for this.

I sigh deeply. "Okay."

After checking my emails to make sure there are no pressing needs, and drats, there aren't any, I put up an auto-responder, then shut down my computer. I glance at the clock. If I go home and quickly pack my bags, I can be in Snowhaven by lunchtime.

I say my goodbyes to my meddling boss, who still looks like she has all the answers to some pop quiz only she knows about. She raises her brows as she gives me a finger wave. "This will be a good thing for you. I can sense it."

I'm not so sure about that, but as I hurry down the street to my apartment, I dig my phone out of my purse.

Gale's last text to me still sits unanswered.

ME

Sorry for the days of no response. I'm coming home today.

GALE

Yes! Do you have enough time for lunch before you go back with the shoes?

> Loads. I'm home for two weeks.

> I need details, but I. CAN'T. WAIT. TO.
> SEE. YOU!

A smile creeps onto my face at my best friends' excitement. Ugh . . . my feelings are such a traitor. I'm not supposed to be excited about going home. But as I think about how the other girls are going to react, and how much I miss them, I realize I am excited. Shane or no Shane.

> See you soon!

I hope you've enjoyed reading **The First Baseman's Grumpy Fan**. Cassie and Shane's book is coming up to bat next in *The Catcher's Childhood Crush*.

Acknowledgments

You've come to the end of the book. I hope you've enjoyed Gale and Finn's love story. You'll see them again as side characters in future stories, so this isn't goodbye.

The First Baseman's Grumpy Fan wouldn't be here without several people, things, and historic baseball events that deserve mentioning.

To Bananaball for existing and making me wonder what would happen if a Bananaballer ended up on a very traditional baseball team. And behold, Finn and the Snowhawks materialized.

To Rollie Fingers and his cleats at the National Baseball Hall of Fame and Museum in Cooperstown, NY. The story of needing them to match your new team (prior to the trade being rejected by the MLB) provided inspiration for what happens to Finn when he gets traded to the Snowhawks. I loved researching your story during my time as a collections intern there. It has stuck with me for the last fifteen years.

To Becky Muth, a fabulous romance and cozy mystery author, who was first a work bestie and is now the person I go to for ideation, procrastination, and conversation. I'm so glad to have met you and become friends. Everyone needs a Becky in their life.

And of course to Rob. We may have met using more conventional means, yet somehow, I could still see this meet cute happening to us in another life. Weird things like that just happen to us. And thank you for making loaded tater tots a thing in our house.

Then to my wonderful family, friends, and publishing team who support me on this journey, even on days when that involves me making stickers or asking for your vote on baseball card designs. It's all part of the process, I swear.

And finally, thank you to *you* for reading this book.

About the Author

Rosalie Pease hails from small-town Rhode Island, where the nearest stoplight was two miles away and she knew to come home when her mom whistled or when the streetlights came on.

Her desk is a mess, but she can find everything on it, so it works for her as long as things aren't falling onto the keyboard when she writes.

When she's not writing, she's living her happily ever after: playing with her daughter, hanging out with her husband, or being amused by her two catnip-loving ginger tabbies.

Come find Rosalie online:
Website: https://rosaliepease.com
Instagram and Threads: @WriteRosiePease
Facebook: @WriteRosaliePease

www.ingramcontent.com/pod-product-compliance
Lightning Source LLC
Chambersburg PA
CBHW051437190726
48289CB00001B/229